Gail knew she would be willing to trust Blake with her life.

The question, though, was whether or not she could trust him with her secret. Being a man of high principles, would he be able to accept her story and believe in her innocence, when so many didn't?

He was beginning to care for her, she could tell. It was in his eyes when he looked at her, in that sudden stillness whenever she got too close to him. Was she throwing away a chance of happiness by keeping him at arm's length?

On the other hand, if she told him her story, she ran the risk of disillusioning him. It would be terrible to see that warm look in his eyes turn cold and watch him struggle to let her down lightly....

D0027627

Dear Reader,

I'm not going to waste any time before I give you the good news: This month begins with a book I know you've all been waiting for. *Nighthawk* is the latest in Rachel Lee's ultrapopular CONARD COUNTY miniseries. Craig Nighthawk has never quite overcome the stigma of the false accusations that have dogged his steps, and now he might not live to get the chance. Because in setting himself up as reclusive Esther Jackson's protector—and lover—he's putting himself right in harm's way.

Amnesia is the theme of Linda Randall Wisdom's *In Memory's Shadow*. Sometimes you *can* go home again—if you're willing to face the danger. Luckily for Keely Harper, Sam Barkley comes as part of the package. Two more favorite authors are back—Doreen Roberts with the suspenseful *Every Waking Moment,* and Kay David with *And Daddy Makes Three,* a book to touch your heart. And welcome a couple of new names, too. Though each has written elsewhere, Maggie Simpson and Wendy Haley make their Intimate Moments debuts with *McCain's Memories* (oh, those cowboys!) and *Gabriel Is No Angel* (expect to laugh), respectively.

So that's it for this time around, but be sure to come back next month for more of the best romance reading around, right here in Silhouette Intimate Moments.

Yours,

Leslie Wainger
Senior Editor and Editorial Coordinator

Please address questions and book requests to:
Silhouette Reader Service
U.S.: 3010 Walden Ave., P.O. Box 1325, Buffalo, NY 14269
Canadian: P.O. Box 609, Fort Erie, Ont. L2A 5X3

EVERY WAKING MOMENT

DOREEN ROBERTS

Silhouette®
INTIMATE™MOMENTS®

Published by Silhouette Books

America's Publisher of Contemporary Romance

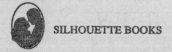

SILHOUETTE BOOKS

ISBN 0-373-07783-1

EVERY WAKING MOMENT

Printed in U.S.A.

Books by Doreen Roberts

DOREEN ROBERTS

has an ambition to visit every one of the United States. She recently added several to her list when she drove across the country to spend a year on the East Coast. She's thinking about setting her future books in each of the states she has visited. She has now returned to settle down in Oregon with her new husband, and to get back to doing what she loves most—writing books about adventurous people who just happen to fall in love.

To Bill, for all your encouragement, faith and unswerving loyalty. You inspire me and sustain me, and your unconditional love fulfills my every waking moment.

Chapter 1

The business section was no more than six blocks long, Blake Foster reckoned as he propped himself against the doorway of the antique store. This small town was exactly as he'd pictured it—a few dismal-looking shop fronts, a small general store with a sub post office, a shabby diner, the inevitable tavern. Yes, that about summed up Mellow Springs.

Right now was probably not a good time to judge whatever doubtful merits the town might possess. Piles of dirty, frozen snow lined the sidewalks, and a bleak gray sky promised more to come. The wind had to be blowing straight off the mountains, Blake thought, as he tugged the fur-lined collar of his jacket up the back of his neck. The cold was enough to freeze his eyeballs.

For a moment he yearned to be back at a cozy table in Delphi's Bar in the heart of downtown Portland, instead of this godforsaken hole in the wilds of the Northwest mountains. This was one assignment he could safely bet he wouldn't enjoy.

He never did enjoy his job when a woman was involved. Especially when she looked as good as the one in the picture nestled in the pocket of his plaid shirt.

It wasn't often a woman stirred his interest anymore. He'd already paid a high price for learning that emotions got in the way of his work and were best ignored. Something about the sad brown eyes and wistful smile of Gail Stevens, however, haunted him in his weaker moments.

Blake frowned at the twinge of uneasiness beneath his belt. He couldn't afford that kind of thinking. He had a job to do, and he was good at it only as long as he remained impartial.

A dark blue compact car turned onto a gravel patch on the other side of the street, and he jerked to attention. The tires crunched noisily across a crisp ridge of mud-stained snow, then rolled to a halt in front of a large barn.

After a second or two, a woman climbed out and slammed the door. She wore a short gray skirt beneath a navy blue reefer jacket, and her dark hair streamed across her face as she hurried across the narrow street, struggling against the wind. She dragged a handful of hair back with her gloved hand when she reached the doorway of the bookstore a few yards away from where he stood.

He could see her profile clearly now—her small, firm chin tucked into the bright red scarf at her throat, although the sweep of her dark hair hid her eyes. Without looking in his direction, she tugged the door open and hurried into the shop.

He would have known her even without that confirmation. He felt a small stab of satisfaction. He'd finally tracked her down. All he had to do now was make contact. And the sooner the better.

He headed back to the hotel, doing his best to ignore the rumblings of apprehension in his gut. It was the daughter, he told himself. She was the one who would get the worst of this lousy deal. Too bad that it was always the kids who had to suffer the consequences of their parents' mistakes. That was the toughest part of his work.

Deliberately, he shoved the thought out of his mind. In an hour he would go back to the bookstore and find out a little more about Gail Stevens. If he did his job right, she would never suspect anything was wrong until it was too late. And by then, it would no longer matter.

On her knees in front of the Mystery shelves, Gail carefully stacked the latest releases, sorting out the authors in alphabetical order. One of the covers caught her eye, and she turned the book over to scan the back blurb. Although she had a pile of books at home to read, she still found it hard to resist an intriguing plot or interesting characters.

The doorbell jingled, announcing a customer. Gail placed the book on the shelf and glanced over at the door. Expecting to see one of the locals, she felt a small jolt when a tall, husky stranger stepped into the tiny shop and looked around him with an expectant air.

Rising to her feet, she watched him as he wandered over to the used books and began idly scanning the various spines. He was dressed in jeans and a dark brown leather jacket, and his dark hair was swept back from a wide forehead to disappear beneath the upturned collar.

She could see only his profile as he stared at the shelves. It was a strong face, dominated by a slightly hooked nose and a stubborn chin. His mouth turned down at the corners, as if he'd weathered more than his share of hardships.

She started, wondering where the illogical thought had come from. At that moment, he turned his head and looked up, straight into her eyes.

She felt the impact of his gaze clear across the room. It was as if a glacier had suddenly scudded over the floor, freezing everything in its path. Shadowed by the bookshelves, his eyes glinted cold gray, and his ruthless mouth looked capable of inflicting verbal pain.

Normally she didn't mind being alone in the store. Polly Wilson, the owner of The Book Nook, didn't usually come in until the lunch hour, but Gail would have been more than happy to see her arrive earlier.

"Good morning," Gail said, keeping her expression pleasant. "Is there something I can find for you?" She'd managed to make the pat phrase sound casual, in spite of her flutter of apprehension. There was just something about the man that unnerved her, although she wasn't sure why.

"I hope so." The customer started toward her. As he moved into the light from the windows she almost laughed at herself. His stern features no longer seemed forbidding. In fact, she decided, he was rather nice to look at. A little more polished than her first impression, but definitely rugged.

When she looked into his eyes, however, she had the strange notion that he was just as wary of her as she was of him.

"I'm touring the area," he said, when she reached him. "I'd like to see some travel books."

His deep voice, with its faintly husky undertone, seemed to seep right into her bones. She could sense the tension in him now, humming just beneath the surface and barely controlled.

Telling herself she'd been reading too many murder mysteries, she turned away from him, and felt the tiny hairs on her nape bristling as he followed close behind her to the back of the store to the travel section.

"Were you interested in a particular area?" she murmured, as she reached for a slim guidebook.

"The mountains, lakes...anything of interest nearby."

Gail nodded, trying to regain her composure. She reached for another book and noticed the slight tremble in her hand. Annoyed with herself, she turned sharply to face him.

His gaze seemed to bore right through her skull, scattering her concentration. Again she sensed a certain edginess about him, and wondered what it was that kept him so uptight.

"These might be of some help," she said. "If you're interested in skiing, there's a lodge and chairlift not too far from here." She tried to recall the name of the resort and for some reason drew a blank.

He took the books from her, his fingers brushing hers. She could feel the reaction from his touch sneak up her arm to tease the back of her neck. She snatched her hand away and pretended to study the spines of the books on the shelf again.

His tension was communicating itself to her, she thought, with a flash of irritation. One minute he seemed threatening, the next he was generating sparks of excitement up and down her body.

"This is a fairly extensive guide of the area," she said, showing him a thick paperback. "It lists all the hiking and ski trails, as well as the fishing lakes and streams. Of course, this time of year, your choices might be limited...."

She stopped, her words faltering as his gaze settled on her mouth. She could almost feel the magnetism radiating from him, drawing her onto dangerous ground. With effort, she pulled herself together. Confused by her conflicting thoughts, she thrust the book at him, saying pointedly, "It's eighteen-fifty."

He took the guidebook from her, his eyes never leaving her face. Flipping through the pages without reading any of them, he murmured, "Thank you. This will do just fine."

Heading back to the counter, she sucked in a long, slow breath. This was utter nonsense. At thirty-four she should know better than to allow her hormones to govern her good sense. Just because an attractive man wandered into a town where there happened to be a considerable shortage of interesting men did not give her a reason to go to pieces.

Her enigmatic customer took his time reaching inside his jacket for his wallet, while his gaze flicked around the store. The absurd thought that he was committing the layout of the premises to memory tempted her to smile at her paranoid fears.

"Do you do much skiing?" he asked abruptly.

Taken by surprise, she sounded flustered as she answered, "Not a lot...I don't really have much time."

"How far away is the ski lodge?"

"About ten miles east of here."

"Does it have accommodations?"

"I believe so. I don't know it well enough to recommend it, though. The book should give you more information about it."

"And the name?"

This time she came up with it. "Fircrest Lodge." How could she have forgotten that? She had taken Heather to the bunny slopes there just two weeks ago. "That will be nineteen-eighty with the tax," she said firmly.

She wasn't sure she cared for the way he fired questions at her. He had a brusque way of talking, as if he were interrogating her. The thought made her uneasy again. She was only too familiar with that kind of cross-examination.

Impatiently, she brushed her fears aside. That was all in the past, and she had nothing to fear anymore.

He handed her a twenty, and she rang up the charge.

"Are there any good restaurants around here?" he asked. "So far I've only seen the diner on the corner and the one in the Alpine Inn."

She gave him his change, dropping it into his open palm. "There's a Chinese restaurant on Fourth Street, across from a steakhouse. I don't know what they're like—I usually eat lunch at the diner. There're also a couple of fast-food places farther down the road. You might have seen them when you came in, unless you came down from Canada?''

He shook his head. ''Seattle. I must have passed them in the dark last night.''

''They close early.'' She dropped his purchase into a bag with the receipt and held it out to him. ''They're kind of set back in the trees.''

''I'll watch out for them.'' He took the bag from her, his fingers once more brushing against hers.

This time she suppressed her reaction, wondering if he had deliberately engineered the contact. Almost immediately she dismissed the notion as ridiculous. She watched him glance around the stacked shelves of books once more.

''What time do you close?'' he asked, as he tucked the book inside his jacket. ''I might want to come back later and look for something to read.''

Her heart skipped, and she dropped her gaze. ''We close at six, except for Friday night when we're open until nine.'' Staring at the receipt book, she concentrated on entering the sale.

''Thank you.''

Without looking up, she gave a slight nod, her fingers gripping the pen until she heard the door close behind him. Finally able to relax, she slowly let out a breath.

She wasn't sure which had disturbed her the most—his subtle sensuality or the faint aura of danger she sensed behind those magnetic eyes. She had to stop imagining the worst, she thought, impatient with her irrational fears.

She'd fought hard to put the past behind her and rid herself of her paranoia. She wasn't about to let one obscure stranger stir up all that anxiety again, and give her more sleepless nights. She'd worked too hard to overcome her insecurity.

The locals were beginning to accept her now, and Heather, just like a typical five-year-old, had adjusted to her new environment almost at once. She hadn't even mentioned her father in weeks.

Only one person knew their real names, and that was Polly. They were safe in this little town.

Wandering back to the Mystery shelves, Gail allowed her mind to return to that fateful day when she'd arrived in Mellow Springs. She'd been pretty desperate at the time. She and Heather had left Portland with little more than the clothes on their backs, and no clear idea where they were going.

They had needed a place to hide, a place to find peace, where Heather could grow up and where Gail could forget the horror of the past. Driven by an urgency she couldn't explain, Gail had stayed at the wheel until she could no longer see. Her exhaustion had caught up with her in Mellow Springs.

She had woken up the next morning in the tiny town that was no more than a dot on the map, and she had decided that Providence had taken a hand. Assuming the name ''Kate Morris,'' she'd rented a house, then looked for a job.

Stepping into the bookstore one day, she'd come face-to-face with a slight woman who wore her iron gray hair scraped back from her face in a bun, making her bony features look even more austere. Nevertheless her bright blue eyes danced merrily behind her rimless glasses, and Gail had taken an immediate liking to the spry, middle-aged owner.

Polly had seemed enchanted with Heather, and upon learning that ''Kate'' was looking for a job, had offered her a position at the store, saying she was tired of working full time and could use the help. There wasn't much to do except read in Mellow Springs, she'd told Gail, and the bookstore did a brisk trade.

Gail had given Polly a plausible story to explain why it was so imperative that no one know her real name. Her in-laws were vindictive and wanted to take their grandchild away from her. They had money and power, and she was worried they would succeed, so she'd taken Heather away to start a new life.

Polly had seemed to take it all in stride and promised to keep their secret. Registering Heather at the local kindergarten under her pet name "Annie," Gail had also located a reliable baby-sitter, Darcie Reynolds, who came highly recommended by Polly.

Her life was now secure for the first time in a good many years. Gail had no reason to worry about a stranger, even if he did disturb her. She and Heather were safe, and she intended to see they stayed that way.

In spite of her resolution to put the customer out of her mind, however, his image seemed to haunt her for the rest of the morning. She found herself wondering why such a dynamic man would choose this lonely place to vacation alone.

Tourists were not that uncommon in Mellow Springs, even in winter, although they were more likely to be retired couples touring the great Northwest, or campers, hikers and mountain climbers—outdoor types.

Not that the stranger didn't seem capable. With his powerful build and aura of hidden strength, he looked energetic enough to tackle the toughest mountain trail. But somehow, he just didn't appear the sort to enjoy scrambling over rocks in the frigid air. He looked as if he would be more at home on a busy street, in a noisy, crowded bar somewhere, or maybe cheering a football team from the stands of a city stadium.

Yet, in spite of his intimidating manner, she hadn't been

able to ignore that undercurrent of potent masculinity. Her body's response to his touch had been unmistakable.

Gail threw down the pile of bookmarks she'd been sorting in disgust. She didn't want to think about him anymore. Who he was and what he was doing in Mellow Springs was entirely his own business and none of hers. She could only hope that she wouldn't be in the shop if and when he chose to come back and look for something else to read.

Polly arrived promptly at noon, and Gail felt a sense of release as she left the store and drove over to the kindergarten to pick up her daughter.

She no longer panicked every time she left Heather somewhere. Even so, she still had moments of uneasiness, and Gail was always relieved to see the little girl happy and smiling when she arrived to collect her.

Heather chatted happily all the way to the baby-sitter's, telling her mother about school. Gail gave her only half her attention. Her thoughts were still grappling with the memory of a sharp-eyed man who had succeeded in disrupting her entire morning.

Darcie Reynolds was a cheerful, industrious young woman who managed to take care of five young children as well as her own two with remarkable serenity. Nothing seemed to upset her, and Gail envied Darcie her calm composure.

Heather always looked forward to playing with the rest of the kids, and she adored the baby-sitter. Gail felt extremely fortunate to have found her.

After chatting with Darcie for a minute or two, Gail stooped to say goodbye to Heather. "You be a good girl, Annie," she said, smoothing back Heather's feathery blond hair from her eyes, "and I'll be back for you later, okay?"

"Okay." Heather gave her a wet kiss on the cheek, then turned back to a little girl who sat on the carpet, hugging a worn teddy bear. "I'm going to paint my dolly's face when I get home," she announced with pride. "You want me to paint your teddy's face?"

Gail sighed and gave Darcie a rueful look. "You'd better lock up your makeup if you don't want it smeared all over the toys."

"Don't worry." Darcie walked with Gail to the door. "I learned a long time ago to keep stuff like that way out of reach."

"I'm beginning to learn," Gail said ruefully.

"You okay? You do look a bit strained. Things aren't getting you down, are they?"

Gail shook her head. "Didn't get much sleep last night, that's all."

"Well, okay. Just let me know if you need a break. You know I'll keep Annie overnight anytime you want. She's a good kid and no trouble. In fact, she keeps my two in line."

"She's bossy, you mean." Gail sighed. "I hope she grows out of that."

Darcie laughed. "You worry too much."

"Yes, I'm afraid I do." Gail opened the door and stepped outside into the cold wind. "Thanks again, Darcie."

"You don't have to thank me. You pay me."

"I mean, thanks for being a friend."

"Sure, pal. Anytime."

Warmed by Darcie's grin, Gail tried to put her morbid thoughts out of her mind as she parked in her usual spot and then walked back to the Corner Café.

Gina, the frazzled-looking blond waitress, greeted her eagerly as she stepped inside the moist warmth of the diner.

"Got my book? Great! I've been looking forward to this one."

"It came in this morning," Gail assured her as she followed the waitress to a table at the window. "You'll be the first in town to read it."

"Well, don't tell anyone, or they'll all want to borrow it. Let them buy their own, that's what I say." Gina handed her the plastic menu. "You want the usual, or do you want to try the special?"

Gail skimmed down the familiar list of food selections. "I think I'll stick with the grilled chicken sandwich."

"So would I." Gina took the menu from her. "I'll bring your coffee." She strutted across the room to the kitchen, tossing a remark at one of the customers that made the man laugh out loud.

Gail smiled and looked out the window. Thick gray clouds coasted across the sky, blotting out the sun. She wondered if it was going to snow again. If so, what would the mysterious tourist do then?

Annoyed with herself for thinking about him again, Gail looked around the diner. All the tables were full. She'd been lucky to get one by the window.

The door opened, letting in a blast of cold air that stung her legs. She wished now that she'd worn pants instead of a skirt and sweater.

Suddenly her heart skipped a couple of beats. Standing just a few yards away, the stranger from earlier stood looking around him for an empty table.

Gail edged back, hoping he wouldn't see her. It was a futile hope, of course. Seated in the window, she was as prominent as Gina, who at that moment was tripping back across the floor with her coffee.

The man's gaze followed the waitress all the way to Gail's table. She barely noticed as Gina put down the steaming cup of coffee in front of her.

"Here, drink this," the waitress ordered. "You look cold."

Gail gave her a vague smile. "Thanks."

"Sure. I'll be back with your sandwich in a few minutes.

Harry's going crazy in there. You know how he is when we get busy.''

Gina turned away, almost bumping into the stranger who stood right behind her. Muttering, ''Excuse me,'' she stepped around him and pranced back to the kitchen.

''Hope you don't mind, but this is the only seat left,'' he said to Gail, dragging the other chair out from her table. Before she could think of an answer, he'd draped his jacket over the back of the chair and sat down.

Yes, she thought irritably, she did mind. The fact that she preferred to eat alone had apparently not even occurred to him.

It was on the tip of her tongue to tell him so, but then she reminded herself that he was, after all, one of Polly's customers. She could hardly be rude to him. Reluctantly, she resigned herself to sharing the table with him. She would just have to do her best to ignore him.

''This gives me the chance to thank you for helping me this morning,'' he said, giving her one of his restrained smiles. ''The guide is extremely helpful.''

''We sell a lot of them in the summertime,'' she murmured, pretending an interest in the dessert menu propped up between the salt and pepper shakers. ''That's when we get most of our tourists.''

''I imagine this is not the best time to explore the mountains.''

''Unless you have a fondness for snow.''

To her surprise he chuckled—a low, pleasant sound that melted some of the reserve she'd built up against him. She looked up, disturbed to find him watching her.

The cold light from the window slanted across his face, accentuating the tiny crevices at the corners of his eyes. She could see a sprinkling of gray in his dark hair at the temples, and faint frown lines between his brows.

"I don't mind snow," he said. "My main priority is peace and quiet."

She felt her shoulders begin to relax. "Well, you'll get plenty of that here. There's not a lot of excitement in Mellow Springs."

She looked up with a start as Gina placed her chicken sandwich in front of her. She hadn't noticed the waitress approach. Gina looked at her companion and bestowed her wide grin on him. "I guess you found the bookstore okay, then."

"Yes, I did. Thank you." He gave the waitress a cursory glance. "I'll have a steak sandwich, medium rare, and coffee."

Gina shrugged, obviously put out by his indifference, then sauntered off in search of more appreciative company.

"I was in here this morning for breakfast," he said, in answer to Gail's questioning look. "I asked where I could find a travel guide and she recommended your store."

"Gina spends a lot of time in The Book Nook."

"She also told me your name. Kate Morris, isn't it?"

Gail nodded, wondering what else the gossipy waitress had told him.

"I'm Blake Foster, and I'm happy to meet you."

He held out his hand, and she tentatively put hers into it. "Nice to meet you, Mr. Foster."

His warm, firm grasp tightened around her fingers. "Blake. You don't mind if I call you Kate?"

She gave a slight shake of her head. What did it matter, anyway? He was just passing through, and names would be easily forgotten. Judging from the vibrations strumming through her fingers, it was just as well.

"This town must seem very small compared to Seattle," she said, after an awkward pause. She would have liked to eat her sandwich and make her escape, but it seemed rude to start without him.

"Quite a contrast, I must admit." Once more his astute gaze roamed the room.

Again she was struck by the undercurrent of tension beneath his cool image. He reminded her of some wild, predatory animal, concentrating on his prey, his violence held at bay by a thin thread.

She felt a quiver in the region of her stomach and wasn't sure if it was anxiety or something more provocative. In spite of all her misgivings, he fascinated her. He was unlike any man she had met before.

She had known more than one predatory man in her life—cruel, insensitive men who were completely without any sense of decency or honor. Somehow she couldn't equate Blake Foster with any of those monsters.

Gina returned with his steak sandwich and coffee, and Gail could finally eat her lunch. After a while, he asked her if she had always lived in Mellow Springs.

Her nerves tightening again, she shook her head. "I moved here from Newberg, Oregon, a few months ago. My husband was killed in a car wreck, and I wanted to get away from the memories. I came upon this town by accident, and decided it would be a good place to start a new life with my daughter."

The lies had come easily enough. After all, she'd been telling the same story ever since she'd arrived in Mellow Springs. Even so, her pulse jumped nervously when she met his intense gaze.

"I'm sorry," he said quietly. "That must have been a tough thing to do."

She shrugged. "It gets easier."

"How old is your daughter?"

"She's five, going on nineteen."

He smiled at that. "Where is she now?"

"With a baby-sitter. She goes to kindergarten in the mornings, then Darcie keeps her the rest of the time I have to work."

"You don't have any family? It must be pretty lonely here on your own."

This time she could tell him the truth. "No family. I grew up in foster homes. I never knew my parents. From the little I know, I guess they weren't married, and my mother was too young to take care of herself, let alone a baby."

He nodded, his gray eyes intent on her face as if afraid to miss a word. "What about your husband's family?"

She shrugged. "I have no contact with them." His questions were getting a little too personal, and she deliberately changed the subject. "So what do you do in Seattle?"

He seemed surprised by the abrupt question, but answered her readily enough. "I'm in real estate. Though I have no idea why they call it that. Any business based less on reality I have yet to meet."

"You sell houses?"

Her voice had risen in astonishment and his face registered amusement. "You seem surprised by that."

"I don't know why.... I just thought— I mean..." Aware she was floundering, she let her voice trail off.

"What did you think I did for a living?"

A lion tamer or a soldier of fortune jumped immediately to mind, but she could hardly admit that. She shrugged, saying nonchalantly, "Oh, I don't know. Something a little less—"

"Mundane?"

She laughed. "I really don't know enough about selling real estate to make a judgment."

"It's a very exacting science," he said solemnly. "For instance, you must be able to judge instantly if furniture you've never seen will fit into a living room you haven't measured, as well as identify every species of green shoot in the yard while they are barely an inch tall."

Grinning, she said, "I can imagine you get some pretty

dumb questions. I've had a few of those myself at the book-store.''

For the next few minutes they traded anecdotes, until Gail gave a guilty start and looked at her watch. "Oh, Lord, I'm going to be late getting back. Polly will wonder where I am.''

Blake looked concerned. "I hope she won't be too upset with you.''

Gail shook her head and reached for her bill. "Polly never gets upset." She stood and slipped her arms into her coat.

Blake got to his feet, and lifted his jacket from the chair. "Thank you for sharing your table with me," he said, as she led the way to the front counter. "I can't remember passing a more enjoyable hour.''

She sent him a quick glance. "I enjoyed it, too.''

"Perhaps we can do it again before I leave town.''

"Perhaps." She paid for her meal, then turned to leave. "Goodbye, Mr. Foster. I hope you enjoy the rest of your trip.''

"So do I. And it's Blake, remember?" Once more his gray eyes invaded her face. "So long...for now, Kate.''

She managed a smile, then slipped through the door. Her cheeks felt hot, in spite of the bite of the cold wind. In fact, her entire body felt invigorated, more alive than she had felt in a very long time. Blake Foster had been great company, with his wry humor and quick, intelligent mind. She had found it so easy to talk to him.

A little too easy, she reflected, as she walked briskly to the bookstore. She couldn't afford to let her guard down like that, particularly with a total stranger. She should know better. She must never forget why she'd run away, and the possible danger that lay in every new acquaintance. No matter how much she had enjoyed his company, she would make a point of avoiding Blake Foster.

She opened the door of the shop and stepped inside, unable to escape the uneasy thought that avoiding a man in a town this size would be practically impossible. Particularly if he was persistent. And something told her that Blake Foster was the persistent type.

That afternoon she found it difficult to concentrate on anything. Twice she missed a question from Polly and had to ask her to repeat it, and then she gave a customer the wrong order and couldn't find the right one. Every time she heard the doorbell she jumped, half expecting the powerful figure of Blake Foster to be standing in the doorway.

Finally Polly demanded to know what was the matter with her. "You've been as twitchy as a cricket all afternoon," she said, her blue eyes full of concern. "What's biting at you, for heaven's sake? Did someone upset you?"

"Not exactly," Gail said, rubbing at a stubborn spot on the front of the glass case she was polishing.

Polly reached out and took the dust cloth from her hand. "You're going to rub a hole in the dang thing if you keep that up. You might as well tell me what's got you all fired up, missy, because I'm not letting you out of here until I know what it is."

Gail sighed. Polly meant well, but there were times when she used her advanced years of experience as an excuse to get downright nosy. In the next instant, she was ashamed of her petty criticism. Polly had been good to her. She'd trusted her, in spite of her less-than-perfect background. Polly was simply being protective.

"I guess it was the tourist who came in this morning," she said lightly. "You know how I get about strangers in town."

"We get a lot of strangers in town," Polly said, giving her a shrewd look. "I don't see any of them giving you the heebie-jeebies the way this guy did." She dropped her voice, even though they were alone. "You don't think he's one of those private detectives, do you? You know, working for your in-laws?"

Gail shook her head, ignoring the quiver of apprehension. "No, I don't think so. He was just...a little intimidating, that's all."

Polly narrowed her eyes. "Good-looking?"

Gail shrugged. "I guess."

"Ah, so that's it." Polly gave her a hefty slap on the shoulder. "Well, it's about time you started hunting for another man. Go for it, gal, that's what I say."

Gail could feel her face growing warm. "He's just a tourist passing through, Polly. I'm not likely to see him again, even if I were interested, which I'm not. So you can forget your matchmaking."

Polly lifted a finger and wagged it at her. "You're much too young to give up on love, Kate Morris. And that daughter of yours could use a father. Little girls need a daddy in their lives. I know your ex was a jerk, but that doesn't mean every man on this good earth is the same way."

"I prefer not to take any more chances on that." Carefully, Gail rearranged a display of diaries on top of the case. "I thought I knew Frank well when I married him. I had no idea that the so-called qualities I admired in him would be so destructive. I thought he was strong and protective, but instead he turned out to be possessive and insanely jealous. I was a virtual prisoner in my own home, and I have no intention of ever being that miserable again."

"Life is about taking risks," Polly said gently. "I hate to see you waste yours because of some bum who didn't know how to love a woman."

Gail held back the bitter response hovering on her tongue. The warmhearted bookseller looked upon Gail as the daughter she'd never had. Polly just didn't know the true story. And Gail was going to make darn sure she never knew. Her life—and Heather's—might very well depend on that some day.

Chapter 2

Alone in his hotel room, Blake sat on the edge of his bed, going over the entire conversation he'd had with Gail Stevens earlier. She wasn't at all what he'd been led to believe. Tight-lipped, of course; but that was to be expected. She also had that indefinable air of class, which surprised him. So was the way she made him feel when she smiled—as if he'd just stepped into a sauna.

She'd made it obvious she didn't trust him, and anyone with an ounce of intelligence could tell she was hiding something. Unfortunately for her, Gail Stevens was not too good at hiding her feelings.

Which made it all the tougher to accept the facts as he knew them. How the devil did a woman like her get involved in the kind of mess she'd ended up in?

Blake shoved himself off the bed and paced uneasily to the window. The wind whipped the branches of the tall firs that lined the parking lot, making them sway like the giant masts of a storm-tossed schooner. He could hear a faint whistling sound coming from the window frame, and when he put his fingers there, he could feel a cold draft.

Already it was getting dark and it wasn't yet five o'clock. The sun set early in this northern winter. He hunched his shoulders, as if he were outside in the wind instead of in the warmth of his room. The more he thought about this assignment, the less he liked it. Something didn't add up.

With a frown he left the window and headed for the courtesy bar next to the television set. Inside, he found a couple of miniature bourbons and a half bottle of soda. He took them out, then grabbed the ice bucket and went in search of the ice machine.

Striding down the silent corridor of the deserted hotel, he faced the source of his uneasiness. For the first time in a good many years, he was attracted to a woman again. He'd started to think he'd outgrown those schoolboy urges, but sitting across the table from Gail Stevens that afternoon, he'd wondered what it would be like to take her to bed and make hot, passionate love to her.

The thought had startled him, and he'd had the devil of a time hiding his reaction. Luckily he was better at covering up his emotions than she was.

Cursing under his breath, Blake shoved the bucket beneath the chute of the ice machine and leaned on the button. He had to admit, if he'd been in that diner for any other reason, he would have thoroughly enjoyed having lunch with her. That wasn't all he might have enjoyed. Just thinking about what might have followed brought beads of sweat to his brow.

He had no illusions about the trouble he was in. Those kinds of feelings were going to make his job that much tougher. And if he had any sense of self-preservation, he had better get his head on straight—stat. He couldn't afford to mess this one up. There was too much at stake.

The ice spilled over the edge of the bucket and again he

muttered a quiet oath. He had a job to do, he told himself, and he was going to do it. And he couldn't let an attractive woman with sad, beautiful eyes and the most seductive body he'd ever been that close to, get in his way.

When Gail left with Heather for school the next morning, she found a new, soft blanket of snow covering the streets. The sun, however, had swallowed up the clouds, leaving a watery blue sky and a hazy view of the white mountain peaks in the distance.

"Can we go sledding again, Mommy?" Heather asked, as Gail bundled her into the car. "I wanna go up the mountain again."

"We'll see," Gail murmured, only half listening to her daughter. She had slept badly, disturbed by dreams that included Frank and a shadowy stranger who looked a lot like Blake Foster.

Unable to shake the unsettling images, she dropped Heather off and headed for The Book Nook. To her relief the morning passed without any sign of the imposing tourist, and she was beginning to relax by the time Polly arrived.

After leaving Heather with Darcie, Gail decided not to go to the diner for lunch. She was reluctant to bump into Blake Foster again. She wasn't at all comfortable with the way he made her feel. Instead, she drove out to the hamburger place on the edge of town.

The snow was melting from the lacy branches of the fir trees that surrounded the tiny ramshackle building. Large white clumps slid from the thawing needles and fell to the ground, where they shattered into tiny pieces.

One of the powdery mounds thudded down almost at Gail's feet as she crossed the parking lot to the restaurant. The jolt it gave her took her breath away. Her heart still pounded as she pulled open the door and went inside.

Several people sat at the sparse tables, but although Gail scanned the entire room, she couldn't see the dark head of Blake Foster. Wondering why she should expect to see him there, she mentally scolded herself for her overactive imagination.

She kept an eye on the door while she ate, and although she saw nothing out of the ordinary, she couldn't seem to lose the odd feeling that she was being watched. While pretending to study the menu, she scrutinized everyone in the place.

Except for a gray-haired man who looked to be too frail to run for a bus, let alone harm her, no one else appeared to be paying the slightest attention to her. Nevertheless, she left some of her hamburger and most of the coffee in her hurry to leave there and return to the relative security of the bookstore.

Polly looked up in surprise when Gail rushed through the door. "My, my," she murmured, glancing up at the clock, "it's nice to see someone so anxious to get back to work. You've still got ten minutes left of your lunch hour."

Gail pretended to be surprised. "I do? Ah, well, I can use it to check out the latest box of books and find out which ones I want to take home with me."

"You picked the right place to work, I must say. I've never known anyone who reads as much as you do."

"There's not much else to do in the evenings after Annie goes to bed."

Polly poked her shoulder with a bony finger. "You never heard of television?"

Gail moved away to hang up her coat. "I don't watch much TV," she said, glancing back at her over her shoulder. "The shows are either too violent or just plain silly. I—" She froze as the door suddenly opened behind Polly and a tall, forbidding figure stepped inside.

"Hello again," Blake Foster said pleasantly.

Polly stared for a long moment at Gail, then turned to greet the customer. "Good afternoon, sir. Is there something I can help you with?"

Blake Foster bestowed a heart-stopping smile on her. "Thank you, but this young lady helped me yesterday, and I'd like to deal with her again, if that's all right with you?"

Polly looked back at Gail with a gleam in her eye. "I guess you're back from lunch now, aren't you, honey?"

Gail nodded weakly. "Of course." She made herself walk forward, and even managed a smile. "Good afternoon, Mr. Foster. What can I do for you?"

"Blake, remember?"

She looked into his light gray eyes, and wondered why she'd ever thought they were cold. "Yes, of course... Blake."

"That's better." His smile dazzled her, and for a moment she forgot she was supposed to be waiting on him.

"'I was wondering if you had any more books on the area," Blake said, glancing at the bookshelves. "The one you recommended was excellent, but rather limited on the local history of the place."

Gail looked at him in surprise. "I didn't realize you were interested in the history. If you'd said yesterday—"

"Oh, I know, it's my fault. I should have mentioned it." He took a step toward her, and before she realized his intention, he'd taken her by the arm in a proprietary gesture and was leading her down the aisle, much to Polly's obvious enjoyment.

Furious with him for his familiarity, Gail pulled away from him. Her reaction to the warm grasp of his fingers on her arm had been predictable and immediate. "The history section," she said coolly, "is the third shelf on the left. I'm sure you'll find what you're looking for there."

She turned on her heel and marched back to the counter, where Polly stood shaking her head at her.

"You're going to frighten him away with that scowl on your face," Polly whispered fiercely. "If I were a few years younger, I'd be showing him every dang history book in the place."

"I told you," Gail whispered back, "I'm not interested."

"Uh-huh." Polly grinned. "Then how come you're wearing a blush on your cheeks and a sparkle in your eyes? Come on, missy, you can't fool old Polly. I've been around too long."

Gail was about to deliver an angry retort forming on her lips when from directly behind her, she heard Blake clear his throat.

"I wonder if I might impose on you one more time?" he said, as she swung around to face him. "I don't seem to be able to find what I want."

Gail pursed her lips. Blake Foster might be many things, but she was willing to bet that helpless wasn't one of them. Polly, however, was nudging her none too discreetly in the back, and there didn't seem much else she could do.

With a cool nod in his direction, Gail led the way back to the history shelves. "What exactly are you looking for?" She started to pull books from the shelf. "A history of the mountains? Gold digging in the area? The silver mines, perhaps? How about a comprehensive guide to the geological outlay of the Cascades? Or a concise history of the Native Americans who first settled the area?"

He smiled at her a little sheepishly. "All right, so I just wanted to get you away from Hawkeye over there. I wanted to tell you how much I enjoyed our lunch yesterday."

Disarmed in spite of herself, Gail let out her breath. "Thank you. I enjoyed it, too."

"I was wondering if you'd care to have dinner with me tonight? They have an excellent dining room at the hotel, and I really would like to discuss the area. I'd like to take in some of the sights, and I've learned from experience that the locals know more about their hometown than any guidebook or map can tell me.''

"I haven't been here very long myself," Gail said quickly, all her defenses springing back to alert. "I'm really not the right person to ask. Now Polly, however, can tell you anything you want to know. She's lived here most of her life.''

Blake pulled his face into a comical one-sided grimace. "No offense, but I'd much rather have dinner with you.''

Gail lifted her chin. "I'm sorry, Mr. Foster, but I'm afraid I can't. I have a daughter to take care of, if you remember.''

He regarded her for a moment in silence. "No babysitter?''

"No baby-sitter.''

"I thought that's where she goes in the afternoons.''

Gail could feel a slight stirring of resentment. He was being a little too insistent. "I don't like to leave her there any longer than I have to. My time with my child is important to me.''

"Of course it is. I can understand that. Why don't you bring her along? I'm sure we can find something on the menu she'd like.''

Gail was starting to feel desperate. "Annie has to be in bed by eight," she said sharply. "She needs her sleep.''

Blake nodded. "I see. In that case, I guess I'll have to eat alone again." He reached out and plucked a book from her hand, although Gail could swear he hadn't so much as glanced at the title. "If you should change your mind, Kate, I'll be in the dining room around seven-thirty. I really hope you decide to come.''

Her hands shook as she stuffed the rest of the books back on the shelf. She could feel his gaze on her when he followed her back to the counter. Polly, thankfully, had moved over to the discount table and was busily stacking books.

Relieved to be putting the counter between them, Gail rang up the purchase and gave Blake the total. He handed her a bill, and at that moment, Gail caught Polly's eye.

The owner's eyelid closed in a lecherous wink, and Gail fumbled the bill, dropping it on the floor. Crouching to retrieve it, she gave herself a mental shake. This was ridiculous. She would have to have a plain talk with Polly once Blake had left.

She could feel her cheeks burning by the time she'd stuffed the bill into the drawer and counted out the change. She dropped the coins into his open palm, taking care not to touch him. She made the mistake of looking up at his face, and his smug smile flustered her even more.

"I'll be back," he murmured, and for an instant she thought it sounded almost like a threat. His affable expression, however, reassured her.

"Enjoy the book," she said automatically.

"I'll try." With a nod at Polly, he left, letting the door close behind him.

Watching him stride past the window, Gail could almost feel the emptiness left by his absence. She looked quickly at Polly, who was watching her with a knowing look on her face.

"Yep," Polly said with great satisfaction. "He got to you, all right. Why the heck didn't you go ahead and say you'd have dinner with him?"

Aware that their conversation had been overheard, Gail smothered her resentment. "I don't have dinner with strangers," she said crisply. "And you know why."

Polly shook her head. "You've got to get the danged past out of your mind." She dusted her hands on her apron, as if to emphasize her point. "If your in-laws haven't tracked you down yet, it's a good bet they're not going to.

You've got to start trusting again, Kate, honey, or you'll end up a lonely old woman, like me.''

"You seem to be doing just fine.''

"Maybe, but there're plenty of cold nights I wish I had a warm body to curl up with.''

"Then I'll get a dog.''

Polly sighed. "You're just too stubborn for your own good,'' she muttered good-naturedly. "One of these days you're going to meet a man who'll blast right through that thick hide of yours, and you won't know what hit you. You mark my words.''

Gail managed a smile. "Maybe. But I can promise you, it won't be Blake Foster. Now I'd better get back to cataloging those trades that came in this morning.''

She had barely started the job when another customer demanded her attention. After finding the book the elderly lady had asked for, Gail rang up the charge and handed her the purchase. The receipt book wasn't lying in its usual place, Gail noticed, as she thanked the customer.

After the woman had left, Gail searched the counter, then all the drawers. The receipt book had apparently vanished. Thinking that Polly might have taken it, Gail hurried to the back of the store, where the owner was busily stacking the children's shelves.

"Have you seen the receipt book?'' Gail asked, when Polly peered down at her from halfway up the ladder.

"It's on the counter where you left it, isn't it?'' Polly climbed down and dusted her hands together. "At least, it was when I last saw it.''

"Perhaps it fell on the floor and went under the counter.'' Gail headed back to the front of the store. "I seem to be all fingers and thumbs today.''

"Don't you, though,'' Polly said from behind her.

Gail ignored her, dropping to her hands and knees to

look under the counter. "It's not here," she announced, as she scrambled back to her feet.

"Didn't that handsome hunk of yours buy a book on local history?"

Gail started. "Yes, but what's that got to do with..." Her voice trailed off as Polly reached over and plucked a book from a pile sitting on the counter.

"Is this the book?"

"Oh, Lord." Gail ran a hand through her hair. "I must have given him the receipt book by mistake. They're the same size and color and—"

"And you were plum twisted inside out by his smile," Polly said, grinning. "I can see how it happened."

"It was more likely from watching you pull all those faces at me." Gail looked at the book in her hand in disgust. "I wonder if he'll bring it back."

"If he even knows he's got it. I got the impression he wasn't real interested in reading that history book. He'll most likely toss the bag aside and not even look in it."

"I guess I'll have to go and get it, then," Gail said, hoping feverishly that Polly would volunteer.

"Good idea." Polly looked up at the clock. "You can leave a half hour early and drop by the hotel on your way to pick up Annie."

There didn't seem to be any way to get out of it, Gail thought, unable to suppress a little spasm of anticipation. She did her best not to think about it, but for the rest of the afternoon she found herself rehearsing over and over what she was going to say when she saw Blake Foster again.

By the time she was ready to leave the store, her stomach felt tied up in knots. Just in case, she called Darcie and warned her that she might be a little late. When she didn't explain why, she could tell Darcie was eaten up with curiosity.

"You want me to keep her for the night?" the baby-sitter asked. "I'll be happy to if you've got a hot date."

Gail rolled her eyes toward the ceiling. Why was everyone in town doing their best to palm her off on some poor, unsuspecting male? "I do not have a date," she said carefully. "This is business."

"Too bad. I was hoping you'd found yourself a new man."

"Sorry to disappoint you. Tell Annie I'll be there as soon as possible."

"Don't worry, she's busy repapering Janice's dollhouse. If you change your mind, I'll be happy to keep her."

"I won't change my mind," Gail said firmly. She hung up and found Polly watching her.

Her face looked quite serious as she said, "I know it's none of my business, Kate, but I think it would do you good to have a night out. You deserve to enjoy yourself a bit more. You haven't had a night out without Annie since you got here. Too much togetherness is not necessarily a good thing, you know."

"You're right." Gail pulled her coat from the hook and thrust her arm in a sleeve. "So how about you and I driving into Parkerville for dinner and a movie one night?"

"Fifty miles there and back for a movie?"

"And dinner."

Polly grinned. "You're on. But I still think you should go tonight."

Gail picked up the book and waved it at her. "Good night, Polly. I'll see you tomorrow."

The headlights of her car reflected on the snow piled high at the sides of the road as she drove toward the hotel. Above the silent trees a carpet of stars shimmered, and she could see a glistening of frost on the pavement ahead of her.

She drove carefully, watching for the Alpine Inn, which

lay around the next curve. Her stomach muscles tensed as she rounded the bend and saw the lights twinkling through the branches of the firs. In spite of her frantic rehearsals all afternoon, she couldn't think of a single phrase to say to Blake that wouldn't sound trite.

Hi, I gave you our receipt book by mistake this afternoon. Can I have it back, please? He was going to think she'd done it on purpose. She wondered if he'd discovered the mistake and was hoping she would bring him his book and stay for dinner. If so, he was in for a big disappointment.

Carefully, she applied the brakes and turned into the parking lot. There were no more than a half-dozen cars parked outside the main doors. By tomorrow night the hotel would be filled with ski enthusiasts but on weekdays, for the most part, the parking lot was practically deserted.

Walking into the warmth of the hotel lobby, Gail unbuttoned her coat. Flames leaped from the crackling logs in the fireplace, and beneath the knotty-pine staircase an enormous vending machine looked out of place in its rustic setting.

A wizened little man sat behind the counter, and he gave her a toothless grin as she approached. "What brings you out to the Alpine on a cold night?"

"Hi, Sam. I'm here on business." She held up the package in her hand. "One of your guests left a book at the store. I'm just dropping it off for him."

Sam narrowed his eyes. "Which one might that be, then?"

"Blake Foster."

Sam nodded. "Oh, him. Quiet, that one. Don't like to talk none."

Refusing to be drawn into a discussion about Blake, Gail smiled. "Is he in?"

"Was, last I know. Wait a minute, I'll call the room."

Gail's heart began to slowly pound as Sam lifted the receiver and punched out a number. After a moment he spoke into the phone. "Mr. Foster? Got a visitor down here for you."

Blake must have asked who it was, as Sam looked at Gail and winked. "It's the pretty lady from The Book Nook. She says she has a book for you."

"Ask him—" Gail began, but Sam had already replaced the receiver.

He jerked his head in the direction of the stairs. "He says to go on up. Room 25, end of the hallway."

Thoroughly flustered, Gail began to stammer. "I...I thought he'd come down here to get it. I mean... Perhaps I should... "

Sam frowned. "Something wrong? He's not bothering you, is he?"

"Oh, no," Gail said hastily. "It's just that I... " She lifted her shoulders in a helpless gesture. "Room 25?"

"Room 25," Sam echoed solemnly.

"Thank you."

"You're entirely welcome."

Conscious of Sam's eyes on her, she slowly climbed the stairs to the second floor.

Polly had told her that the Alpine Inn had been built long before the modern motels came into being. Although an elevator had been added in later years, it was hidden at the rear of the building. The ski crowd preferred the primitive charm of the magnificent staircase.

Gail was beginning to wish she'd used the elevator by the time she reached the top of the stairs. She seemed to have lost all the strength from her legs.

Reaching the door numbered twenty-five, she paused in front of it, willing her heart to quit thumping against her ribs. Blake was just a man, she told herself fiercely. And she was a grown woman, well able to deal with anything he might throw at her. Defiantly, she raised her hand and knocked on the door.

It opened almost at once. She was unprepared for the little rush of pleasure she felt at the sight of him. He wore dark gray slacks with a black-and-gray sweater, and looked as if he'd just come off the slopes.

"I gave you the wrong book this afternoon," she blurted out, before he could say anything. "I believe you have our receipt book by mistake."

His expression didn't change, except for an almost-imperceptible twitch of his eyebrow. "You disappoint me," he said, opening the door wider. "I was hoping you'd changed your mind about dinner."

She shook her head. "Sorry. My daughter is waiting for me."

"Downstairs?"

"At the baby-sitter's."

"Ah, then surely you can have a drink with me. It's the least I can do after you came all this way to give me my book."

"And to pick up the receipt book," she reminded him. It seemed important to make sure that was clear.

"And to pick up the receipt book." The slight inflection in his voice suggested he was amused. "I'll get it."

She waited awkwardly by the door until he reappeared, the receipt book in his hand.

"I suppose there's no point in asking you to come in," he said, as he handed it to her.

She did her best to sound indifferent. "Thanks, but I have to pick up Annie."

"Ah, yes...Annie. Surely she wouldn't mind if you were a few minutes late? I'd like to buy you that drink."

"I really shouldn't...." Her voice trailed off as he gave her a wistful smile.

"I hate drinking alone. I promise I won't keep you long.

You can call your baby-sitter from here, if you like, and let her know you'll be detained for a few minutes."

She'd already done that, but she wasn't about to admit it to him. "Well..."

"It would mean a very great deal to a lonely stranger in a strange town who doesn't know a soul and who's bored with TV and is dying for some intelligent conversation." He pressed his hand over his heart in a dramatic gesture of despair.

He looked so comically pitiful she had to laugh. "I had no idea it was that bad."

His smile reminded her why she was wary of him. He was just a little too charming. He unsettled her, made her feel hopelessly gauche—something she'd never felt before. She didn't like losing her composure this way.

Still, she thought, it wouldn't hurt to have a quick drink with him. Polly was right; it had been a very long time since she'd had any kind of social life. Blake Foster might disturb her self-assurance, but he was fun to talk to, and as long as she remained impervious to his unmistakable charisma, no harm could come of it.

"I guess I could manage a few minutes," she said, trying to ignore her little spasm of excitement.

"Great. Do you want to call?"

"No, I really don't plan on being that long."

He didn't give her any argument. Stepping into the hallway, he closed the door behind him. "Shall we go?"

Walking side by side down the quiet corridor gave her an absurd sense of intimacy. Already she was beginning to regret her decision. She should have left right away. She would have been halfway to Darcie's by now. She shouldn't have—

"I hope that scowl doesn't mean you've changed your mind," Blake said, startling her out of her thoughts.

Flustered, she shook her head. Luckily the elevator doors opened just then, giving her an excuse not to answer him.

"Have you done much sight-seeing yet?" she asked, when they were seated in the corner of the dimly lit bar. It seemed safer to ask the questions; then he couldn't ask any of his own.

"Not yet." Blake smiled at the waitress who hovered at his elbow. "I'll have a light beer." He glanced across at Gail.

"Just a soda," she said. "I'm driving."

The waitress disappeared, and Gail looked back at Blake. He was watching her, with an odd expression on his face that vanished a second after she'd registered it.

"So tell me about the local attractions," he said, leaning back in his chair. "So far, all I've found of interest in the guidebook is hiking trails, or fishing in the lakes, neither of which appeals to me much in this weather."

She hesitated, wondering why he had come to this tiny backwoods town if he was looking for excitement. "There isn't much more. Most people who come here like to ski or climb mountains. Or simply commune with nature, I guess. A lot of people like to get away from their hectic lives and just do nothing but sit around and contemplate their navel."

He laughed at that, and the sound of it washed over her, relaxing her tension. "That's more or less what I had in mind, though I'd prefer to do it somewhere other than a hotel room. Are there any bus tours of the area? I'd like to get a closer look at the mountains."

"Not that I know of. You'd have to go into Parkerville for that kind of thing."

"That's the nearest big town, right?"

"Right. It's about fifty miles east of here." She told him what little she knew of the town and mentioned Fircrest Lodge again. He seemed genuinely interested in her job at the bookstore, and she gladly answered his questions. She enjoyed her work and didn't often have a chance to talk about it.

Glancing at her watch a while later, she was startled to see how quickly the time had passed. "I must be going," she said, gathering up her purse. "I had no idea it was so late."

"Too late to go home and cook, right?" Blake smiled at her across the table. "Please let me buy you dinner. I feel guilty for keeping you so long, and I would really enjoy your company. I hate eating alone even more than I hate drinking alone."

She was enjoying herself, she had to admit. The more she was with him, the more relaxed she felt. He no longer seemed threatening. In fact, she couldn't imagine why she had ever felt that way about him. The only danger lay in the fact that his masculine appeal was hard to resist, something she would have to guard against. She was reasonably sure that she could manage that.

Looking up, she found him watching her with a hopeful expression on his face she found impossible to resist. "I'd like that," she said finally, rising to her feet. "But I must call my baby-sitter and ask her to keep Annie overnight."

"Of course. Can I order you a drink?"

She hesitated. Perhaps one wouldn't hurt. "I'll have a glass of Chardonnay with dinner," she replied, then left the room to look for a phone.

She found one in the lobby, and quickly dialed Darcie's number. The sitter was only too happy to keep Heather. "I gave her a plate of spaghetti for supper," she said, "so don't worry. Go ahead and have a good time. Anyone I know?"

"I told you, it's business."

Gail winced when she heard Darcie's soft laugh. "Yeah, sure. Have a good time anyway, okay?"

Promising to call again when she got home, Gail hung up and went back to the bar. Blake was waiting for her, and together they walked into the dining room, where they were seated at a table by the window.

Only one other table was occupied—by an elderly couple who paid no attention to the new arrivals. After ordering the salmon, Gail settled back in her chair to enjoy her wine.

An old-fashioned oil lamp cast a soft glow across the cream tablecloth. The view from the window was obscured by the darkness, except for the lanterns hung in the lower branches of the pines.

A log fire crackled in the corner fireplace, adding a cozy warmth to the room, the flames reflecting in the antique brass ornaments that hung on the walls.

Gail could feel her tension slipping away as she took another sip of wine. Blake had ordered bourbon for himself and sat gazing into the glass as if deep in thought. Looking at the strong sweep of his jaw, Gail felt a tiny quiver of awareness. Blake Foster was a good-looking man.

He glanced up, and to her embarrassment caught her staring at him. "This is nice," he said, smiling at her.

She nodded. "How did you hear about Mellow Springs? It's not exactly on the tourist map. I should have thought you'd find mountains a lot closer to home than this."

For an instant she thought she saw a wary look in his eyes, but then he smiled. "A couple of friends of mine stayed here in the summer. They warned me it wasn't a good time of year to come, but I was looking for some peace and quiet, and this little town sounded perfect."

"Do you often travel alone?"

"Yes, I do."

The emphatic answer surprised her. She didn't respond right away, and after a moment he added, "Have you always worked in a bookstore? Before you came here, I mean."

She could feel her nerves tightening again. "No, though I've worked in other stores. I really like working with books. I've always loved reading and I enjoy talking to the customers. I'm amazed at what I've learned in the few months I've been at The Book Nook."

To her relief the waitress arrived just then with their order. The conversation drifted to safer ground while they ate. Gail particularly enjoyed a lively discussion on the rising stars of country music, a topic on which she could hold her own.

In fact, she was intrigued to discover that she had several things in common with Blake. They both liked classic movies and country music; they shared an indifference to Chinese food while both liked Mexican, and although Blake admitted he didn't have time to do much reading, the few books he had read were among Gail's favorites.

Relaxing with a cup of coffee after the dishes had been cleared away, Gail had to admit she hadn't enjoyed herself this much in years. The wine, together with Blake's easygoing manner, had softened the edges of her uneasiness and she was sorry to see the evening come to an end.

"I've really enjoyed this," Blake said, echoing her thoughts. "We must do it again."

She gave him a vague smile, reluctant to commit herself, in spite of the good time she'd had. "How long will you be staying here?"

He shrugged. "That depends."

He didn't elaborate, although she had the distinct feeling that she would have a great deal to do with the length of his visit. The thought made her uncomfortable. She couldn't afford to forget for one minute why she was in Mellow Springs. She felt guilty, aware that she was encouraging this nice man when she had no intention of doing so.

"What made you pick Mellow Springs to start over?"

he asked, breaking into her thoughts. "I'm surprised that someone with your vitality would want to bury herself in a backwoods town like this one."

The question had caught her off guard. For a moment she couldn't remember what she'd already told him. She played with her teaspoon, trying to compose her thoughts. "I came from a small town," she said at last. "I liked the feel of this one. I think you can have a certain sense of belonging in a small town that isn't there in the city. In a town like Mellow Springs you get to know the people. In a city you can live for years in one place and never know your neighbors."

"It sounds as if you've lived in a city at some time in your life."

She could feel her tension returning. The questions were casual enough, but still they were questions she didn't want to answer.

"For a while," she said lightly. "What about you? Do you like living in the city?"

"It has its moments. I like the convenience of having everything practically on the doorstep. When a man lives alone, as I do, ordering in meals becomes a necessity."

"I can imagine. Your job must keep you fairly busy, though."

"It can get pretty hectic at times. That's why I wanted to get away to the great outdoors. I needed to unwind."

Gail laughed. "That, at least, you should be able to do in Mellow Springs."

"It must be lonely for you, though, especially with a small daughter. What do you do for amusement?"

"Oh, Annie's easy to please. Give her crayons or finger paints and she'll be happy for hours. Sometimes I take her into Parkerville. They have a children's museum there and that's her favorite place in the whole world. She can play with all those neat gadgets and gizmos without me constantly warning her not to touch."

He smiled. "Sounds like a kids' paradise."

"And mine. I don't have to worry about her hurting anything." She decided to ask the question that had been on her mind all evening. "Do you have kids?"

He shook his head. "No. I was married once, but it didn't last long. My biggest regret in life is missing out on being a father. I'd really like to meet Annie. I think we'd get along just great."

That was something she couldn't allow to happen, Gail thought nervously. Heather could easily let slip her real name. Here in Mellow Springs, no one was ever likely to recognize the name. But Blake lived in Seattle. Frank had been a recognized businessman in Portland. The case had made headlines in the papers and on television—big enough that the story could easily have been carried by the Seattle media.

Apart from the fact that she wanted to keep her whereabouts secret, she was uncomfortably aware of another reason she wanted to keep the truth from him. His approval of her was beginning to matter to her. And that could very well prove dangerous for them both.

Chapter 3

Aware that Blake was waiting for her response, Gail struggled to pull her thoughts together. It seemed safer just to ignore the subject of her daughter. She reached for her coffee, searching for a question to ask him. "How long have you lived in Seattle? I lived near Green Lake for a while when I was a kid. It's grown considerably by now, I imagine."

For a moment he looked taken aback, and she felt guilty for cutting him off the topic of meeting Heather. But then he answered her easily enough. "I haven't lived there very long at all, as a matter of fact. I'm still finding my way around the city. I haven't had much time to explore. My job keeps me pretty busy."

"Where did you live before that?"

"The East Coast." He grinned at her. "I'm ready for some dessert. How about you?"

She shook her head. "Oh, I couldn't. I've eaten too much already."

It wasn't until later, as she was driving home, that she wondered if he'd deliberately changed the subject when she'd questioned him about where he'd lived before Seattle. It seemed odd that someone in real estate wouldn't know his way around the city, now that she thought about it. And he didn't sound as if he'd come from the East Coast.

Impatient with her suspicions, she reminded herself that a lot of people from the East Coast didn't have that much of an accent. It just depended where in the East they'd lived. As for Blake finding his way around Seattle, it was a sprawling city and not easy to become familiar with. She was overreacting again.

After letting herself into the house, she gave Darcie a quick call to satisfy herself that Heather had settled down for the night. Reluctant to field any more of Darcie's questions, she cut the conversation short and hung up.

In spite of her weariness, she didn't feel like going to bed. She made herself a cup of warm milk and took it into the living room, where she sank into her favorite armchair and tried not to think about Blake.

After flipping through the pages of a magazine, she had to admit she wasn't having much success in keeping him out of her mind. She kept remembering his deep chuckle, the way his eyes rested warmly on her face, the appealing twitch at the corner of his mouth whenever he was amused by something she said.

He was good company. He'd made her feel more alive, more aware of herself. She'd never had much of a sense of humor—there had been little to laugh at in her life. Yet she'd found herself trading quips with Blake as if she'd always been the life and soul of the party. It was fun and exhilarating to know she could make him laugh.

She leaned back in her chair and closed her eyes. She could see him so clearly in her mind—his gray eyes, sometimes guarded, mostly warm and sympathetic, and his thick, dark hair curling slightly on his nape.

She could picture his mouth, the hard lines softened by his smile. She could imagine what it must be like to be kissed by him. If only she could let things go that far, instead of having to hide behind a different identity.

Her eyes snapped open and she sat up. This was insane. Blake was simply amusing himself while on vacation. He was simply passing through her life and would soon be on his way back to Seattle.

Which was just as well. There could never be a future for her with someone like Blake Foster—or with any man, for that matter. If he learned the truth, he would soon back off. How could any man be interested in a woman suspected of having plotted to kill her own husband?

Leaving her milk untouched, she hauled herself to her feet. Perhaps, once she was in bed, she would feel more like sleeping. She wandered into the bedroom, her gaze moving instinctively to the dark space under the bed.

She hesitated, then gave in to the impulse. Reaching underneath the bed, she found the box she'd hidden there.

It was all there inside.

As she took out the newspaper clippings, she could feel the horror of those days creep over her. Almost against her will, she began to read, sitting there on the edge of the bed alone in the empty house.

The headlines shrieked from the front page. Local Retailer Brutally Murdered. Wife Suspected in Love Triangle.

Even now, months later, the shock of those words numbed her. She'd found Frank dead in the office of the furniture store he'd owned. He'd been lying in the corner, covered with blood from the gunshot wound that had killed him.

Frank's brother, Mike, had been arrested the next day.

The day after that, the police had come for her. Mike Stevens had implicated her in the murder.

In spite of her frantic denials of any wrongdoing or conspiracy, Mike had insisted that she had helped plan the murder. The prosecution did its best to link her romantically with him—a man she despised almost as much as she hated her husband. There were witnesses who claimed they'd overheard Frank arguing with her over Mike.

Thanks to an astute lawyer, she'd been released for lack of evidence before the trial. But not before Mike had promised her that she would never be free. In his twisted mind she'd tempted him, then rejected and betrayed him. He'd killed his brother because of her and she would have to pay. He had friends on the outside who would help him, he told her. He would destroy what mattered to her the most. Her daughter.

The trial had caused a sensation in what was, after all, a fairly small city. The final verdict was declared and Mike was convicted, still swearing she had helped him. Then came the recriminations—the sidelong glances, the suspicious looks. She knew what they were thinking...that she was guilty. They'd let her go because they couldn't prove anything, but she was guilty.

The phone calls in the night had started soon after the trial. Certain that she was being followed, and terrified for Heather's safety, she'd told the police about Mike's threat. They'd dismissed it as a lovers' quarrel, making it clear they still believed his story that she was romantically involved with him.

Knowing she could expect no help from them, and afraid that Mike might somehow find a way to harm Heather, she had sold all her personal possessions, packed up what little she'd kept and headed out of town. She hadn't stopped until she'd hit Mellow Springs.

Carefully, Gail put the newspaper clippings away and

locked the box again. Her hands trembled as she pushed
the box far back under the bed. Heather must never know.
If Gail had to spend the rest of her life living a lie, she
could never let her daughter know the truth.

As long as Heather was Annie Morris, she was safe. It
was better she didn't know the truth. Not only that, if
Heather ever heard about Mike's accusations, there would
always be a shadow of doubt in her mind about her mother.
Gail was not about to risk losing her daughter because of
Mike's lies.

Pacing back and forth across the carpet of his hotel room,
Blake tried to put things into perspective. So he was attracted to the woman. He'd been attracted to women before
and hadn't done anything about it.

He wasn't sure why she appealed to him more than any
other woman. True, she was nice to look at, as well as
intelligent and warmhearted. But it was more than that.
Maybe it was because she was such a damn good listener.

He'd told her more about himself than he'd meant to,
and once or twice he'd let his guard down enough to blow
his cover. Luckily she hadn't picked up on it.

She had a way of slipping past his defenses, making him
forget everything except how much he wanted her in his
bed.

Cursing, Blake strode to the window and opened it. Cold
air rushed in at him, laced with flakes of snow. He drew
in deep gulps of it, trying to erase the heat of his erotic
yearnings.

He had to get off this merry-go-round, he thought in
desperation. The longer he was around her, the more intense his feelings were likely to grow.

He should quit while he was still ahead, or he would
botch up the job when the time came. He couldn't allow
his emotions to sway his judgment—it was the number-one

rule in his profession. He'd learned that the hard away, a few years back.

He closed his mind to the memory of dead bodies strewn across a dark wet street. They'd assured him it wasn't his fault. He'd known better. He hadn't done his job right. He'd trained them, and they should have been able to handle it. But they hadn't. And they'd died. No matter what anyone said, deep down he knew he had to answer for that, some day. He could only hope that the chips weren't being called in now.

The truth was, he told himself, he had one hell of a problem. He had to stick with her until he could make his move. The best way he could do that was to pretend he was interested in her. Not that he had to do much pretending. How the hell was he supposed to ignore what she was doing to his mind, let alone his body?

He slammed the window shut and reached for the bourbon he'd taken from the bar earlier that evening. He would have to make sure he ignored her effect on him—that was the bottom line. She had lived in Seattle; she could easily trip him up. He would have to keep his mind clear of everything except his cover, and the reason he was here. Heaven help him.

All the next day Gail did her best to concentrate on her job. It wasn't easy. Every time the door opened her heart skipped crazily, while she half hoped, half dreaded she would see Blake's tall figure striding into the store.

Polly gave up teasing her after the first few dry comments, apparently sensing that Gail was in no mood for joking.

Once more she avoided the diner at lunchtime, then spent the afternoon wishing she'd had the courage to go there. When the last customer had finally left for the day, she thankfully helped Polly close up shop. In spite of her best efforts, she couldn't ignore the dull ache of disappointment.

Despite her apprehension, she'd felt quite sure Blake would find an excuse to call in to see her, and the fact that he hadn't, told her that he wasn't as interested as he'd appeared.

It didn't help to remind herself that he was on vacation, after all, and had better things to do than hang around town on the off chance he might spend a few minutes with her.

He was most likely spending his day exploring the mountains, she decided, and had forgotten all about the casual acquaintance he'd had dinner with the night before. He'd more or less told her he'd invited her out of boredom, and had grasped the opportunity to pass some time with someone to keep from feeling lonely.

It didn't help, either, to remind herself that it was for the best. She kept going over their conversation, wondering if she'd said something to offend him. She could think of nothing except, perhaps, ignoring his wanting to meet Heather. And that was definitely for the best.

She spent the evening playing with Heather to make up for the night before. After putting her daughter to bed, she decided to go to bed early herself. Again she dreamed of two men fighting each other.

At first she thought they were Mike and Frank, but then she realized Mike was fighting Blake. They were struggling over a gun, and she knew that any second it was going to fire and someone would die. She must have cried out, as she awoke to find Heather standing by the bed, her eyes wide with fear, shaking her by the arm and mumbling her name over and over.

"Oh, honey, I'm sorry, did I wake you?" Gail drew the trembling body into her arms and cuddled her. "Mommy just had a bad dream, that's all. You have bad dreams sometimes, don't you?"

Heather sniffed. "Sometimes."

"Well, then you know that it's only a dream and it goes away when you wake up, right?"

Heather slowly nodded. "Are you frightened, Mommy?"

"No, I'm not frightened. But tell you what, why don't you keep me company tonight and sleep in my bed with me? Would you like that?"

Heather's face brightened. "Can we go sledding tomorrow? I don't have to go to school and you don't have to go to work."

Still feeling guilty for waking her daughter, Gail relented. Thank heavens for a boss who gave her weekends off, she thought gratefully. "We have to go buy you some new shoes in the morning, but if you like, we'll go up to the mountains after that."

"Yeah!" Heather bounced up and down in the bed. "Can I take Fuzzy?"

Gail smiled. Fuzzy was a well-worn bear with one tattered ear, and Heather never went anywhere without it. Darcie had once joked that she thought Fuzzy was permanently attached to Heather's hand.

"Of course, you can take Fuzzy." She snuggled down with her daughter under the covers. "But you'd better go back to sleep right away if you want to have lots of energy for the bunny slopes tomorrow."

To her relief, the little girl drifted off to sleep almost at once, although it was some time before Gail could relax enough to join her.

She woke up the next morning feeling exhausted, and if it hadn't been for her promise to her daughter, she might have spent the day in front of the fire with a good book.

The shopping trip didn't help matters. Heather tried on several pairs of shoes, none of which she liked, so Gail had to choose for her, which resulted in an argument with her daughter.

Gail threatened to call off the trip to the mountains if Heather didn't behave. The shoes finally bought and wrapped, Gail took her daughter by the hand and thankfully left the store.

Dark gray clouds piled high above the mountain peaks warned of yet another storm brewing in the distance. In spite of the sunshine bathing the sidewalks, Gail could smell snow in the air as she crossed the street to the car. The chilly wind tugged at her hair, sweeping it across her face. She brushed it back with her gloved hand, and as she did so, caught sight of a familiar figure striding purposefully toward her.

For an instant her heart leaped, then she remembered Heather at her side. There didn't seem to be any way to avoid the meeting, short of being downright rude.

Blake halted in front of her, his carefree grin causing her pulse to quicken. "I was hoping I'd see you. Hawkeye told me you don't work on the weekends."

She had to smile. "I have Saturdays off, and Polly closes the store on Sundays."

"So she told me."

Gail's heart skipped a beat as he looked down at Heather, who was staring up at him, Fuzzy clutched firmly in her hand. "This must be Annie." He hunkered down in front of the little girl, his head just about on a level with hers.

Heather regarded him gravely, but didn't speak.

"This is Mr. Foster, Annie," Gail said, striving to sound offhand. "Say hello to him."

"Hello," Heather said shyly.

"You can call me Uncle Blake." He glanced up at Gail, his eyes crinkling at the corners. "Is that all right with you?"

"Of course." Conscious of her faded jeans and red

jacket that had been washed once too often, she wished she'd worn something a bit more presentable.

Although Blake wore jeans with his leather jacket, somehow he still managed to maintain his downtown image.

"We bought some new shoes," Heather announced, apparently deciding that it was okay to confide in the stranger.

"Is that right? Can I see them?"

Heather pointed to the package Gail held. "They're in there."

Blake took the bag from her, drew out the shoe box and opened it. "Very nice," he murmured, studying the black patent-leather shoes. "I bet you look real grown-up in these."

He must have said the right thing, as Heather bestowed on him the ultimate honor. "This is Fuzzy," she said, thrusting the bear at him. "You can kiss him."

In spite of her anxiety, a tiny thrill teased Gail's heart as she watched Blake touch the bear's nose with his lips. "Hey, Fuzzy," he said softly. "I'm very happy to meet you."

Heather giggled. "Fuzzy's going sledding with us. Can you come, too?"

Gail's uneasy smile vanished. "Honey, Uncle Blake has better things to do, I'm sure. Perhaps we'll ask him another time."

Heather looked up at her, her lower lip jutting ominously. "I want him to come now."

Blake got slowly to his feet. "I'd like to come," he said, winking at Heather. "That's if I won't be in the way?"

"Can he come, Mommy? Can he?"

She couldn't think of a single reason to refuse. Blake was watching her, a half smile on his face and his eyes full of hope.

"Well, if you're sure you want to compete on the slopes

with hordes of screaming children intent on mowing you down..."

"I'd love it." He took hold of Heather's hand. "Come on, we can go in my car."

"But—" Gail got no further. Heart pounding with apprehension, she watched Blake lead her daughter back across to the road to where a black sedan sat at the curb.

"Oh, boy, look how big it is!" Heather exclaimed, as Blake opened the door and she scrambled into the front seat.

"We'll sit in the back." Gail reached for her daughter, but Blake closed his fingers around her arm.

"We can all sit up front. There's plenty of room."

Gail wasn't so sure about that. Even with Heather fidgeting with excitement between them, she was intensely aware of Blake sitting mere inches away.

She felt a little like one of the heroines in the Saturday-matinee movies, tied to the tracks waiting for the train to thunder into view. Any moment she expected Heather to say something that would tell Blake she'd lied to him.

Apparently unaware of her agitation, Blake chatted easily with Heather, asking about her school and her friends at the baby-sitter's. Heather was only too happy to give him all the numerous details that made up her day, while Gail listened with every nerve quivering, ready to jump in if her daughter said the wrong thing.

After a while, when it appeared that the worst wasn't about to happen, Gail forced herself to ease her fears. Even if Heather did mention her real name, it would be easy enough to explain it away as childish imagination. In any case, it was unlikely that Blake would pick up on it.

In fact, the more she thought about it, the more she managed to convince herself that she was being melodramatic about the entire thing. What did it matter, anyway? Within the next few days, Blake would be on his way back to

Seattle, and she would never see him again. She might as well enjoy the time she had with him, and stop worrying about something that might never happen.

Settling back in her seat, she allowed her tense muscles to relax. She always enjoyed the drive to the mountain, and now that she wasn't behind the wheel she could really appreciate it.

The view was quite spectacular. As the car climbed the gentle incline up the mountain, the roadside gradually fell away, allowing glimpses through the trees of the valley below. Thick stands of firs, their branches weighed down by glistening snow, dotted the slopes as far as the eye could see.

Although the sun was gradually disappearing behind a haze of high cloud, reflection from the deepening snow on the sides of the road was still bright enough to dazzle her eyes.

Heather chatted nonstop, pointing out squirrels and blue jays, and shrieked with delight when she caught a brief glimpse of a deer moving through the woods.

Gail was conscious of Blake sending her a sidelong glance now and again, but she was content to let him keep Heather amused with his comments, while she absorbed the quiet beauty of the mountainside.

They arrived at the parking lot just as the sun slipped behind an enormous black cloud. Gail climbed out of the car and pulled on a white wool cap, shivering in the keen bite of the wind. Screams and shouts of laughter echoed across the snow as brave souls raced down the slopes on large metal disks.

Heather scrambled out, her cheeks turning red with excitement. "Come on, Mommy!" she cried, tugging on Gail's hand. "Let's hurry!"

Gail caught sight of Blake's face as he watched the revelers on the slopes. He looked as if he were about to step off a cliff into a raging torrent.

"You've never done this before, have you?" she said, hazarding a guess.

He looked at her, his expression rueful. "Never. But it looks like fun."

"It is, and much easier than it looks. You just sit tight and hang on."

"You really ride those things?"

She laughed. "I don't have much choice. I don't like Heather going up there alone and I have to get down again once I'm up there."

"You can't just walk down?"

"I can, but that means leaving Heather alone at the bottom until I get back." She tilted her head to one side and gave him a sly look. "Don't tell me you're afraid to ride the bunny slopes, Mr. Foster?"

"Afraid?" He grabbed hold of Heather's hand. "I'm more worried about making a fool of myself. Let's go. Anything this little squirt can do, I can do, too."

He was putting on a show for her benefit, Gail decided, as she followed the big man and her daughter to the rental office. She simply couldn't imagine Blake Foster being afraid of anything. Or caring about his image, for that matter.

They rented three disks, and Heather eagerly dragged hers toward the hill, followed more slowly by Gail and Blake. "If I break my leg," Blake commented, "I'm counting on you to rescue me off the mountain."

Gail laughed. "You'll be too close to the ground to worry about breaking your leg—unless you're really unlucky."

"I'll take your word for it." He glanced at her. "I hope you didn't mind me coming along."

"Not at all," she said lightly. "I'm glad of the company. And you're a big hit with Fuzzy."

He smiled at that. "Thanks, but I'm more concerned about you. You were so quiet coming up in the car, I wondered if you were mad at me for engineering an invitation."

"'Engineering'? I thought it was Annie doing all the pressuring."

"Well, I didn't exactly discourage the idea. I guess I jumped at the chance to spend more time with you. Not to mention the opportunity to risk life and limb on the slopes."

She gave him a quizzical look. "I guess you didn't take advantage of all the skiing opportunities on the East Coast."

He shook his head. "This is the closest I've ever been to a mountain. I just hope I don't disgrace myself."

He looked so worried she had to laugh. "Come on," she said, dragging her disk ahead of him. "Just follow Annie. You'll be fine."

She had to admit to a moment or two of apprehension as she watched him climb aboard the disk. Huge flakes of snow began feathering down as he sat poised at the top of the slope with his long legs tucked under his chin, both hands gripping the sides and his shoulders hunched against the cold.

The wind tumbled his hair across his forehead, and he looked up at her with a grin. In that moment he lost his slick, city attitude. He looked more like a cowboy getting ready to ride a rambunctious bull.

Heather, who had been waiting impatiently for her turn, shoved off with a loud shriek. Blake watched her go, and shuddered. Gail climbed onto her disk and gave him the thumbs-up sign.

He raised his hand in answer. "See you at the bottom." The next instant he was gone, hurtling down the slope after Heather as if he'd grown up on the mountain.

He managed perfectly, as she'd known he would, sliding to a graceful stop as the slope leveled out. She'd been right. All that apprehension had been contrived to get her sympathy. Shaking her head in amusement, she launched herself down the hill.

The rush of wind in her face took her breath away. Trees flashed by in a blur of green as she sped down the slope, and she leaned back slightly to control the bucking disk. Too far and she would flip over backward; not far enough and she could spin sideways and tip over.

She reached the bottom and skidded to a halt just a few feet from where Heather and Blake waited for her. Breathless and laughing, she started to her feet. Blake offered her his hand and she took it, feeling the strong tug of his fingers as he pulled her up.

"Congratulations, Mr. Foster," she said breathlessly. "You made it."

As she straightened, her foot slipped and she almost lost her balance. Without thinking, she made a grab for his jacket just as his hands caught her under the arms.

For one searing moment he held her close as he steadied her on her feet. She looked up to thank him, and all at once it seemed as if the entire world had gone still. The shrieks of laughter faded into oblivion as his intense gaze held her motionless.

He was near enough for her to smell the faint fragrance of his musky aftershave. She was acutely conscious of his hands gripping her sides, his thumbs brushing her breasts. The cold air froze her breath as she looked into his eyes, and her heartbeat quickened when she saw her own turmoil mirrored there.

She imagined for an instant that she saw a need as potent as her own, and then it was gone. In its place she saw subtle-but-unmistakable warning.

Shaken, she pulled away from him, and his hands

dropped to his sides. Turning to Heather, he patted her lightly on the head. "That was fun. Wanna do it again?"

"Yeah!" Heather yelled, and rushed off, Fuzzy still tucked securely under her arm.

For the rest of the afternoon Gail struggled with the memory of that charged moment. She must have imagined the warning, she told herself, as she watched her daughter throw snowballs at Blake while he gamely ducked to avoid them. She had to stop seeing a threat lurking in every corner. She would never have any peace until she rid herself of her senseless fears.

She had to smile in spite of herself as Blake received a snowball smack in the face. Heather rushed off, shrieking at the top of her lungs as he stooped to gather a handful of snow. Then, instead of throwing the snowball at her daughter, he twisted his body at the last minute and aimed it at her.

She ducked, and the snowball whizzed past her ear, barely grazing her shoulder. Forgetting her uneasiness, she marshaled her own ammunition and joined in the fight.

The snow fell thick and fast by the time Gail called a halt to the merriment. Heather's hair was plastered to her face around the edges of her wool cap, and Blake looked as if he'd just stepped out of a shower.

Disturbed by the image conjured up by that particular thought, Gail concentrated on bundling Heather back into the car. "A hot bath for you when we get home, young lady," she said, as Blake climbed in behind the wheel.

"That sounds like a great idea." Blake started the engine and backed the car out. "I have to stop on the way home for gas." He peered up at the sky. "Let's hope this doesn't keep up for long."

Snow covered the windshield as they started down the incline. The wipers swept it aside to leave it bunched at the outer edges of the window. Watching the icy mass pile up,

Gail said anxiously, "I hope we aren't leaving too late to come off the mountain."

"Don't worry, I'm good at this." Blake glanced at her over Heather's head. "I'll take it easy."

She nodded, weariness creeping over her now that she was relaxing in the warmth of the car.

Heather was already half asleep. She stirred, however, when Blake asked, "Is anyone hungry?"

"Me," Heather said sleepily.

"You're always hungry." Gail smiled at her. "I'll fix you a hamburger when we get home."

"I've got a better idea," Blake said, his gaze concentrated on the road ahead. "How about I buy everyone hamburgers on the way home?"

"I think I'd better get her home. She's had a long day and she's awfully wet." Gail hesitated, tempted to invite him back to the house for dinner. Before she could voice the thought, however, he nodded.

"Okay. You're probably right. So how about this, then? Suppose I pick you both up tomorrow morning, and we'll drive into Parkerville. I'd like to take a look at that children's museum you were telling me about."

Heather opened her eyes wide. "Yeah! Can we, Mommy? Can we go?"

She should refuse, Gail thought, eyeing her daughter's pleading face. Not only would it be hard for her to see Blake leave if she continued to spend time with him, it would be hard on Heather, too, if she became very fond of him.

"I don't know, honey," she said carefully. "There's so much that needs doing at home. Perhaps we should just stay home tomorrow and take care of the chores."

"Oh, please, Mommy, please, please, please? I really want to go to the children's museum."

Gail sighed. He couldn't have picked a more tempting proposition as far as Heather was concerned. She glanced over at him, but he seemed absorbed in the road ahead, his eyes half narrowed against the glare of the headlights on the snow.

For once he hadn't tried to pressure her. She appreciated that. She tried not to notice his hands, sure and strong on the wheel. She noticed a few dark hairs sprinkled across the backs of his wrists, and her shiver had nothing to do with the cold. Almost without conscious thought she heard herself say, "I guess it wouldn't hurt this once."

He gave her a quick glance of approval. "I'll pick you up at eleven in the morning. We'll have lunch in town. It will make a change from the diner."

She looked away, wondering if he'd waited for her there the past two days. "That would be nice."

Heather, it seemed, had drifted off to sleep, as she made no sound.

"I'll look forward to it." He was quiet for a moment, then added, "You'll have to tell me where you live, since I'll be dropping you off at your car. Unless I follow you home."

Her pulse fluttered, and she kept her gaze on the swirling snow. "That might be easier. Though it's not difficult to find."

"I'd rather follow you. Then I'll know you arrived home safely."

"I'll be fine. I'm getting used to driving in the snow."

The silence seemed to stretch between them, while Gail tried desperately to think of something to say. All at once she felt awkward with him again, as if something were expected of her, yet she couldn't think what it could be.

Blake stopped for gas just outside of town, and Heather didn't even wake up. "I had a great time this afternoon," he said, as they were pulling out of the gas station. "Thank you for allowing me to join you. I know how much your weekends with your daughter must mean to you."

"We had fun, too." Gail smiled down at the sleeping

child, whose head nestled against her shoulder. "Annie loves to have someone new to play with."

"She's quite fearless, isn't she?" Blake shook his head. "The way she flung herself down that slope just about gave me a heart attack."

Gail laughed. "Kids bounce off the ground a lot easier than adults. Though I have to admit, the first time she went on her own, I held my breath all the way until she reached the bottom. Up until then, I'd ridden with her, but she kept insisting she wanted to go down by herself. That was one of the toughest moments of my life, watching her take off on that sled all alone. She looked so small and defenseless, I was quite sure she would break her neck."

"She must take after your husband."

For a moment shock blanked out her mind. "Why do you say that?" Aware that her voice had sounded sharp, she made an effort to soften it. "I mean, I've never talked about him. How could you know what he's like?"

He sent her a swift glance. "Take it easy," he said softly. "I'm sorry, I didn't mean to stir up painful memories. It's too soon to talk about him, I should have realized that. It was stupid of me. Please, forgive me?"

She waited until the pounding of her heart subsided before answering him. "It's all right. My husband and I were not... I mean, I'm sad that he died, of course, but I'm not..." Her voice trailed off into an uneasy silence.

Blake didn't speak again until he pulled up behind her car in Main Street. He shut off the engine, and the silence between them seemed to thicken even more.

"I'm sorry," he said quietly. "I only meant that you seem to be the kind of person who weighs everything carefully before crossing the bridge, while Annie charges across without a second thought."

The metaphor was so apt she had to smile. "Please, don't apologize. I try not to think about my husband anymore, that's all.'' She gave Heather a gentle nudge. "I guess I should wake up my daughter."

Heather stirred, murmuring a sleepy protest.

"I hope we're still on for tomorrow?"

She looked at him across Heather's head. In the shadowy light from the streetlamp his features looked softer, his expression wistful. She quickly suppressed the warmth that rushed over her. "Of course we're still on. I'll see you at eleven."

"I'll follow you home."

The wave of tenderness had taken her by surprise. Had Heather not been there, she realized, she might have given in to the impulse to kiss his cheek. Confused by her sudden surge of emotion, she busied herself getting Heather out of the car and into her own compact.

The bone-chilling cold, after the warmth of Blake's sedan, seemed to numb her mind. She switched on the engine and turned up the heat, while Heather grumbled in the seat next to her.

Glancing into the rearview mirror as she drove off, she saw Blake pull out behind her. It gave her a comforting feeling to know he was there, and suddenly she didn't feel cold anymore.

She was crazy to worry about this situation, she told herself as she headed for home. Maybe she was walking down a dead-end street, but at least she could enjoy the trip. And as long as she kept her head, no one would get hurt.

Heather was young enough to soon forget the handsome stranger who had popped briefly in and out of her life. Once more, Gail's glance strayed to the rearview mirror. As for herself, she knew well enough the limitations of this relationship. All she had to do was remember them.

Chapter 4

The next morning Heather impatiently hopped up and down in front of the window long before Blake was due to pick them up.

After answering for the fifth time the question, "Is he coming yet?" Gail suggested that Heather draw a picture for Blake as a thank-you gift for taking them out.

Gail herself couldn't seem to settle down. It had taken her almost an hour to decide what to wear, during which time she'd changed her outfit twice, and even now she wasn't sure she'd made the right choice.

Her yellow sweater seemed okay with her black stretch pants, but she couldn't choose between her dark blue wool reefer and a green quilted jacket she hadn't worn since leaving Portland. She finally decided on the green jacket, then debated whether or not to leave her hair loose or tie it back.

That question was answered when Heather's shriek announced that Blake had arrived, a good fifteen minutes early. Now she didn't have time to tie her hair.

Hurrying to the door to meet him, she almost fell over Heather, who was determined to be the first to greet the visitor. In fact, Blake looked taken aback when the child hurled herself at him the minute Gail had the door open.

Folding his arms around the small body, he gave her a hug. "Guess you're all ready to go, squirt."

He grinned at Gail, and her heart seemed to turn over. At that moment she would have given anything to trade places with her small daughter. "She's been ready to go since the crack of dawn," she said lightly. "I wish I had her vitality."

His gaze flicked over her in a way that warmed her from head to toe. "You do just fine, from what I can see."

"Thanks." The awkwardness that he always seemed to generate in her surfaced once more as she turned away to hunt for her purse.

After locking the front door, she paused for a moment to draw in that first invigorating breath of clean, crisp mountain air. Ever since she'd arrived in Mellow Springs, she had never failed to appreciate the contrast to the city smog she'd left behind. Although Portland was fairly pristine compared to some of the larger cities, its smell of exhaust fumes and fast food was a far cry from the sweet fragrance of snow-covered fir and cedar.

"Come on, Mommy!" Heather complained as she ran down to the black car at the curb.

"Would you like me to drive," Gail offered, "since you did all the driving yesterday?"

"Thanks, but I don't mind driving." He opened the door for her. "I'll need you to navigate, though."

"Of course. It's easy to find. I'm sure Annie could tell you how to get there."

Heather, however, had opted to sit in the back seat. She was still working on her "secret project" and needed the space to spread out her paper and crayons.

That left Gail seated next to Blake in the front. Somehow, without Heather sitting between them, she found it much harder to relax.

The best way to avoid feeling self-conscious with someone, she'd learned long ago, was to ask that person questions about himself. She'd tried that tactic before with Blake, and he'd avoided answering her. Maybe now that he knew her better, he would answer some of the questions she was dying to ask.

She waited until Heather had settled down with her drawing, then asked the obvious question first. "How long have you been in real estate?"

He didn't answer right away. For a long, awkward moment she thought he wasn't going to answer at all. She stole a look at his profile. He stared straight ahead at the road winding in front of them, his hands resting squarely on the wheel.

Finally, after the pause had gone on much too long, he said quietly, "Not very long. I found my previous job too stressful, and I finally quit. It took me a while to find something else."

"What was your previous job?"

He must have expected the question, yet his jaw tensed, as if he resented having to reply. "I was a teacher."

She sensed there was more behind his words than he was saying. She wondered if he'd been in some kind of trouble, and if that was why he was reluctant to talk about his past.

"What did you do before you sold books?" he asked suddenly, startling her out of her thoughts.

Now it was her turn to act evasive. Her mind floundered while she sought for an answer. "I was an accounts clerk for a...department store. I wrote up contracts on purchases, processed credit cards, that kind of thing. All very boring."

She glanced at Heather over her shoulder. The little girl was still absorbed in her drawing. "So tell me about the

East Coast. Whereabouts did you live? You don't have much of an accent."

"I've lived in a lot of places." His laugh sounded a little strained.

"Really? Which place did you like best?"

"I guess it depends on what you consider a perfect environment. For me, that's always been the Northwest."

"I've never been farther east than Montana, but so far I haven't seen anyplace I'd rather live." She sat forward, scanning the highway. "There's a turnoff up here on the left. If you take that you'll cut off about ten miles."

He slowed the car and made the left turn. "You must find Mellow Springs pretty dull after living in a city."

Her pulse skipped. She stared at him, but saw nothing in his expression to alarm her. "I didn't live in a city," she said, her voice rising just a little. "I lived in Newberg. It's a very small town about thirty miles southwest of Portland."

He glanced at her. "You told me you lived in Seattle once."

"Oh." She felt foolish for jumping on his innocent remark. "Well, that was a long time ago, when I was growing up. I left Seattle as soon as I was old enough to fend for myself."

"That must have been tough, growing up in foster homes."

"It was." For an instant a picture of a small child flashed across her mind. The child was herself, and she was crying, clinging to the broad hips of a woman with a kind face and a sad smile.

She felt the lump forming in her throat and forced back the memories. Twisting around, she reached out a hand and ruffled her daughter's hair. "How is everything going back there, honey?"

"Fine." Heather picked up the sheet of paper and studied it. "I'm all done."

"That's good. You want to come up front with me now?"

"Okay." Heather scrambled over the seat and slid between Gail and Blake.

If he realized that she had deliberately ended the conversation, Gail thought, he showed no signs of it. He chatted with Heather, making her laugh with silly jokes, until finally Gail joined in.

The rest of the journey went much faster than usual. In no time at all, it seemed, they were driving down the main street of Parkerville, looking for a place to eat lunch.

Heather, for once, was on her best behavior. Although eager to get to the children's museum, she sat quietly, wading through an enormous plate of spaghetti, while Gail did her best not to notice the way Blake's eyes lit up every time the child spoke to him.

How sad that he'd had no children of his own, she thought, feeling an ache in her heart for him. He would have made a wonderful father. She wondered why he hadn't married again, then remembered his terse reply to her question. *"I was a teacher."*

Again she wondered what kind of tragedy lay behind those brief words. Obviously something he didn't want to talk about. It seemed as though they both had secrets they wanted to keep.

The afternoon passed by much too quickly. Usually Gail kept one eye on the clock, judging how long Heather could stay without overtiring both of them. With Blake there, however, the visit to the museum took on an entirely new spirit of adventure for both Gail and her daughter.

Blake had enough energy for all three of them, it seemed. He appeared to be tireless as he explored prehistoric jungles with Heather, played computer games and taught her how to play "Jingle Bells" with her feet on a giant keyboard.

Heather was ecstatic she'd found such an enthusiastic playmate. As for Gail, she had never before found the exhibits quite so interesting.

When Blake challenged her to a race through an intricate system of mirrored mazes, she eagerly accepted. Heather dashed ahead, though, experience giving her an easy victory.

Gail found herself alone in a narrow corridor facing three possible openings, with dozens of her reflections staring back at her from every conceivable angle.

From somewhere on her left she heard Blake chuckle, and hurled herself at the opening—straight into his arms. Whether he had planned it or not, she couldn't be sure. He held her for a brief instant, then let her go. Unnerved by her reaction to the unexpected contact, she jerked back, out of his reach.

His gaze seemed to burn into her soul, then his features relaxed in a grin. "I win."

Grateful to him for being sensitive enough to ignore the awkward moment, she raised her chin in a challenge. "We're not out yet." She darted past him and plunged once more into the maze of mirrors.

Seconds later she saw the exit and headed for it, well aware that he could easily have outdistanced her. Heather cheered when she saw her mother emerge victorious from the garishly painted exit, followed closely by "Uncle" Blake.

"You let me win," Gail protested, laughing.

"No way." His smile suggested otherwise, however, and once more she had to fight the urge to throw her arms around him and give him a warm hug.

When she finally checked her watch, she was horrified to see that it was almost closing time. "We should leave," she told Blake, over Heather's loud protests. "It's a school day tomorrow."

"Quite right." Blake swung Heather up to sit on his shoulders. "Come on, squirt, let's race Mommy to the car."

Heather slept most of the way home in the back seat, while Gail did her best to sort through her chaotic thoughts. The more time she spent with Blake, the more she was learning to trust him.

She sensed that he was a man of high principles, and whatever trouble he'd faced in the past, it had hurt him badly. It could have been his divorce, or something to do with his abandoned teaching profession. Whatever it was, she was certain he was above reproach.

She had thought she could never trust another person again as long as she lived. She'd been wrong. She knew now that she would be willing to trust Blake with her life.

The question, though, was whether or not she could trust him with her secret. Being a man of high principles, would he be able to accept her story and believe in her innocence, when so many didn't?

He was beginning to care for her, she could tell. It was in his eyes when he looked at her, and in that sudden stillness whenever she got too close to him. Was she throwing away a chance of happiness by keeping him at arm's length?

On the other hand, if she told him her story, she ran the risk of disillusioning him. It would be terrible to see that warm look in his eyes turn cool and watch him struggle to let her down gently.

"I hope I'm not the reason for that scowl," he remarked, scattering her thoughts.

She glanced at him, feeling a little self-conscious. "Of course not. I was thinking about all the chores that didn't get done this weekend."

"I guess I should apologize for that. I've monopolized your time."

"Not at all. I had a wonderful time, and so did Annie. She'll be talking about it for days. It was definitely worth a few missed chores."

"I'm glad about that."

She stared back at the road, trying to make up her mind if it would be a mistake to invite him back to dinner. It would seem ungracious if she didn't, under the circumstances, she decided.

"I have a couple of steaks in the freezer," she said, trying to sound indifferent. "If you haven't anything better to do, you're welcome to stay and have dinner with us."

Again she waited through one of his long pauses, her heart racing with apprehension. Perhaps it hadn't been such a good idea after all.

"I'd love to join you for dinner, if you're sure it's no trouble."

She swallowed. "No trouble at all. Annie will be delighted."

"I'm pretty good at washing dishes."

"Then it's settled. I never turn down an offer to help with the dishes." She'd managed to sound casual enough. Now all she had to do was get through the rest of the evening without messing things up.

Heather chatted incessantly throughout dinner, much to Gail's relief. It saved her from having to field any more questions from Blake. Just as she was beginning to relax, however, Heather complicated matters again by asking "Uncle" Blake if he would read her a bedtime story.

"Honey, I don't think so," Gail said, before Blake could answer. "You've just about worn out Uncle Blake today. I think it's time we gave him a rest."

Heather pouted. "I *want* him to read me a story."

Blake pushed himself away from the table. "I'll be

happy to read a story. I'm not exactly experienced in this sort of thing but I'm willing to give it a shot.''

"You really don't have to—'' Gail began.

"I'd like to,'' he interrupted. "Now, why don't you get Annie ready for bed while I do the dishes?''

She struggled for a moment longer with her doubts. "You've just made me an offer I can't refuse,'' she said at last. "But I don't want to be left out of the fun, so if you don't mind, I'll sit in on the story, too.''

Solemnly Blake leaned toward Heather and whispered, "Do you think we should let her listen to the story, too?''

Heather looked a little worried. "I think she heard you,'' she whispered back.

"I guess we'd better let her listen, then. Huh?''

Heather nodded, and looked anxiously at her mother. "You can listen if you like, Mommy.''

"Oh, thank you.'' Gail raised her eyebrows at Blake. "This is indeed an honor.''

"I hope you appreciate the performance.'' He pushed himself away from the table. "Now I'd better get to those dishes.''

"Come on, Mommy.'' Heather jumped down from her chair. "I have to get to bed so's I can hear the story.''

Amused, Gail followed her eager daughter to the bathroom. It was usually a major struggle to get Heather to bed on time.

Blake had finished stacking the dishwasher when she returned to the living room a short while later.

"That was the shortest bath on record,'' she told him, when he looked up from the section of the Sunday newspaper he was reading.

"Ah, I take it my eager audience awaits.'' He folded the paper and stood, looking taller and more imposing than she remembered.

She'd had trouble all evening dealing with his magnetic

presence in her home. Now that they were alone in the room, she could feel her tension increasing again. "Thanks for doing the dishes." She glanced over at the kitchen. "I'm impressed. Not many men can do such an efficient job."

"Comes from years of practice." He gestured toward the bedrooms. "Shall we go?"

She nodded and awkwardly led the way to Heather's room.

Her daughter sat up in bed, her damp hair curling over her ears as she waited expectantly for her visitor.

"We've chosen the book," Gail said, handing it to him. "It's one of Annie's favorites." She pulled a small bedside chair forward and motioned him to sit down.

He was beginning to look self-conscious now that he was onstage, she couldn't help noticing. The children's book she'd chosen was just a few pages long, but he leafed through it as if it were a two-hundred-page tome on ancient civilization.

Heather sat watching him, her lively eyes brimming with excitement. "It's the story of the Three Little Pigs," she told him. "And you have to huff and puff and blow the house down."

Blake looked up, his face brightening. "Oh, I know that one." Settling back, he began to read. "'Once upon a time…'"

Gail settled herself on the edge of the bed, helpless to prevent the sweet ache of longing that gripped her as he read the story with all the sincerity of a born storyteller. Heather lay quite still, her gaze unwavering on his face. Seeing the two of them together like that was almost more than Gail could bear.

As he turned the last page, Heather sighed, and gave up the battle to force her eyelids open. Blake leaned forward and kissed the child lightly on the forehead. "Sleep tight," he whispered.

In the second before he composed his expression, Gail saw such a searing pain in his face, she almost cried out. Now she new what it was that hurt him. He was thinking about his ex-wife, and the child they'd never had.

Her illogical stab of jealousy shocked her. It was a measure of how deep her feelings for him had grown. She stood abruptly and drew the covers over Heather's bare shoulder.

The chair creaked as Blake got to his feet. He moved quietly toward the door and she followed him, her heart beginning to pound.

The quiet intimacy of the moment had stripped her of all her defenses. She wanted this man, and she wasn't ashamed to admit it.

She followed him into the living room, her gaze traveling over his broad shoulders. The maroon knit shirt he wore stretched tight across his back, and she had an almost-uncontrollable urge to slip her hand beneath it.

The erotic impulse stole her breath, and she felt as if she were suffocating. She longed to be outside, feeling the cold air on her cheeks, yet at the same time she wanted to keep him there for as long as possible.

He reached for his jacket, which lay across the back of the couch. "Well, I guess I'd better get going."

"Would you like a cup of coffee?"

She wasn't sure if she was relieved or disappointed when he shook his head.

"Thanks, but I think I'll move along. I don't want to overstay my welcome."

"You'll never do that. You'll always be welcome in this house." She crossed the room with him, taking care to keep a distance between them.

He paused at the door, and she made herself look up at him. To her dismay she saw a shadow of the sadness she'd seen earlier. "Thank you," she said gently. "You gave one little girl a truly wonderful weekend, which I'm sure she'll never forget."

"I'll never forget it, either." His gaze rested intently on her face, and once again she was conscious of the world around her fading into insignificance.

It was almost hypnotic, the effect he had on her. Never before had she felt so vulnerable in someone's presence without so much as being touched by him. His hold over her was purely emotional. It was as if he could reach a deeper part of her that had never been invaded before.

He both frightened and exhilarated her to an almost-unbearable pitch. Every atom of her being yearned to be touched by him—to know the feel of his hands on her, of his mouth hard on hers, demanding satisfaction.

She was terrified he would be able to read her thoughts, yet she was helpless to prevent them from tumbling through her mind. She couldn't stop the trembling that shook her body. He must see. He must know how much she wanted him.

Perhaps he did, for she saw his mouth tighten, his jaw tense. His eyes narrowed to slits, and the light that burned in them seemed to sear her soul.

Nervously she moistened her lips while his gaze moved down over her mouth, her neck, her breasts, as intimate as an actual caress of his fingers.

Her body responded at once, tingling with anticipation.

"Kate," he said softly, "I..."

She drew in a sharp breath. The sound seemed to intensify the fire in his gray eyes. His nostrils flared, and he made a tiny movement toward her.

Her head swam with the force of her passion. Her entire body felt as if it were alight. If he touched her now, she thought desperately, she would explode.

"Damn."

The fiercely muttered curse jolted her. Still fighting the urgent demands of her body, she watched him spin around and grope for the door handle. "Good night, Kate," he muttered, and disappeared out the door.

She thought she would never get to sleep that night. He'd aroused a need in her that couldn't be denied. She tossed and turned, trying to ignore the gnawing ache deep in her belly.

She could almost feel his fingers tracing fiery patterns on her bare skin, and the rasp of his long legs entwining with hers. Her lips trembled with the burning need to kiss his shoulders, his back, his chest...until he reached for her with an urgency as intense as her own.

She had heard about women relieving themselves when something like this happened, yet she had never been driven to try it herself. Now, for the first time, she understood. For some reason, that made her cry.

Blake had driven the two miles to the hotel in a haze of aching, relentless need. Now, lying in bed and unable to sleep, he cursed himself over and over for succumbing to his physical desires. It had been so long since he'd wanted a woman this badly. If ever.

Groaning, he pummeled the pillow and jammed it back under his head. He'd seen it coming. He'd been helpless to prevent it. Despite all his efforts, all his hard-earned experience, he'd fallen into the oldest trap in history. He'd let her get under his skin, and now he was paying the price.

Now he had to figure out what the hell he was going to do about it. It was no use trying to ignore it any longer. He was finding it damn near impossible to keep his hands off her.

What he should do was stay as far away from her as he could until he'd cooled off. But that was impossible. He had a job to do, and he had to see it through. No matter how much she heated up his blood. No matter how much he wished he didn't have to go through with it. Because whatever happened, he was going to get burned—but good.

Gail fell asleep at last and awoke abruptly the next morning out of a nightmare. Heather seemed to be even more stubborn than usual, taking forever to get dressed for school. At long last she was ready, and Gail dropped her off at the kindergarten, barely making it on time.

Her dream still with her, she drove to the bookstore, aware of a prickly feeling at the back of her neck, as if someone were following her. Several times she stared into the rearview mirror, half expecting to see Blake's car behind her.

All she saw was a beat-up old Chevy truck with a broken fender hanging down on one side. She had to smile. Blake wouldn't be caught dead in a car like that.

The feeling of being watched stayed with her all morning, and she wished she could banish the bad dream. Every time she passed the window she looked out, hoping to see Blake's dark head across the street. Memories of the weekend constantly slid unbidden into her mind, making her smile.

The morning seemed to drag, made even more unbearable by her constant glancing at the clock. Half an hour before she was due to pick up Heather from kindergarten, she made up her mind she would eat lunch at the diner again. Maybe he would be there, hoping to see her but not wanting to pester her. That would be just like him.

If so, she thought, she would find a way to tell him about her past. She couldn't go on like this, afraid of what he would think of her. She had to trust her instincts sometime.

All her life she'd been afraid to take risks. She'd married Frank because he'd offered her security, and she'd thought she knew him well. She'd gone for the sure thing and that had backfired on her. So she might just as well take some risks now.

She would lay it all on the line, explain about Mike's lies, and hope that Blake would understand. She prayed, with all her heart, that he wouldn't let her down.

The minutes ticked agonizingly by. She busied herself at the back of the store, determined to stay away from the window so that she wouldn't be constantly distracted.

When the shop doorbell jangled, she almost jumped out of her skin. Her heart seemed to stop beating. Then, as she caught sight of the figure standing by the counter, joy filled her heart in a rush of relief. He'd come after all.

Blake smiled when he saw her. "Ready for lunch? I'm starving. I thought you might like to keep me company at the diner today."

"You read my thoughts." She looked up at the clock. "I have to wait for Polly to get here, though. She shouldn't be too long."

"Right. Then we have to pick up Annie and take her to the baby-sitter's, right?"

"Right. She'll be thrilled to see you."

For a moment she thought she saw a shadow cross his face. "I'm looking forward to seeing her, too. That's quite a kid you have there."

"Thanks. I think so, too." She dragged her gaze away from his face as the doorbell rang again and Polly hurried in.

"Sorry I'm late," she said breathlessly. "I had to stop at the post office—" She broke off, her eyes brightening when she saw Blake standing by the counter. "Well, if it isn't our faithful tourist. How's the sight-seeing going?"

"Couldn't be better." He smiled at Gail. "I found this incredible tour guide, and she's been absolutely wonderful."

"Has she, indeed?" Polly murmured. "I'll have to recommend her to my other customers."

Still caught by his gaze, Gail laughed. "This is an exclusive tour. A once-only deal."

"I'm honored." He inclined his head in a mock bow.

She returned the gesture. "My pleasure."

"Excuse me if I'm interrupting something," Polly said, moving behind the counter, "but isn't it your lunchtime?"

"Yes!" Gail snatched up her purse and headed for the door. "Annie will be wondering where I am."

"I'll drive." Blake grabbed hold of her arm and steered her toward his car.

For once his arbitrary attitude didn't offend her. In fact, she rather enjoyed him taking charge. It had been tough having to be responsible for her life and Heather's. It was nice to lean on someone for a change.

She had to smile at herself. That was quite an admission after everything she'd put up with from Frank. Blake Foster had to be quite a man to turn her thinking around to that extent. She settled herself in the front seat of his car, enjoying the prospect of being alone with him for a little while.

But then she felt a little letdown when he barely spoke on the way to the kindergarten. In fact, he seemed deeply preoccupied, and she felt a stab of uneasiness as she studied his uncompromising expression.

"Is something wrong?" she said at last, when she could bear the suspense no longer.

He glanced at her with a start. "Wrong? No, of course not. Why would you think that?"

"You look a little forbidding."

"I'm sorry." He paused long enough for her to start worrying, then added, "I guess I was just thinking about having to go back to work, that's all. It's always tough when a vacation ends."

Her heart seemed to drop right down to her heels. "You're leaving?"

"Soon." The hard edges of his mouth had returned. "All good things come to an end sooner or later, I guess."

She'd always known he would go back to Seattle. She just hadn't let herself think about the actual day. The ache in her throat was so bad she found it difficult to swallow. "So when will you be leaving?"

"I haven't decided yet, but I can't stick around much longer."

Why not? For a moment she was afraid she'd spoken out loud. He hadn't mentioned anything about being sorry to leave, or that he would miss her.

When he did speak the words, it was as if he'd echoed her thoughts. "I'll miss you...both."

"I'll miss you, too. I know Annie will miss you, as well."

She didn't know how she felt as he drew up in front of Heather's school. Her mind was numb, and the ache under her ribs was almost unbearable. She was afraid to think beyond that moment, terrified she would break down and beg him not to leave her.

Heather chatted all the way to Darcie's house, making meaningful conversation impossible. She would just have to wait until they were at the diner, Gail thought, only half listening to her daughter's breathless account of the morning's activities.

Darcie opened the door when Heather rang the bell a few minutes later. Her gaze flew immediately to Blake sitting behind the wheel of his car. "Well," she said softly, "I can see now why you've been so secretive about your dinner dates."

Gail pretended to be occupied with kissing Heather goodbye. "You be a good girl," she told her daughter, "and I'll see you tonight."

"Okay, Mommy." Heather flapped her hand at Blake, then vanished inside the house.

Darcie smiled at Blake, and he lifted his hand in a casual wave. "He's quite a hunk," she murmured. "Can I meet him, or are you keeping him all to yourself?"

"It's not like that," Gail protested. At least it wasn't for Blake, she added silently.

She led the baby-sitter to the car and introduced her.

Darcie stuck out her hand. "I imagine you're the reason Kate has been walking on clouds lately?"

Blake grinned and shook her hand. "I've heard a lot about you from Annie. She thinks the world of you."

"Yeah, well, what do kids know? As a matter of fact, I'm crazy about her, too."

Darcie turned back to Gail and mouthed, *"Nice!"* Out loud, she added, "Don't forget, if you want me to keep her overnight again, just let me know."

"Thanks, Darcie," Gail said awkwardly. "I'm sure that won't be necessary."

Darcie had the audacity to wink at her. "You never know."

Hoping Blake hadn't seen the wink, Gail scrambled back into the car. She kept her distance, sitting closer to the door as they drove to the diner. Full of indecision now, she tried to think what to do. There didn't seem any point in baring her soul if he was leaving without looking back.

The car came to a halt in the parking lot behind the diner. She hadn't even noticed they'd arrived.

Blake looked at her as she unfastened her seat belt. "Are you okay? You're awfully quiet."

"Just tired. I didn't sleep well last night."

"I know how that goes."

She risked a glance at him and noticed the tension along his jaw. In spite of his apparent good mood, she could sense something different about him. Knowing him as well as she did now, she could tell something was on his mind. He might have been telling the truth, and it was just the thought of his vacation coming to an end that bothered him. Or maybe it was something else.

She tried to think back to the last moments they'd spent together. He'd left in a hurry. Had she been too transparent? Perhaps he'd realized how he affected her, and was wary of taking it any further.

If he'd had any inkling of her fantasies about him, it was small wonder he was on guard. She could feel her flush of embarrassment as she followed him into the diner.

As usual the tables were crowded, and they had to wait for a seat. Crammed in between a rowdy group of youths and a middle-aged woman with a voice that carried clear across the room, Gail knew there would be no opportunity to tell Blake about her past.

She wasn't sure she wanted to tell him now. Maybe it was just as well, she told herself, as she picked at her chicken salad. At least she would still have her pride left. It seemed a poor consolation.

Blake appeared determined to keep the conversation going, in spite of her halfhearted attempts to answer him. "That was some museum yesterday." He broke up a cracker and dropped it into his soup with painstaking precision. "A great place for kids."

She barely took in what he was saying, the ache under her ribs was so acute. She nodded automatically. "Heather always has a good time there." She caught her breath, feeling as if she'd plunged into an icy fog.

"I'm not surprised. She's intelligent enough to get the most out of it. She's a very bright little girl."

She couldn't answer him. A cold hard knot was forming in her stomach and her throat felt as if someone's fingers were slowly squeezing all the air from her lungs.

Heather. In her muddled state of mind she'd made the

ultimate slip. She'd called her daughter "Heather." And he hadn't picked up on it.

He'd known whom she meant. He'd known something he couldn't possibly have known—*unless he already knew who she was.*

Chapter 5

She didn't know what to do. She couldn't force another bite of food down her throat, yet she dared not let him know she'd caught him out.

Frantically her mind groped for answers. Maybe he hadn't heard her correctly and just assumed she was talking about Annie. But did "Heather" sound enough like "Annie" to make that mistake? She didn't think so.

She had to be overreacting, she told herself desperately. She tried to think how she would have responded if he'd called someone they both knew by a strange name. She would have wondered who he was talking about. She would have at least questioned him about it.

"Kate? Are you ill? You look as white as that snow out there."

Startled out of her wits, she stared at him, making a vain attempt to hide her agitation. He'd given her the opening and she was going to take it. She needed time to think, time away from him so she could make sense of her chaotic thoughts. She wouldn't jump to conclusions. She needed to think it all through carefully, and more than likely she would come up with the right answer.

"I...I don't feel all that good," she said, making no attempt to hide the trembling in her voice. "I...have a very bad headache. I get them sometimes. I...I'm sorry. I think I'd better get back to the shop. Polly has some medication that always seems to work. Do you mind?"

"Not at all." He looked worried now, deep furrows forming between his brows. He scraped back his chair and stood.

She got shakily to her feet and let him help her on with her coat, although every nerve in her body screamed out to him not to touch her.

Don't think, she told herself. She must wait until she was alone, without the distraction of his hand on her arm and that deep look of concern in his eyes.

He helped her into the car as if she were made of glass, and then drove quickly to the bookstore. He didn't speak, nor did he look at her until they were parked at the curb.

"Wait there, I'll open the door."

"No!" She'd almost shouted it. She saw the puzzled look on his face and lowered her voice. "There's really no need for you to get out in the cold again. I'm fine. Really."

"Are you sure?" He leaned over and peered up at her as she started to close the door. "Call me later and let me know how you are?"

She nodded. "Thanks, Blake. Sorry to be such a drag."

"Take care of yourself, will you?"

She slammed the door shut and ran into the shop. She didn't look around, but she knew he'd watched her until she'd pulled the door closed behind her. Leaning her back against it, she drew in a long, shaky breath.

Polly gave her one look and then rushed over to her.

"What happened? Are you hurt? Did you have an accident? It's not Annie, is it?"

Gail just stood there shaking her head, fighting the threat of tears.

Polly grabbed her hands and started rubbing them. "Look at you," she muttered. "You look frozen. Didn't run over a dog or something, did you?"

With a tremendous effort, Gail pulled herself together. "I...have a headache." She looked at Polly, silently begging her to understand. "I'd like to go home. Can you manage without me?"

"Of course." Polly's frown deepened. "This doesn't have anything to do with our tourist, does it?"

It was uncanny how Polly could always pick up on her thoughts. Deliberately, Gail shook her head. She wasn't ready to discuss it yet. Or even think about it until she had it sorted out in her mind. She could be wrong. She could be overreacting. It could have been an innocent lack of attention on Blake's part.

And it could be something else. He could have been sent by Mike.

Her mind veered away from the horror of that possibility. She managed a tight smile as she pulled her hands from Polly's grasp. "Nothing's wrong. I've just got this terrible headache, that's all. I guess I didn't sleep much last night."

"Daydreaming about that handsome tourist, no doubt." Polly shook her head. "He's quite a looker, I must admit, but I hope you don't get yourself all in a tizzy over him. He's only passing through, you know, and you know nothing about him. You could end up getting hurt."

Gail's own laugh sounded shrill in her ears. "Don't worry, Polly. I haven't got any illusions about him. I promise you, if I can just go home and rest this afternoon, I'm sure I'll be fine tomorrow."

"You'll call me if you need me, won't you," Polly said,

making it sound like an order. "I don't like to think of you in that house all alone. And what about Annie? Who's going to pick her up?"

Gail's stomach dropped. Heather. *He knew where she was.* "I'll pick her up." She pulled in a steadying breath. "If I don't feel well enough to go out, Darcie will keep her overnight."

Now she felt an overwhelming urge to see her daughter. She dragged open the door, belatedly checking to see if Blake was there. The curb was bare, and she felt sick. Had he gone back to Darcie's? Heather adored him. She trusted him. She would go with him.

"Excuse me." Brushing past Polly, she headed for the counter and grabbed up the phone. Her fingers shook so much she misdialed and had to start again. All the time she was aware of Polly's curious gaze on her, but she couldn't worry about that now. Finally the line clicked as someone picked up the phone.

"Darcie?" Her voice cracked, and she had to pause a moment before adding, "Is Annie there?"

"She's right here. You want to speak to her?"

Her heady rush of relief brought tears to her eyes. "Please," she said unsteadily.

She closed her eyes briefly when she heard Heather's voice. Carefully she calmed her voice to answer her daughter. "Hi, honey. I just wanted to know if you're having fun."

She listened, her fingers gripping the phone, while Heather told her about the game she was playing.

"You have to spin the little wheel, and then move the counter where the wheel tells you to," Heather's childish voice explained.

"That's nice, honey. You be good, okay? Now tell Darcie I want to speak to her. I'll see you later."

Darcie came back on the phone. "What was all that about?" She sounded mystified.

Gail struggled to answer her. "I just felt lonely, I guess. Must be my hormones acting up. I'll see you at the usual time, okay?"

"Okay. I'll have her ready. Did you have a nice lunch with Mr. Gorgeous?"

"Very nice." Gail swallowed. "Darcie, you wouldn't let Annie go home with anyone except me, right?"

"Of course not. What—?"

"Even if you knew them?"

There was a long pause on the end of the line while Gail's heart thumped against her ribs. She could almost feel Polly's shrewd gaze boring into her back.

"What's up, Kate? Is something wrong?"

Darcie's anxiety came through loud and clear, and Gail hurried to reassure her. "It's just me being silly, that's all. I'll see you tonight." She hung up and headed for the door, but Polly barred her way.

"Don't you think you'd better tell me about it?"

Gail felt like weeping. "I...I'm all right, Polly. I promise you. I'll call you later."

"Are you in trouble, Kate?"

"I'm suffering from an overactive imagination, that's all." Her voice had regained a little of its strength and she even managed to smile. "I'll be fine after a good night's sleep. Okay?"

Polly shrugged. "If you say so." It was clear, however, that she wasn't entirely convinced.

Hating the need to lie to her friend, Gail escaped thankfully into the frosty wind. She welcomed the chill on her warm face. Now that she knew Heather was safe, she was beginning to calm down.

She couldn't seem to get warm, however, and couldn't wait until she could get into the house and turn up the heat.

Perhaps she had been mistaken, after all, she told herself as she drove slowly home. It didn't seem possible that the big, friendly, sympathetic man she'd grown so close to could somehow be connected to the vicious criminal locked away behind bars.

She could picture Blake in a dozen ways. Smiling down at her with the mountain soaring behind him and thick, fluffy snowflakes brushing his nose. Laughing with Heather at the museum while he showed her how to paint clowns on the computer. The searing, hungry look in his eyes when he'd left her last night.

Her throat ached. She had to be wrong. She had to be. It was a stupid mistake, that was all. Maybe she hadn't actually said the name "Heather," but had just thought she had. But then she remembered clearly the cold feeling of certainty the moment she'd spoken her daughter's name.

There was one way to find out if Blake was who he said he was. And it should be easy enough.

She made herself wait until she'd taken some medication for the headache, and had settled down enough to stop shaking. Finally, when she could put it off no longer, she lifted the phone. It took several calls before she reached the number she wanted.

The woman on the other end informed her that she was talking to the Real Estate Association in Seattle.

"I'm trying to find an agent by the name of Blake Foster," Gail said, her shoulders hunched with tension as she gripped the phone to her ear.

"Do you know which agency he's with?" the voice inquired.

"No, I'm afraid I don't. I only know he's in real estate in the Seattle area."

"Just a moment, please, I'll try to find that information for you."

She waited, her fingers numb, her mind blank. Finally,

after an agonizing wait, the voice spoke again. "Mrs. Morris? I'm afraid I was unable to find an agent by that name in our records."

Gail swallowed. "He hasn't been there long. Is there a chance he's not listed yet?"

"No, I don't think so. We have the computer records of every registered real-estate agent in Washington. If your Mr. Foster is selling real estate here, he's doing so without a license."

She could hardly speak. Her lips felt frozen as she formed an answer. "I see. Well, I guess I must have made a mistake then. Thank you for your trouble."

"No problem."

She hung on to the phone for several moments after the woman hung up, willing herself to stay calm. Maybe it wasn't what she thought, she argued with herself. Perhaps he was married and had given her a different name. There could be a dozen reasons why he hadn't told her the truth about himself.

Carefully, she replaced the receiver in its cradle. He'd lied to her. He'd been vague about Seattle, admitting that he wasn't too familiar with the city.

Pacing around the worn carpet of her small living room, she recalled the first day she'd met him. He'd unnerved her with his sharp questions, as though he were grilling her.

She'd felt an almost-tangible sensation of a formidable and dangerous power that had frightened her. Then there was her feeling that she was being watched all the time. His persistence in wanting her company. In fact, she realized, with a stab of cold dread, she'd hardly been out of his sight since she'd met him.

It all added up. He had deliberately tracked her down. And there was only one person who could have sent him. Mike Stevens. Mike had promised to destroy her. He'd threatened Heather's life. He was out to get her, and if he

couldn't do it himself, he'd told her, he would send someone else to do the job. That someone was Blake Foster.

Panic, swift and debilitating, caught her by the throat.
She spun around in the middle of the room and whimpered.
What could she do? Whom could she turn to? The police?
They would laugh at her, the way they had in Portland.

No doubt Blake would have all the necessary identity to
fool them. It was her word against his—the word of a
woman suspected of conspiracy in her husband's murder.

Once more she willed herself to stay calm. She had to
think what to do. She would have to leave town, get as far
away as possible as fast as she could. She would take
Heather and go up into Canada for a while. At least until
she could find out who Blake Foster really was and what
he wanted from her.

The phone rang suddenly and she froze, staring at it as
if it would blow up in her face. She let it ring a second
time, then snatched it up, hysterical with fear, afraid that it
might be Darcie on the other end.

Her whispered, "Hello?" must have sounded odd.

"Kate? It's Blake. Polly told me you'd gone home. She
said you looked awful. I was worried about you."

He sounded concerned and just a little guarded.

In spite of her fear, she hadn't been able to stop the
tingling pleasure she always felt at the sound of his voice.

Horrified at the treachery of her body, she forced herself
to stay calm. She couldn't let him know she was on to him.

"Polly worries too much." Her laugh sounded forced,
even to her. "I'm quite all right."

"I'd like to come over and see for myself. You shouldn't
be alone if you're sick."

Panic hit her, robbing her of speech for a moment. "No,
I... Really, I'm fine. I'm feeling much better. I took some
aspirin and they did the trick, so you have absolutely no

need to worry. I'm going to take a little nap before I pick up Annie.''

It occurred to her that he didn't even realize what he'd done. Again the stubborn hope that refused to die flickered to life again. This could all be a stupid mistake. She'd become paranoid again, imagining threats and dangers that weren't there. If only she could tell him the truth—lean on his broad shoulders and take comfort in his arms.

''Well, as long as you're feeling better, how about having dinner with me this evening? You know how I hate eating alone.''

She felt herself weakening. With an effort, she pulled herself together. He had lied to her. He wasn't a real-estate agent from Seattle. Whatever his reason for lying, he couldn't be trusted. And if there was the slightest chance that he could be working for Mike Stevens, then she wasn't about to wait around and put Heather's life, and probably her own, in danger.

She pressed her fingers to her forehead, trying to think clearly. ''I...I'm sorry, Blake. I have a...meeting with Annie's teachers at seven-thirty this evening. I won't be able to make dinner.''

''Oh, that's too bad. How about coffee afterward, then? I'll buy Annie a milk shake. I know she'd like that.''

Gail closed her eyes as a shaft of pain hit her. How could she have fallen for that deceptive warmth and phony consideration? How could she have forgotten her first impressions of him so easily? She'd trusted so readily again, when all her life she'd been betrayed by those she'd believed in.

She should have known better. God knows, she'd had enough experience.

''Kate?''

The suspicion in the sharp query alerted her. ''I'm sorry, Blake. I think I'll have to take a rain check. I don't want Annie to be too late to bed. She gets so cranky the next morning. Perhaps we can do it later in the week?'' She hesitated. ''That's if you'll be around that long?''

''I'll be around.''

Had she imagined it or had she heard a threat in that remark? She was shivering, she realized, in spite of the heat blowing from the vents at her feet. She said goodbye to him, barely suppressing the catch in her voice when she realized it would be the last time she spoke to him.

It was easier to think of him as the enemy, sent to get her and her daughter. Only she couldn't quite make herself believe that. And that could be a dangerous mistake.

She called Polly, and gave her a long story about the cold weather getting her down. ''It's not just me, it's Annie, too. She hasn't been at all well lately. I think a week of California sunshine would do us both the world of good. Can you manage without me for a while?''

''Of course I can. Have a good trip and...Kate?''

She knew Polly wasn't deceived for one moment. Apparently she'd decided to respect her wish to keep her troubles to herself. Grateful for her friend's understanding, Gail answered her with a rush of affection. ''Yes?''

''Take good care of yourself. And that little gal of yours.'' Polly's voice broke, and she hung up.

Gail replaced the receiver, feeling more lonely than she ever remembered. Polly and Darcie had been her only real friends. It was hard to say goodbye.

Darcie was surprised when Gail turned up an hour early to pick up Heather. ''She's upstairs,'' she told Gail. ''I think they're holding a teddy bears' picnic. I let them take cookies upstairs but I drew the line at filling their teapot with hot tea.''

''I've decided to take a trip to California,'' Gail told her. ''I think Annie might enjoy Disneyland.'' She hated having to lie, but if Blake was hired to find her and questioned her friends, they would point him in the opposite direction, and she and Heather would be safe.

"Really?" Darcie grinned at her. "When are you going? Are you going to meet the hunk there?"

"No, I'm not going to meet anyone," Gail said, just a little too sharply.

Darcie's grin vanished. "Hey, I'm sorry. I didn't mean—"

"It's okay. It's my headache making me cranky." Gail forced a smile. "As a matter of fact, I'm leaving tomorrow. We'll be gone for a week or two, but I'll let you know when we get back."

Darcie frowned. "Bit sudden, isn't it?"

"Not really. I've been thinking about it for some time. Oh, one more thing. Don't mention Disneyland to Annie. I want to surprise her."

Darcie still looked doubtful, but she nodded. "Okay, I won't say a word. You two have a good time, okay?"

Gail smiled. "Thanks, Darcie. Now I'll go get my daughter."

Heather wasn't at all happy at being dragged away from her picnic, and Gail had to promise her a hot fudge sundae to pacify her resentful daughter.

"First off, though, we have to go home and pack our cases," she told Heather, as she drove as fast as she dared on the frosty highway.

"Where are we going?" Heather sounded sulky, and Gail hoped she wasn't going to be difficult.

"We're going on a trip, all the way to Canada."

"Where's Canada?"

"A long way from here." She was answering automatically, her gaze on the rearview mirror. She couldn't see Blake's car, but it was hard to tell now that it was getting dark.

The headlights from the battered-looking car behind hit

the mirror, dazzling her, and she switched her gaze back to the road. Something about the car seemed familiar. She frowned, trying to catch another glimpse of it, but it had dropped back, and all she could see was the lights.

Maybe it had been the broken fender, she thought, but then she'd seen a lot of broken fenders lately. One thing she did know, the fender on Blake's car was intact. Besides, his car was black, not light gray, and it was in a lot better shape than the one behind her.

Which meant that so far, Blake was not on her trail. Which was all she had to worry about right then.

She parked her car in the driveway, then opened the front door to the house. She wished now that she'd left a light on. Walking into a dark house gave her the creeps.

Impatient with herself, she felt for the light switch in the hall and flipped it on. She was letting all this upheaval get on her nerves. She didn't know for sure that Blake had been sent by Mike. In fact, the more she thought about it now, the more ludicrous it seemed.

She was half tempted to call Blake and confront him with what she knew. But that would be taking too much of a risk. It would be far better to wait until she was safely into Canada before attempting to find out more about Blake Foster.

She would not let herself think about the past few days as she threw clothes into a suitcase. To do so would weaken her resolve. She hated herself for still wanting him, for being unable to cut off the feelings that had so recently blossomed into life.

It was just her lousy luck, she told herself, that she should find the one man in the world who was able to make her feel like a desirable woman, only to learn that he was a criminal who'd hunted her down in order to kill her and her daughter. It was the story of her life.

* * *

In his hotel room, Blake sank onto the side of the bed and reached for the phone. He dialed for an outside line, then quickly punched out the numbers he knew off by heart.

He waited through three rings before the line clicked, then relaxed as he heard the familiar voice in his ear. He spoke quietly into the mouthpiece, a habit ingrained in him many years ago. "It's me."

"So what's up?"

"Not much. I'm maintaining contact with her, but so far nothing's gone down."

"Where is she now?"

He could picture her so easily. Her brown eyes laughing up at him, her dark hair blowing in the wind, her lips parted in an unconscious invitation that just about drove him crazy. He closed his eyes, willing the images to fade. "She's at home with a headache. She's supposed to be going to a school meeting tonight, so this could be it. If so, I'll be there, right behind her."

"Be careful, Blake."

"Don't worry. I know what I'm doing."

"Do you? I sure hope so. It's imperative she doesn't figure you out."

Blake frowned. The man on the other end of the line knew him well. Perhaps too well. Maybe something in his voice had betrayed his fascination with Gail Stevens. Angry with himself, Blake cleared his mind of the tormenting memories. "She has no idea who I am, or that I'm on to her. She can't make a move without me knowing about it. I'll stick with her like a bad cold until this job is done."

"Just make sure you do the job. You wouldn't be the first one to be fooled by her."

His temper flared, and he fought to subdue it. "I just find it damn difficult to believe that she could have anything to do with that creep."

"She married his brother," the voice reminded him.

Blake swore. "What in blazes do women see in bastards like the Stevens brothers? It just blows my mind."

"She's getting to you, too, huh?"

"No, she's not getting to me. I'm not that stupid."

"Well, I could hardly blame you if you did fall for that innocent, wronged-woman act. After all, we were never able to prove she conspired with Mike Stevens. Or that she was ever involved with him."

"Yeah, well, she just doesn't seem the type to me. Maybe the feds were wrong. It wouldn't be the first time."

The voice on the line sharpened. "You can't take a chance on that, Blake. Mike Stevens has been on the loose for almost a week now. He's on the run and he's armed and dangerous. If our sources are genuine, he's on his way to join up with his woman in the boondocks out there. Why else would she hang around some dreary backwoods town in the mountains?"

Blake sighed. "Okay, you're right. It just seems such a damn waste, that's all."

"Look," the voice said, sounding more sympathetic, "I know it's tough. No one likes to hound a woman. Especially one who looks like she does. Just remember that as U.S. Marshal, your job is to bring Stevens back to jail. The woman is free to go, unless she tries to get in your way. Then you know what you have to do."

"Yeah, yeah, I know." Blake wiped the back of his hand across his forehead. "Don't worry, I'll take care of it. I'll be in touch as soon as anything breaks."

He dropped the receiver into the cradle and glanced at the clock. He had at least three hours to kill before he drove over to Gail's house and tailed her to the meeting.

He did his best to get comfortable in the inadequate armchair and flicked the remote through all six channels on the television. Images flickered across the screen, but he paid little attention to them. His treacherous mind would not let him alone.

Damn it, he wanted her in the worst way. His hands itched to cup her tantalizing breasts, and his mouth burned to taste her body. He got hard just thinking about her.

Groaning, he tilted his head back and closed his eyes. He should know better. He was a cop, for God's sake. He, of all people, should know that the most innocent-looking were often the most guilty. Why couldn't he keep that in his mind? What was it about her that made him forget everything that had been drummed into him for the past twenty years?

Cursing viciously, he thrust himself out of the chair and walked to the window. Drawing back the drapes, he peered out at the darkened parking lot. It was snowing again. He could see the snowflakes whirling around in the glow from the streetlamps.

Would she still go to the meeting if it snowed? Probably, he told himself. She took her daughter's education very seriously. She was a good mother.

His stab of pain cut off his breath. What would happen to Heather if he messed this up and Gail took off with Mike Stevens? It didn't bear thinking about. Always on the run, living in one hole after another... That was no life for a kid.

He had better remember that, he told himself, the next time he felt himself getting hot over Gail Stevens. If he found this job repulsive, he could at least tell himself he was doing it for the kid.

He let the drapes fall back into place, and went back to the armchair. An earnest-looking man peered back at him from the TV set, attempting to explain to him how to get rid of his graying hair.

Blake ran his fingers across his temples. This job would probably turn him completely white, he thought in disgust.

Here he was, fantasizing over a woman who was planning to go on the run with a convicted killer. Not only that, she was going to drag her kid into the whole ugly mess.

He could forgive her just about anything but that. She had no right to destroy her daughter's life in that way. It was a purely selfish move, and that was why he found it so damn hard to understand. She just didn't seem the type.

He wished to God that it was all over, and that he was on his way to Parkerville with Stevens in cuffs. Maybe then he would get some peace of mind. He couldn't go on with this cover much longer. The way she affected him, sooner or later he would slip up. And then he would probably have to get rough. That was the last thing he wanted to do.

He thought he might have let something slip at lunch earlier, judging from the scared look on her face. But then she'd explained about the headache—

Blake's feet hit the carpet as he shoved himself upright. That headache had come on pretty damn suddenly. Now that he thought about it, she'd sounded real uptight when he'd spoken to her on the phone.

The back of his neck started tingling, the way it always did when he sensed something out of whack. He glanced up at the clock. Almost five. She should be picking up Heather right about now.

He grabbed the phone book, struggling with his elusive memory. Dammit, he'd only been introduced to her that morning. Richards... Redford... Reynolds. That was it.

He found it listed, much to his relief. Punching out the numbers, he prayed he was wrong. She answered on the first ring.

"Hi, Darcie," he said pleasantly. "I was wondering if Kate has picked up Annie yet? I thought I'd take them both out to dinner."

His stomach dropped when Darcie said warily, "Kate was here an hour ago."

He fought to keep his voice calm. "She took Annie home?"

"Yes, she went home to pack. She's taking Annie to California. She didn't tell you?"

He thought fast. "Yes, she did, but I didn't think she was leaving until tomorrow." His shot in the dark worked. Darcie sounded obviously relieved when she answered.

"Oh, so she did tell you. She said she was leaving in the morning, but I guess she wanted Annie to help her pack."

"More than likely. I'll catch them at home. Thanks, Darcie." He dropped the phone. An hour ago. He could only pray he made it in time. Cursing, he grabbed his jacket and slammed out of the room.

"Can I take my dolly's house?" Heather dragged the house out from the cupboard, spilling doll's furniture across the floor.

"Oh, no, honey, we won't have room in the car. We'll just take Fuzzy, and some books to look at." Gail squatted down to pick up the toys.

"What about my tricycle?"

"No, honey, just the books."

Heather started to whine. "I want to take my tricycle."

Worried that her tension might be communicating itself to the little girl, Gail did her best to smile. "I'll tell you what. We'll take your camera and you can take lots of pictures. And we'll take your talking farm with us, too. I think we've got room for that."

Reluctantly Heather gave up her hold on the tricycle. "When are we going to get a sundae?"

"We'll stop on the way out. I promise." Gail pushed her daughter's arms into her jacket, then pulled on her woolly cap. "There. That should keep you warm. I've made up a bed for you in the back seat of the car, so that you can go to sleep there. We have a long, long way to go and you'll be really sleepy before we get there."

"I don't wanna go to sleep." Heather yawned. "I'm hungry."

And tired enough to fall asleep quickly, Gail thought hopefully. "We'll get a hamburger and you can eat it in the car."

Heather's eyes lit up at this unexpected treat. Normally she wasn't allowed to eat in the car. "And a sundae?"

Gail sighed. "Yes, and a sundae. But you'll have to be extra careful not to spill it. Mommy's going to be driving and I won't have time to clean you up."

She grabbed Heather's hand and led her out to the car. The snow was barely covering the pavement. With any luck she would reach the freeway before it got too bad.

Shivering from nervousness more than from the cold, she opened the back door of the car and settled Heather inside. The cases were already stowed in the trunk. All she had to do now was turn off the lights, grab her purse and they could be on their way.

"Now you wait here for a minute, honey," she told Heather as she tucked the blanket around her. "I just have to go back into the house for a minute, then we can go get your hamburger."

"I have to go potty," Heather announced.

Gail held on to her failing patience. "You can go when we get to the hamburger place," she said firmly. "Now wait there a minute while I go and lock up."

Back inside the house, she felt an aching sense of loss as she took a last look around the neat living room. The bright yellow cushions she'd made for the shabby brown couch and the matching curtains she'd painstakingly sewn for the windows, Heather's dollhouse she'd bought for her birthday, and which had cost her half a week's salary, the little cross-stitch pictures on the walls—she might never see any of those things again.

This had been her home for less than a year, but it had become very special to her. She would miss Mellow Springs. She had been happy here—happier than she ever remembered. It was so hard to leave.

A surge of bitter resentment brought tears to her eyes. Damn Mike Stevens. Damn herself for ever getting involved with the Stevens brothers. And damn Blake Foster for tearing apart her life once more. Would it never be over?

Sniffing, she turned off the light and headed for the front door. This time she didn't look back as she stepped outside once more into the swirling snowflakes and slammed the door behind her.

She couldn't seem to stop the tears from pooling in her eyes, and she kept her face turned away from Heather as she climbed behind the wheel.

"Hello, Mommy," Heather said, in the voice she always used when she was into mischief.

Too dispirited to deal with her daughter right then, Gail decided that she couldn't do too much harm in the back there. "Okay," she said unsteadily, "we're off."

Heather giggled behind her, and Gail forced herself to relax. She might be overreacting to this whole situation, she told herself, but now that she was actually on the road, she felt a good deal more at ease.

If she was wrong about Blake, and he wasn't working for Mike, then he would probably be hurt to find out that she'd just taken off without telling him.

But then he'd told her he was planning on going back to Seattle soon, without saying anything about keeping in touch with her. He would miss her, he'd said. Like he would miss the snow, or the mountain air. She was nothing more than a pleasant interlude in his life, as quickly forgotten as his first sled ride down the bunny slopes.

Heather giggled again behind her. Gail flicked a glance in the rearview mirror, but her daughter's head was below the level of the reflected image. "What are you doing back there?" she demanded, trying to remember what she'd put in the back seat with Heather. Nothing destructible, she was sure about that.

"I'm not doing nothing, Mommy."

"Anything," Gail corrected automatically. Heather had sounded entirely too innocent, and she frowned. She couldn't imagine what mischief Heather could be up to, but she knew her daughter's tone of voice. "We'll stop for a hamburger down the street," she said, "but only if you are good. Mommy has to watch the road, so I hope you are being a good girl back there."

"Yes, Mommy," Heather replied, giggling again.

Gail was beginning to squirm. Something was going on back there with her daughter, and she needed to know what it was. She waited until she reached a straight stretch of road, then slowed the car enough so that she could turn far enough around to see what Heather was doing.

Shock slammed into her chest when she saw the shadowy figure seated in the corner directly behind her. He must have been leaning close to the door to avoid being seen in the rearview mirror.

Her breath stopped in her throat, and she felt as though she'd plunged into an icy lake. Her foot automatically slammed on the brake, sending the car fishtailing across the road.

Momentarily distracted, she fought the wheel, her stomach heaving with shock. Regaining control of the car, she shifted her gaze back to the rearview mirror. One single thought drummed in her brain. Her daughter was strapped into the back seat next to a man who could very well be a cold-blooded killer.

Chapter 6

She could see his face now, glowing for an instant in the reflection from the oncoming lights. "Hi," he said softly, his familiar voice sending chills down her spine. "You, of all people, should know better than to get into a car without checking out the back seat."

"I knowed he was there all the time," Heather announced, sounding as if she was thoroughly enjoying the game. "I promised I wouldn't tell, and I didn't, did I, Uncle Blake?"

Gail stared into Blake's cold gray eyes reflected in the mirror, her heart hammering wildly against her ribs. Her mind skittered about, trying to make sense of what was happening.

He couldn't intend to hurt Heather, he just couldn't. In spite of all her doubts, now that she was face-to-face with him again, nothing in the world would make her believe that.

The snowflakes seemed thicker now, chasing each other

across the windshield to escape the sweep of the wipers. She could feel the back wheels slipping on the curves, but she kept her foot on the accelerator, praying she could keep the car under control.

Once more her gaze flicked up at the mirror. Blake's grim expression chilled her to the bone. She was acutely aware of his strength and power. She would be no match for him if he did make a move to hurt her.

She made herself meet his gaze. "Who are you?" she muttered. "What the hell do you want with me?"

Apparently sensing something wrong, Heather said in a worried voice, "He's Uncle Blake, Mommy. He got in here to s'rprise us."

"Well, he surprised me, all right." She glared at him in the mirror. "Is your name really Blake Foster, or was that strictly for my benefit?"

Blake's smile looked bleak, and she was totally unprepared for his answer.

"My name is really Blake Foster," he said, with just a trace of irony. "U.S. Marshal, to be precise. Since you're on your way to meet Mike Stevens, I thought I'd invite myself to the joyful reunion. I wouldn't advise any tricks, by the way. I didn't exactly come empty-handed, if you know what I mean."

The obvious reference to the fact that he was armed only vaguely registered. Stunned, she simply stared at his reflection in the mirror. She saw him turn to Heather and smile down at her, transforming his face into that of the man she'd thought she knew.

"You did a great job, Heather," he said softly. "I'm real proud of you."

Heather sounded puzzled when she said, "My name's Annie. Nobody calls me Heather anymore."

"I'm sorry. Annie."

Gail heard the exchange, but barely comprehended it.

Her mind whirled with the implications of what he'd just told her.

Dear God, he wasn't the enemy. He was a cop. Her heart leaped with a relief that made her giddy. She hadn't been wrong about him after all. He was everything she'd thought he was. And so much more.

Even as she basked in his startling confession, her mind slowly absorbed the last part of his statement. Her joy evaporated like melting snow. It wasn't over, after all. He was just like the rest of them—he thought she was involved with Mike Stevens.

Drawing in a long, deep breath, she slowed the car and pulled off onto the shoulder. She couldn't see his face quite so clearly now that they were out of the glare of lights, and she needed to see him. She needed him to see her, as well.

Reaching up, she flicked on the overhead light, then turned in her seat to face him.

He watched her, his eyes full of suspicion, his mouth a tight, grim line. "I'd advise you to keep going," he said, his voice low and full of quiet menace. "Don't make me do something I'll regret."

Conscious of Heather seated beside him, she took a moment or two to rehearse her words carefully in her mind. "I think you and I need to get something straight," she said at last. "I'm not going anywhere until I've had my say."

His narrowed gaze warned her clearly that he didn't want to discuss it.

"Mike Stevens," she said, ignoring the threat, "is behind bars in an Oregon prison. He is the very last man on this earth I would want to see."

"Is that right?"

She saw the look of skepticism flicker across his face. Obviously he didn't believe her. Well, that was nothing new. Nobody had believed her story. But this was different.

Somehow she had to convince him of her innocence. It was desperately important to her.

She felt a swift rush of relief at the realization that she could go home again, after all. "I think we should go back to the house," she said, sending a meaningful glance in Heather's direction. "I would like the chance to explain."

"Oh, you'll explain, all right."

"This isn't exactly a good place or time to do that." Again she glanced at Heather, who was now fidgeting in her seat.

Blake stared at her, his eyes mere slits of steel gray. Her heart ached when she saw the cold indifference on his face. He had to believe her. She had to make him believe her.

She smiled at her daughter, who was watching her with apprehension on her small face. "I think it's time we went back and got that hamburger and hot fudge sundae, don't you?"

Heather, apparently reassured, nodded vigorously. "Is Uncle Blake coming with us to Canada?"

Gail noticed Blake's swift reaction to her question. "No," she said quickly. "I think it's a little late to drive all that way tonight, and it's beginning to snow quite hard."

"I wanna go to Canada." Heather yawned. "I want Uncle Blake to come with us to Canada."

"I think we should all go to Canada," Blake said, a little too quietly.

His insistence puzzled her. Did he seriously think she was going to meet Frank's brother? Surely he knew that Mike was in prison?

Or was he? The frightening implications of that thought shot her newfound security to shreds. Anxious now to learn the truth, she met his gaze. "I think we should go home and discuss this in private."

He sat for a long time, obviously weighing things over in his mind. Finally, he gave her a quick nod. "All right, we'll go back. But it won't make any difference. We'll get him just the same.''

She frowned, a very real fear once more beginning to take root at his terse comment.

Blake turned to Heather and tucked the blanket around her shoulders. "Okay, squirt, let's go get that hamburger." He looked back at Gail, and the warning was clear in his eyes. "Drive carefully, and no side trips. Got it?"

She felt as if ice were forming around her heart. He sounded so cold, so indifferent. She was reminded of the first time she'd seen him, and her impression of him—deep, dark and dangerous.

She knew now where that power came from. He was the law. And because of that, maybe he was still the enemy, after all. Her heart sank at the thought.

Her mind wrestled with the problem all the way back to the house. How could she hope to convince him when she hadn't been able to convince the rest of them, not even the people she'd worked with, or Frank's associates—the people who knew her well?

She had to try, she told herself. She was tired of turning the other cheek. She was sick of running away. This time she was going to stand and fight—for her integrity, and self-esteem. Because, for the first time in her life, it really mattered to her what people thought of her. And, one special man's opinion of her mattered a great deal.

Somehow, she vowed silently as she drove back through the steadily falling snow, she would make Blake believe in her. Maybe then, she could finally believe in herself.

She stopped the car at the drive-in restaurant and after taking Heather to the bathroom, picked up a hamburger and sundae for her. Blake refused her offer to order him something and she was too strung out to eat anything.

They reached the house at last, having spent several minutes in silence. Heather, who had eaten half the hamburger and a spoonful of the sundae, was fast asleep in the back, and barely managed a groggy protest as Blake carried her into the house.

Gail followed close behind him, her heart thumping with uncertain fear. It had occurred to her that he must have had a very good reason to come all the way out here after her. It couldn't be just a case of trying to prove she'd lied about Frank's death. After all, she'd been acquitted on that score and she was pretty sure she couldn't be tried again.

It had to be something far more serious. She tried not to think about it as she tucked Heather into her bed and kissed her good-night.

Blake was waiting for her in the living room when she went back downstairs. Somehow, seeing him sitting on her couch now, his hands tucked between his knees and his expression uncompromising, he seemed a stranger—a formidable, dangerous stranger. It was as if the days they'd spent together had never been.

She hovered in the doorway, passionately hoping that she was wrong in her suspicion. "Would you like coffee? Something to eat?"

"Nothing. Thank you." He looked up at her, his gray eyes glinting like frost on pavement. The glow from the lamp beside him threw shadows across his face, and his harsh expression unnerved her.

She crossed the room in front of him and sat down on the edge of the armchair. "I am *not,* nor have I ever been, involved with Mike Stevens," she said quietly.

"Is that why you lied to me? A meeting with Annie's teachers, you told me. Instead you were planning to run off to Canada. Why Canada, for pity's sake? Does that sound like the actions of a person with nothing to hide?"

She sighed. "No, it doesn't. You're right. I didn't tell you the truth. For a very good reason. I was running away. Canada seemed like a good place to disappear for a while."

He narrowed his eyes. "Running away? From Stevens?"

She shook her head, wondering how he could be so damn indifferent. "Of course not. I was running away from you."

She'd shaken him. She could see it in the way he blinked, as if he wasn't quite sure what had hit him. "Why in the hell would you run away from me?" He paused, his expression suddenly sharpening. "Unless you figured out I was a cop and would stop you from meeting Stevens?"

She fought back her resentment. She had to keep a clear mind and stay in control. "For the last time, Blake, I was not going to meet Mike. I thought he had sent you to find me. I thought he'd hired you to...hurt Heather."

There was a long silence, broken only by Blake's harsh breathing. Finally he made a sound of disgust in the back of his throat. "Why, in God's name, would you think that? How could you possibly think that I would hurt Heather? Dammit, Gail, you're not making sense."

She couldn't answer him for a moment. He'd called her by her real name, for the first time. If only it had been said the way she wanted to hear it—from his lips softly and caressingly.

She drew in a trembling breath. "Why is it that you are all so ready to take the word of a criminal against mine? I'm telling the truth, Blake. Mike threatened to send someone to kill Heather. I wasn't the only one who lied. You lied to me, too. I knew you weren't a real-estate agent from Seattle. Even before I caught you out, I think I knew. I thought Mike had sent you. How was I to know you were an undercover cop?"

"You could have leveled with me. You could have told me the truth about your past, instead of making up lies. That's what an innocent person would have done."

"Blake, please, listen to me and try to understand what I'm saying. When Mike was sent to prison, he swore he would find a way to get even with me. He tried to blame me for Frank's death. He said I'd driven him to it. Apparently Frank had flown into one of his jealous rages and accused Mike of having an affair with me. They fought, and Mike pulled a gun on him. I don't know if he meant to shoot him or not. I only know the gun went off and Frank died.''

She shuddered, thinking of that terrible moment when she'd walked into Frank's office and had seen his broken, bleeding body on the floor. "After the police had left,'' she said unsteadily, ''Mike came to me and told me he'd gotten rid of my jealous husband. He said I owed him my life, and that now I should repay him.

"I was horrified at what he'd done, and terrified of what he might do to me and Heather. I managed to talk him into leaving, telling him it wouldn't look good if the police saw him with me so soon after Frank's death. As soon as he was out of the house I called the police.''

Blake nodded, his expression hard and unrelenting. "Yeah, I heard. Your testimony's on record. For what it's worth.''

Resentment burned hot for a moment, and she waited for the reaction to pass. ''It happens to be the truth. When Mike was arrested he knew I'd told the police that he'd killed Frank. He accused me of leading him on, and then rejecting him. He swore to get back at me for betraying him. He said he would...destroy the one thing that meant anything to me—my daughter....'' Without warning her voice had wobbled, and she fought to regain her composure.

"Take it easy,'' Blake said gruffly.

It was the first faint indication that he was affected by her story, and her pulse leaped with hope. She took a steadying breath. ''Mike swore to the police that I'd planned the whole thing with him. They believed him. Everyone believed him.''

Again her voice broke, but intent on finishing now, she

struggled on. "Frank was insanely jealous and possessive. He was convinced that every man who came into the store had come for the sole purpose of coming on to me. Even though I told him over and over that I hated the way Mike acted around me, he still believed that I encouraged him. I guess he made everyone else believe it, too."

She hunted in the pocket of her jeans for a tissue. "I hadn't any close friends, Frank had seen to that, but I thought that among the people I knew, at least one or two would know me well enough to believe me about what happened. Instead they betrayed me, telling the police about the fights I'd had with Frank over Mike's sickening behavior when he was around me."

"Well, I hand it to the guy, he's persistent."

She felt cold when she saw Blake's grim expression. Nothing she'd said had made the slightest difference to him. He'd made up his mind she was guilty and that was that.

All at once she'd had enough. There was no more fight left in her. She got up from the chair and walked over to the door. "I can see that you're determined not to believe me," she said bitterly. "Whatever happened to justice and the concept that someone is innocent until proved guilty?"

She pulled the door open and looked back at him. She'd done her best. She wasn't about to beg. "I'm tired," she muttered. "I'd like you to leave now."

He stood slowly, as if he found it painful to move. Her heart skipped a beat when he studied her for several seconds without speaking. Then he said softly, "You don't understand. I'm not going anywhere. Your lover boy escaped from jail last week. He's on his way here to meet you. Or maybe he's waiting for you in Canada?"

So her worst fears were realized. It was a moment before she could speak. "How did he know where to find me?"

"He had you watched. Someone tailed you from the

minute you left Portland. Mike Stevens has a lot of connections. He pulled in a couple of favors. His contact hung around here long enough to make sure you were putting down roots, then he reported back to Stevens.''

So her fears hadn't been all that paranoid. Her sense of being followed when she'd first arrived in Mellow Springs had been genuine. As for the past few days, she knew now that it was Blake who had given her that same feeling. He must have been behind her all the time, without her ever seeing him.

Her fear spread, almost choking her. ''How did *you* know where to find me?''

Blake shrugged, and dug his hands into the pockets of his jeans. ''When Mike went over the fence he was supposed to take his cellmate with him. He must have decided he'd be better off on his own. So his cellmate got ticked and snitched on him. Apparently in a rash moment Stevens had told him he was going to meet up with you in Mellow Springs.''

''He didn't happen to say what he intended to do with me when he caught up with me, I suppose?'' She held out her hands in a gesture of appeal. ''Can't you see, Blake? He's coming here to make good his threat. He's going to try and get at Heather, and he'll almost certainly hurt me. The man is crazy. He's determined to make me pay for turning him in.''

She stood there while the seconds ticked by, willing him to believe her. He looked so cynical, so damned superior. She just couldn't stand it anymore. Hurt beyond belief at his distrust of her, she finally let go of her temper.

''Damn you,'' she muttered fiercely. ''Every word I've spoken is the truth. But you're just too arrogant to even consider that you could be wrong. You and all your damn colleagues. Well, I can't make you believe what you don't want to believe. But I'll tell you right now, I'm not waiting around here for Mike to come after my daughter while the cops stand around twiddling their thumbs and feeding their egos.''

She slammed the door shut on the last word and rushed across the room. To her utter dismay, Blake calmly stretched out an arm and blocked her way.

''Where do you think you're going?''

''I'm getting my daughter and myself the hell out of here.'' She shoved on his arm, struggling to get free. ''I don't give a damn if you believe me or not, but you're not stopping me from taking my daughter somewhere where she'll be safe.''

He shifted his grip and grasped both her arms. ''Gail—''

Incensed beyond measure, she shoved against his chest. ''Let go of me, dammit. You can't keep me here. I'm not under arrest. So go to hell, Mr. U.S. Marshal. Leave me alone!''

She glared up at him, and saw an answering spark of anger in his eyes. She saw something else—the unmistakable heat of passion. For a moment she wasn't sure if he would yell at her or thrust her away from him.

He did neither.

Before she could draw a full breath he jerked her hard against his chest and smothered her startled cry with his warm, hard mouth. ''I do believe you,'' he muttered thickly, punctuating his words with short, urgent kisses. ''You're damn well not going anywhere without me.'' He opened his mouth, and she was powerless to prevent her own lips from parting.

Her mind warned her to pull away from him, but her body wasn't listening. Crushed against the hard wall of his chest, she clung to his shoulders and gave herself up to the sheer pleasure of being in his arms.

The power that she had sensed in him was transmitted now as a searing, urgent need. She had thought that nothing could move this man and break down his formidable armor. She'd been wrong.

Lost in the heat of his kiss, her body caught fire as his hands moved roughly over her hips, pulling her closer to him. She dug her fingers into his back and met his passion with a fiery need of her own. She wanted this man as she'd never wanted anything in her life. Her body ached with it.

Feverishly she sought his tongue, and felt his shudder in response. She forgot about the fear of the past few hours. She forgot about Mike and the possibility of him turning up in Mellow Springs. All she could think about was Blake's body, hard against hers, his hands triggering spasms of pleasure everywhere they touched, and his mouth, urgent and hot on hers.

She almost forgot about Heather, too, until somewhere in the fog that clouded her mind a tiny warning sounded. She couldn't do this. Not now. Not with Heather sleeping down the hallway. It was sheer agony to pull herself out of his arms.

The second she resisted, he let her go. Dropping his arms to his sides, he dragged in his breath. His voice sounded a little hoarse when he finally spoke. "I'm sorry. That shouldn't have happened. I guess I got carried away."

All her pent-up emotion seemed to drain out of her. He didn't have to make it quite so plain that he regretted his weak moment.

"Forget it," she said tightly. "We're both tired. I think we should both get some sleep." She crossed the room to the door and pulled it open. "I'll call you first thing in the morning."

"Gail, I have to stay here tonight. If what you say is true, and Stevens is out for revenge, both you and Heather are in danger. I can't leave you alone now."

She looked at him, torn between wanting him out of the

house so that she could forget what had happened, and needing him there because she was afraid to be alone.

"What I say is the truth," she said wearily. "I'll make up a bed for you on the couch."

"Just give me a blanket. I'll manage with that."

She found him a pillow and a couple of blankets, and laid them on the couch. Ignoring his insistence that he wasn't hungry, she heated a frozen pizza and opened a beer for him.

Watching him attack the food made her glad she'd offered it. Surprisingly, she was hungry enough to join him. "Where do you think Mike is now?" she asked him, as they both sat at her coffee table munching on the pizza. "I suppose the local police are watching out for him?"

"We've got an APB out on him, but in this neck of the woods he'd be tough to spot. There just aren't enough cops to go around to keep watch on all the roads."

She couldn't look at him without remembering how she'd felt, crushed against his body. "You were planning on arresting him single-handedly?"

His casual shrug didn't quite match the tension in his face. "It's my job."

She shook her head at the trite remark. It didn't begin to cover what was involved. "So what happens now? Now that you don't have me to lead you to him, I mean."

"I guess I just sit tight here and wait for him to show up."

"I hope you realize just how dangerous Mike can be. I have no doubt that he would kill all three of us just to get back at me."

His glance flicked over her face, as indifferent now as if the kiss between them had been nothing but a fantasy. "I'm well prepared for that. I have to admit, though, it will make things easier knowing I don't have to fight off a vicious girlfriend."

She raised her eyebrows at that. "You thought I was vicious?"

There was no humor in his eyes when he looked at her. "From what I'd been told, you'd helped your lover blow away your husband. That put you in the 'vicious' category."

She thought about that for a minute. "What changed your mind about me?"

This time he avoided her gaze. "After twenty years on the force, I'm a pretty good judge of character."

"But right up until tonight, you still suspected me of planning to meet Mike."

"That was before I heard your side of it. Besides, there's always been a doubt in my mind."

"Why? What made you think I could be telling the truth when no one else believed me?"

He picked up his beer and twirled it, making a miniature whirlpool in the glass. "I asked myself why you would turn Mike Stevens in if you'd helped him murder his brother. You certainly couldn't have expected him to keep quiet about your part in it."

"I asked the policeman who arrested me the same question." She uttered a bitter laugh. "Apparently, the police believed that I led Mike on long enough to persuade him to kill Frank, and then I turned him in to be rid of him."

"That occurred to me, too." He tilted his head back and drained his glass, while she fought the resentment still smoldering deep inside her. How could she blame him, when everyone else thought the same?

"But then," Blake said, setting down his glass, "I had to ask myself another question. If you hated the guy enough to send him down for murder, why were you planning to meet him now that he was on the run? It didn't make sense."

She felt a warm rush of gratitude. "Thank you," she

said unsteadily. "You have no idea what that means to me."

"Don't thank me. I'm a cop. I'm supposed to question everything."

Was it her imagination, or was he being deliberately remote? She was tired, she told herself, and letting her imagination get the best of her again. She had his trust once more, and that was all she could ask—for now.

Later, when she could think more clearly, she would decide what that kiss had meant. One thing she did know— he hadn't been unaffected by it, either physically or emotionally. He'd left her in no doubt of that.

A little shiver of excitement coursed down her back. Blake Foster was very good at masking his thoughts and feelings. But in those few moments when she'd been locked in his arms, he'd abandoned all pretense of indifference.

The prospect of all that power and pent-up need being fully released in an explosive display of raw passion melted her insides. Making love with Blake Foster would have to be an awesome experience. Just the thought of it made her weak with anticipation.

She'd found something with him that she hadn't believed existed. For the first time in her life she knew what it was to fall in love. It was terrifying and exciting, all at the same time. It was like flying down the bunny slopes on a disk— the ride was daunting, and there was always the chance of getting hurt, but you couldn't wait to get up and try it again.

Half smiling at her metaphor, she got to her feet. "I'm really tired. I think I'd better go to bed."

He nodded, his gaze fixed firmly on his empty glass.

"Help yourself to anything you want," she added.

When he didn't answer she hesitated, longing for him to say something, anything, that would give her an indication of what was going on in his mind. "I'm...glad you're staying," she said awkwardly. "I feel much safer knowing you'll be here. I have to admit, I'm scared, knowing that Mike is out there somewhere."

"You should be. He's a nasty piece of work."

"Can't you send for reinforcements?"

He shook his head. "This is one I get to handle all on my own. Unless things get ugly, and then I'll call in the local boys."

She shivered. "Well, let's hope he doesn't turn up here tonight."

The look he sent her was hard to read. "As far as I'm concerned, the sooner the better."

Not quite sure why that sounded so ominous, Gail told him good-night and went to bed.

Long after she'd gone, Blake continued to sit on the couch, twisting the empty glass around and around in his hands. He had committed the unforgivable sin. He'd let his emotions get the better of him.

Dammit, he'd wanted her. He'd never wanted a woman quite so badly. He still wanted her. His body hurt with a raw craving that wouldn't subside. Just knowing she was lying in bed, only a few yards away, tied his gut in knots.

She would have made it easy for him, too. He knew that.

He'd felt her responding—her hips grinding against his, her breasts thrusting into his chest, her warm, soft mouth eagerly exploring his. He'd been surprised at her eagerness—surprised and utterly aroused.

God, what he would give to set her down on a soft bed and cover her naked body with his own. She fitted against him just right; he could imagine how it would be to lie naked with her while he used all his skill to bring out the primitive passion that boiled just below the surface.

She was driving him crazy with her soft, seductive laugh and her beautiful eyes glowing with subtle invitation.

He was in trouble, and he knew it. The problem was, this wasn't simply physical. If it had been just a case of the hots for her body, a cold shower would have taken care of it.

He not only wanted her physically, he enjoyed her emotionally, as well. He liked her intelligence, her spirit, her warm, generous eagerness to please. He liked the way she handled her daughter, with a firm yet loving hand. She was a woman who was capable of caring very deeply—the kind of woman he'd often dreamed about.

And that was where the danger lay. He felt as if he was being caught up in something that threatened to carry him to where he didn't really want to go. Couldn't go. He hadn't the faintest idea where all this was going to take him, but one thing he did know for sure—he was not going to be satisfied until he'd thoroughly and passionately made love with Gail Stevens.

Uttering a soft curse, he got to his feet and took his glass out into the kitchen. In the meantime he still had a job to do—a dangerous one. The method might have changed, but the goal was still the same: to apprehend Mike Stevens and take him back where he belonged, safely behind bars.

Only now the job was more complicated. Instead of relying on Gail Stevens to lead him to his quarry, if what she told him was true—and he believed that it was—it was very likely that he would be called upon to protect her and her daughter against a crazed killer before this was all over.

Given his feelings for Gail, that prospect was fraught with pitfalls. Above all, he couldn't allow Stevens to know how he felt about her. If things went wrong, the bastard could and probably would use it against him.

One wrong move on his part, one careless moment of distraction, and he could blow this whole mission and lose both Gail and Heather in the process.

The only way to make sure he stayed on top of things was to forget what had happened tonight. Forget how he felt about her. Ignore what happened to his body every time she came close to him, at least until this was all over. Only then would he be free to deal with the craving that would give him no rest.

His blood raced at the thought. Shaking his head, he made himself ignore the pangs of desire. No more. From now on, Gail Stevens and her daughter were just clients, a means to an end. He only hoped to God it would be over soon.

Down the hallway Gail lay wide-awake in the darkened room. Over and over again she'd relived those few wonderful, passionate moments in Blake's arms. How she wished she could have taken that fiery path to its logical end.

Right now, she could be lying there with Blake, knowing at last how it felt to be fully satisfied by a man. She had never even experienced an orgasm. She wasn't sure what it was supposed to feel like.

Her nights with Frank had been tense and uncomfortable. She never remembered feeling anything like the kinds of sensations that Blake had aroused in her.

Restlessly, she tossed around in the bed. Her desperate need of him frightened her. She'd trusted before and been betrayed. Yet in spite of her fears, she was beginning to trust Blake Foster. She felt safe and secure with him, both emotionally and physically.

She didn't doubt that he could protect them against Mike Stevens. She wasn't so sure about her feelings for him. That took a considerable amount of trust for someone who had sworn never to trust again. For she knew, without a shadow of a doubt, that if she was betrayed this time, it would destroy her forever.

She slept fitfully throughout the night, coming awake at the slightest sound to lie still in the dark, her heart racing and ears straining, until she was sure that all was well.

More than once she was tempted to go to Heather or out

into the living room to check on Blake. She didn't want to disturb her daughter unnecessarily, and she was afraid that Blake might think she was trying to entice him. She'd had more than enough of that kind of misunderstanding.

Eventually it was light enough to get up. She showered and dressed in jeans and a warm, red sweater, then went to wake up Heather before venturing into the living room.

The blankets were piled neatly on the end of the couch, and Blake sat at the other end, reading the morning newspaper, when she followed Heather into the room.

Blake greeted the little girl with a hug and listened patiently to her excited chatter while Gail put on a pot of coffee.

Listening with amusement to their conversation, Gail poured milk into a bowl of cereal and set it on the dinette table for Heather.

"I don't have much in the way of breakfast," she told Blake when she went into the living room to get her daughter. "I think I can find a couple of eggs and an English muffin."

"You could have some of my cereal," Heather offered, beaming at him. "I have lots of cereal."

"Cereal will be fine," Blake said, allowing Heather to tug him to his feet. "I like cereal."

"Come and choose which one you want." She dragged him into the kitchen, while Gail tried in vain to visualize Blake actually enjoying a serving of Froot Loops.

Watching him with Heather at the table that looked too small for him, she felt a tug of tenderness that took her breath away. Heather laughed up at him, her eyes sparkling with a delight that Gail had never seen before.

He had captured both their hearts, it seemed. If only this moment right now could never end.

"I don't want to go to school today," Heather announced, as she scooped up milk from her bowl with her spoon. "I want to stay home and play with Uncle Blake."

"Well, you're not going to school today." Gail picked up the dish and carried it to the sink. "We're going to Canada, remember?"

"I don't wanna go to Canada. I want to stay here."

"No one's going to Canada," Blake said quietly.

Gail stared at him. "What do you mean?"

"What I said. No one's going to Canada. We're all staying right here, where I can keep an eye on you."

She couldn't believe she'd heard him correctly. Very carefully, she placed the bowl in the sink. "Heather, I want you to go and brush your teeth."

"Aw, Mommy, do I have to?"

"Yes, you do have to. And right now."

She waited for Heather to leave the kitchen, aware of the tension starting to build in the tiny room. Only now did it occur to her that Blake hadn't looked at her directly once since she'd come into the living room.

She walked over to the table and picked up his empty bowl. "Are you telling me I *can't* go to Canada?"

For the first time his gaze flicked briefly over her face. "That's about the size of it, yes."

She felt colder now than she'd ever felt in her life. Looking at the cool indifference on his face, it was as though she'd imagined the barely leashed passion she'd sensed was tormenting his body only a few hours ago. How could he be so unemotional after the hot kisses they'd shared?

"But why?" she demanded. "Heather and I would be much safer there."

He looked up at her then, and her heart ached at the remote expression in his eyes. "Because," he said deliberately, "my job is to apprehend Mike Stevens. He's looking for you here, and that's where you're going to be until he shows up."

She lifted her chin. "In other words," she said coldly, "you want Heather and me to act as bait. Isn't that just a tad dangerous?"

"That," he said, with a careless shrug, "is a risk I guess we'll just have to take."

She understood—now—what she should have known all along. She was nothing more than an assignment to him. The only reason he'd been so charming, so supportive, so damned accommodating to both her and her daughter, was for the sole purpose of capturing Mike Stevens. How could she have been so stupid?

PLAY "LUCKY 7" AND GET
FIVE FREE GIFTS!

HOW TO PLAY:

1. With a coin, carefully scratch off the silver box at the right. Then check the claim char to see what we have for you—**FREE BOOKS** and a gift—**ALL YOURS! ALL FREE!**

2. Send back this card and you'll receive brand-new Silhouette Intimate Moments® novel These books have a cover price of $4.50 each, but they are yours to keep absolutely free

3. There's no catch. You're under no obligation to buy anything. We charge nothing—
ZERO—for your first shipmen
And you don't have to make
any minimum number of
purchases—not even one!

4. The fact is thousands of readers enjoy receiving books by mail from the Silhouette Reader Service™ months before they're available in stores. They like the convenience o home delivery and they love our discount prices!

5. We hope that after receiving your free books you'll want to remain a subscriber. But the choice is yours—to continue or cancel, any time at all! So why not take us up on ou invitation, with no risk of any kind. You'll be glad you did!

YOURS FREE!

This beautiful porcelain
box is topped with a lovely
bouquet of porcelain flowers,
perfect for holding rings, pins
or other precious trinkets—
and is yours ABSOLUTELY
FREE when you accept our
NO-RISK offer!

NOT ACTUAL SIZE

NO COST! NO OBLIGATION TO BUY!
NO PURCHASE NECESSARY!

The Silhouette Reader Service™—Here's how it works

Accepting free books places you under no obligation to buy anything. You may keep the books and gift and return the shipping statement marked "cancel." If you do not cancel, about a month later we'll send you 6 additional novels, and bill you just $3.71 each, plus 25¢ delivery per book and GST. * That's the complete price—and compared to cover prices of $4.50 each—quite a bargain! You may cancel at any time, but if you choose to continue, every month we'll send you 6 more books, which you may either purchase at the discount price...or return to us and cancel your subscription.

*Terms and prices subject to change without notice.

Canadian residents will be charged applicable provincial taxes and GST.

If offer card is missing, write to: Silhouette Reader Service, P.O. Box 609, Fort Erie, Ontario L2A 5X3

0195619199-L2A5X3-BR01

SILHOUETTE READER SERVICE
PO BOX 609
FORT ERIE ON   L2A 9Z9

MAIL ▷ POSTE
Canada Post Corporation / Société canadienne des postes

Postage paid   Port payé
If mailed in Canada   si posté au Canada

Business   Réponse
Reply   d'affaires

0195619199   01

Chapter 7

Gail straightened her back, preparing for battle. It might be just duty to Blake Foster, but her daughter's life was at stake, and she wasn't about to jeopardize Heather's safety simply so he could go home and get his back slapped for doing a great job.

"Look," she said, matching his cool tone, "I don't know what kind of jurisdiction you have in this town, but I do know you can't keep me here against my will. Not unless you arrest me. And I haven't done anything wrong. So, if it's all the same to you, I'm going to put Heather back in the car and I'm heading for Canada where we'll be safe."

She turned to go, but before she had taken two steps he was out of his chair and standing between her and the door. Jamming his hands onto his hips, he said with just a trace of menace in his voice, "No, it's not all right with me."

The bowl slipped from her nerveless fingers and crashed to the floor. For a moment she wondered if she'd made a mistake believing his story about being a U.S. Marshal.

After all, he'd given her no proof. She stared at the scattered pieces of crockery, willing herself not to cry.

"Dammit, Gail."

She heard the catch in his voice and caught her breath, but didn't dare look up at him.

"Look," he said, his voice softening just a little. "If I let you run off to Canada, what happens if Stevens finds out about it? He could bypass here altogether and take off after you, leaving me sitting here like a cat at an empty mouse hole. No matter what happens, you won't be safe from him until he's back behind bars. Do you really want to spend the rest of your life running from him? Is that what you want for Heather?"

She shook her head, her gaze still concentrated on the floor. She knew that what he said made sense. Besides, she didn't have the money to stay for long in Canada. Sooner or later she would have to come back to the States and get a job.

"I'm not afraid for myself," she muttered, stooping to pick up the pieces of the bowl. "I'm terrified he'll get to Heather before either of us can stop him."

"I've been thinking about that." He paused, waiting until she'd gathered up all of the pieces and deposited them in the trash. "Can we sit down and talk about this without you running out of the house?"

She felt tired, as if she hadn't slept for a month. Everything seemed to be crowding in on her, and she felt as if she were in the middle of the mirror maze again, with a dozen different ways to go and all of them wrong.

"All right," she said wearily. "But I don't want to frighten Heather. She'll be back here any minute."

"I know." He pulled out a chair and waited for her to sit down. Taking the one opposite her, he leaned his elbows on the table. "How would you feel about letting her stay with Darcie until this is all over? Would Darcie be willing to take her without asking too many questions? Could you think of a reasonable excuse without telling her the whole story?''

"I guess I could," Gail said doubtfully. "Though it'll be tough explaining why I don't want her to go to school."

"It would also mean not going to see her, of course. Stevens might follow you there. He could easily wait until you've left and then take her away from Darcie."

"Oh, God. I don't want to even think about that." She covered her face with her hands in order to think more clearly. It would be best for Heather, of course, but she couldn't stand the thought of being out of sight of her daughter without knowing what was going on or how long it would be. "I suppose there isn't any alternative?"

"Not that I can see. If you try to leave town, he could be right behind you."

She dropped her hands. "You think he's here now?"

Blake shrugged. "He's had plenty of time to get here. I thought he'd arranged a meeting place and was waiting there for you to join him. But now I know that's not happening, I figure he's got to be in the area somewhere. More than likely, he's waiting for the right chance to grab either you or Heather."

The idea that Mike could be that close terrified her. "Do you think he's seen you with me?"

Blake's set expression didn't help to calm her fears. "I don't know," he said slowly. "I can only hope he doesn't get any ideas about that. If he's got the slightest suspicion that there's a cop in the picture, he could decide it's not worth the risk and take off."

"And I'll never know where and when he's going to turn up again."

"Exactly."

She considered his words. "It looks as if I'm damned either way, doesn't it?"

"Not necessarily. As long as Heather is safe with Darcie, that only leaves you to watch out for, which will make my job a good deal easier. I'll be there ready to grab him if and when he makes a move. Though I can't be seen with you outside this house anymore."

"Then how can you protect me?"

"You'll have to stay right here in the house."

She gave an emphatic shake of her head. "No way. I'm going back to work."

"You can't go back to work. It's out of the question."

"I can't sit around here on the off chance that Mike may or may not show up. I have a living to make. Besides, I'd go crazy hanging around here with nothing to do."

"Then you'll have to find something to amuse yourself. It's the only way I can guarantee to protect you. Even then, it's not a sure thing."

She met his gaze, feeling remarkably calm all of a sudden. "I'm going back to work. And that's final."

Blake swore. "It's too dangerous for you to be at the store. He's bound to know you work there. It's the first place he'll head for."

"Well, isn't that what we want? Isn't it better to make it look as if I have no idea he's out of jail? That way he'll figure you're just someone I know if he sees you. If I stay locked up in the house he'll guess I've heard about his escape. He could figure out you're a cop then, and that you're hanging around me just to grab him."

For a long moment her gaze clashed with his, neither of them willing to back down. Finally she detected a glimmer of uncertainty in his almost-colorless eyes.

"Damn!" he said at last. "I know you're right. I just don't like it. I don't like it one little bit."

"Neither do I," Gail said, getting to her feet. "But I want this over as soon as possible. If my going to the bookstore as if nothing had happened will encourage Mike to make a move, then dammit, that's where I'm going. I'm not sure how much longer I can take all this tension, anyway, without completely falling apart.''

"Hey, you're doing just great." She jumped when Blake reached out and covered her hand with his for a brief instant. "I'm sorry, Gail. I'd give anything not to put you through all this. But without you to draw him in, he could easily give us all the slip and disappear. It could be months, even years before we caught up with him again. And in that time he'd have plenty of opportunities to find you and carry out his threat."

"I know." She could feel the fear again like a cold, hard knot in her stomach. At least Blake believed her story now, and that was something. At least now, she wasn't on her own.

The thought gave her bittersweet comfort. How much more comforting it would have been had she had the satisfaction of knowing that Blake had a personal interest in her safety. That was something she would have to deal with later, when this was all over and he had gone back to Portland, or wherever he was from.

She made an effort to give him a weak smile. "I'll go make those calls."

"Wait a minute. There's something I want to ask you."

Her pulse skipped, and she silently cursed herself for being so susceptible to every word he spoke. "What is it?"

"What exactly did I say to give myself away?"

This time she did smile. "I may call my daughter 'Annie' all the time, but I always think of her as 'Heather.' Yesterday I slipped up and called her 'Heather' out loud. You didn't react. You knew who I was talking about. I figured you had to know who we were."

He shook his head in mock disgust. "Some cop I am."

"I think you're a very good cop," Gail said sincerely.

He started to say something, but just then the door opened abruptly, and Heather rushed into the kitchen.

"Is Uncle Blake coming to Canada with us?"

Gail sighed. "She really does have a one-track mind, doesn't she?" Squatting down in front of Heather, she took hold of her daughter's hands. They felt unbearably fragile in her fingers, and she felt a lump forming in her throat. She was responsible for what happened to her daughter. She had to make sure she was safe.

"Honey," she said unsteadily, "Mommy's decided not to go to Canada just yet. You did say you didn't really want to go, didn't you?"

Heather nodded. "I get to stay home and play with Uncle Blake?"

"Well, no." Gail smiled at her, willing her to understand. "I have something much better for you. A big surprise. How would you like to stay with Darcie for a few days? You'd get to play with Brendan and Janice, and sleep in Janice's room every night. Would you like that?"

Heather looked doubtful. "Will you be there, too?"

Gail prayed for the right words. "No, honey. Mommy is going to be pretty busy for the next few days. Too busy to take care of you properly. That's why I want you to stay with Darcie. I'll be able to talk to you on the phone every day, though." She glanced at Blake for confirmation and received a quick nod. "You can tell me everything you and Janice and Brendan have been doing, okay?"

"Okay." Heather gave the prospect some serious consideration. "Can I take my dolly's house?"

"You can take whatever you want." Gail straightened her knees and stood. "Now, will you stay here and talk to Uncle Blake while I make a couple of phone calls?"

"Okay." Looking just a tad worried, Heather sat down at the kitchen table. "I don't have to go to school?"

"No," Gail replied, wondering how she was going to

get through the days without her daughter. "You don't have to go to school. At least for a little while, anyway."

She left Heather alone with Blake and went into the living room to make the calls in private. Somehow she would have to make up a believable story for Darcie. It wouldn't be easy. The baby-sitter was too perceptive to accept anything but a very convincing reason why Gail would dump her daughter on her.

Darcie answered the phone right away, and sounded astonished to hear Gail's voice. "I thought you were in California by now. What happened?"

"I had a...complication," Gail said carefully.

"Aha. It wouldn't happen to be a very tall complication, with come-hither gray eyes and a sexy smile, by any chance?"

Gail managed an uneasy laugh. Now that she'd been given an opening, she might as well run with it, she decided. "Something like that."

"Well, good for you. You deserve a little fun in your life. Go for it, that's what I say."

Gail took a deep breath and crossed her fingers. "Darcie, I was wondering... Would you mind keeping Annie for me for a while? I'd like to spend some time...alone with him, if you know what I mean."

She could feel the warmth creeping over her cheeks as Darcie murmured, "Oh, like that, is it. Of course I'll keep her. For how long?"

Thank goodness Blake couldn't hear the conversation, Gail thought, casting an anxious eye at the closed living-room door. "A few days? I'm not absolutely sure, to be honest. I'll pay you, however long it is."

There was a lengthy pause at the other end of the line, and she held her breath.

"Uh-oh," Darcie said softly. "You really are getting involved. Are you sure about this?"

"Never been more sure."

Darcie chuckled. "All right, it's okay by me. The kids will love the company. She might even create a miracle and stop them from fighting with each other all the time. Make sure you bring plenty of clothes and some of her favorite toys. Then you can forget about her and have yourself a darn good time. You deserve it."

"Bless you, Darcie. You're the best friend anyone could ask for."

"Hey, this is a business arrangement. No need to get mushy on me."

She'd sounded gratified, though, and Gail smiled. "There's just one more thing," she said, hoping she wasn't pushing her luck too far. "I'd rather Annie didn't go to kindergarten while she's there. I think she might feel the separation more if she's in school. I don't think it will hurt her to miss a few days. Do you mind? I'll pay you for the extra time, of course."

"No, you won't. You'll pay me the usual rate and of course I'll keep her."

Thanking her, Gail hung up. She dialed the number of the bookstore, hoping that some day she would be able to repay her friends.

Polly sounded just as surprised as Darcie had been to learn that Gail was still in town.

"I had a change of plans," Gail told her. "I'll explain when I get there." She wondered if Polly would believe the story that she'd given Darcie. Probably not. Knowing Polly, though, she wouldn't ask questions.

Starting to feel a little better, Gail went back to the kitchen to get her daughter ready to go to Darcie's. "All set," she said, in answer to Blake's questioning look.

She turned to Heather, who was looking at the comic strips in the newspaper. "Honey, you'd better gather up what toys you want to take to Darcie's house. Just don't get too many, though, or they might get lost, and you don't want that to happen.''

"I can't pick up my dolly's house," Heather said, looking hopefully at Blake.

"I'll come and get it for you when you're ready to leave," he promised her.

The little girl ran out of the kitchen, while Gail busied herself rinsing off the dishes.

"What did you tell Darcie?" Blake asked, just when she was beginning to hope he wasn't going to mention it.

"I told her I'd changed my mind about taking Heather to California and that I wanted her to stay there for a few days, because I wanted some time alone."

"Darcie didn't ask why?"

"I think she formed her own ideas about that." Gail could feel her cheeks growing warm again as a lengthy silence greeted that statement.

"I hope I'm not ruining your reputation," Blake finally said, his voice sounding strained.

"Darcie's not a gossip."

"Well, when this is over, you can tell her the truth."

And what was the truth? Gail wondered, as she stacked the last plate in the dishwasher. That she'd fallen for a tough, charismatic cop, dedicated enough to his job to be capable of turning his boyish charm on and off whenever the occasion called for it, managing in the process to break her heart? She didn't think she wanted to confess that to Darcie.

"What about your friend at the bookstore?"

She dried her hands on a kitchen towel before answering him. "I'll think of something to tell Polly."

He was silent for a moment, apparently deep in thought. Then he said quietly, "I think you should tell her the truth."

Startled, she looked at him. "The truth?"

"The whole story. That way she can be on guard, too. Especially if Stevens decides to grab you in the bookstore. At least one other person will know what's going on. As long as you can trust her not to say anything to anyone else."

She shrugged. "Why not? It's not going to make a whole lot of difference anyway, is it? I mean, once you've done your duty and captured Mike, everyone's going to know the whole story. This is a small town. You can hardly go around handcuffing an escaped convict and hauling him back to jail without someone sitting up and taking notice. I'm sure it will make headlines in the local newspaper, at the very least."

"I'm sorry. I realize this is the last thing on earth you wanted, but I can't see that we have any other choice."

She wondered if he would realize that her bitterness was directed as much at him as it was the situation she found herself in. "Well, I'm not sure how Polly will feel about having a possible target for a killer working with her, but I know she will do everything she can to help. And she won't say anything to anyone else. I can assure you of that."

"Good, that makes me feel a little better."

He sat drumming his fingers on the table, and she stole a glance at him. If only she could forget how he'd made her feel in his arms. If only she hadn't spent all those wonderful hours getting to know him. If only she hadn't met him at all, and had remained ignorant of what she could be missing.

But then she would never have known some of the most precious moments of her life. For a little while he'd made her feel like a desirable, attractive woman, instead of a mere possession to be owned, used and abused. For a little while, she'd known what it was like to really want a man.

"I left my car down the road a block or two," Blake

said, disrupting her unsettling thoughts. "I came in the back way yesterday afternoon. I'll watch you leave this morning with Heather, just to make certain no one is following you, then I'll wait for you to call before I pick up the car and take it back to the hotel."

Gail's heart skipped nervously. "You'll be staying at the hotel?"

"No, I'll be staying right here until this is over. After you've dropped off Heather at Darcie's, I'd like you to swing by the hotel and pick me up. I'll go with you to the bookstore, and then find some place to hang around without being too conspicuous."

"All right." He was issuing orders in the same dispassionate tone he might use for his fellow officers, instead of the woman he'd kissed so passionately the night before.

Damn, she thought fiercely. She had to forget all about that. It was nothing more than a moment's weakness on his part, and it was unlikely to happen again. In fact, she would make darn sure it didn't happen again.

For the first time in her life she'd felt the intense, sensual urges of an aroused woman. His rejection had been subtle, but it was rejection all the same.

She may have been the one to call a halt last night, but he'd made it crystal clear that he regretted what had happened. He'd been driven by impulse, the way any man would respond to a woman who'd made it pretty obvious she enjoyed his company. Now that she was cooperating with him, he no longer needed to put on the charm.

Even so, she couldn't quite stop the shivery spasm of anticipation she felt at the thought of being alone with him in the house all night. It was just as well he was indifferent. She had the distinct feeling that if she ever made love with Blake Foster, it would be an experience from which she might never recover.

Her nerves twitched when she bundled Heather into the

car a few minutes later. It took all her willpower to keep from looking around over her shoulder. Act naturally, Blake had told her. The more normal things appeared, the more likely they would catch Mike off guard. Even so, she couldn't help staring into the rearview mirror as she drove away from the house, half expecting a car to come careening around the corner in hot pursuit.

Blake, she knew, was hovering behind the drapes in the living-room window. He would watch her all the way down the road until she turned the corner.

If she thought she saw anyone following her, he'd told her, she was to double back to the house. Otherwise, she was to call him the minute she got to Darcie's. Then he would leave the house and meet her back at the hotel.

To her immense relief, no one followed her on the way to Darcie's house. But Heather, to her dismay, became tearful when she got ready to say goodbye.

"I promise I'll call you, honey," Gail said, as she hugged the little girl tight. "And you can call me any time you want, either at the bookstore or at home. Darcie will help you, won't you, Darcie?"

"Of course I will. And I have a special treat for Annie after you've gone."

Heather's face brightened. "Really? Can I have it now?"

"Not until your mommy's gone." Darcie held out her hand. "So you'd better say goodbye to her real quick, now."

Heather clung for a moment longer, then let go. "I'll miss you, Mommy."

"I'll miss you, too, honey. Be good, okay?" Gail hurried down the path, feeling as if she were abandoning her child. Reaching the sidewalk, she turned and gave her daughter a quick wave, then climbed into the car and took off before she could change her mind about leaving her alone with Darcie.

Driving into the hotel parking lot a few minutes later, Gail began to feel a nervous fluttering in her stomach. All this time Heather had been there to act as a buffer between her and Blake. Except for those few brief moments last night, there had been no opportunity to be alone together.

Now there would be no one to defuse this somewhat volatile situation. Although Blake had chosen to ignore what had happened between them, the memory would still be there, hovering over them like a thunderbolt just waiting to strike when they least expected it.

No matter how much he wished it hadn't happened, the fact remained that things had changed between them. There was no going back. The memory was bound to increase the tension between them. She shivered, wondering what would happen, should that tension break.

The foyer was empty when she went inside the Alpine Inn. Sam had disappeared, and after waiting a moment or two, Gail decided just to go on up to Blake's room.

Tapping on his door a moment or two later, she looked furtively up and down the hallway. She felt as if she were engaging in a secret meeting with an illicit lover. The thought brought a flush to her cheeks and she jumped when Blake flung open the door.

"All clear?"

She nodded. "So far." She was trembling, but whether it was from the cold, or fear, or simply the thought of being alone with this man unchaperoned by her daughter, she wasn't sure.

"Okay, let's go."

He was carrying an overnight bag with him, which intensified the feeling of being involved in a clandestine arrangement. She tried not to look at it as they entered the elevator and rode it down to the ground floor.

She was relieved when Blake told her to go out ahead of him, and even more relieved to notice that Sam was still away from his post behind the counter. He was probably taking a lunch break, she thought, surprised to discover it was already midday.

Blake joined her in the car a few minutes later, and she drove quickly into town, parking in her usual spot opposite the bookstore. Polly's car sat a few feet away, next to the two cars that belonged to the women in the antique store next door.

"I'll stay here for now," Blake said, when she sent him a questioning look. "What time will you leave this evening?"

"Around six, when Polly closes the shop."

"I'll be waiting for you here in the car."

Her heart skipped a beat. "All right. I'll need to stop at the store on the way home." Already she was worrying what she should cook for dinner.

"Tell me what you want and I'll pick it up for you. That way, we can go straight home."

Home. This entire conversation sounded so domestic, and disturbingly intimate. She couldn't look at him as she said, "I don't know. What do you like to eat?"

Again she heard that odd note in his voice when he answered, "Why don't I pick up a couple of steaks?"

"Sounds good to me. Can you grab some salad?"

"Sure. French bread?"

"Please." She put her hand on the door handle.

"Gail."

She paused, dreading what was coming, certain she wasn't going to like it.

"You don't have to be so nervous of me."

"I'm not," she said quickly. "I'm scared that Mike will hold up the store or something when you're not around."

"I'm not going to be that far away."

She risked a glance at him. His face was carefully

guarded, and she wished she knew what he was really thinking. "I'm glad to hear that."

"Gail... I'm sorry about last night. I just want to reassure you that it won't happen again."

She felt a sudden spurt of resentment as she looked at him. How could he be so damn insensitive? How could he not know how she felt about him? Now, all at once, she wanted to hurt him back. "I'm glad to hear that, too," she said coolly.

The swift sting of hurt pride reflecting in his eyes brought her no pleasure. Angry at herself, at him, at Mike and the world in general, she opened the door and climbed out. "I'll see you tonight," she said, and slammed the door.

The wind caught her hair as she crossed the road, blowing it across her face. She was glad of the excuse to brush it away. Now he would never have to know that she'd brushed a tear or two away with it.

Seated straight-backed in the car, Blake watched her until she'd gone inside the bookstore and closed the door behind her. He counted to twenty, his gaze fixed on the shop window, until he saw Gail appear briefly and give him a wave of her hand. Then he relaxed his tense body with a long, slow breath.

He still smarted over that well-aimed barb she'd delivered just before she'd scrambled out of the car. He recognized the tension she was under, and no matter what she said, he couldn't quite convince himself that he wasn't at least partly to blame for it.

He'd promised himself he wouldn't get emotional over what had happened the night before. He'd done everything he could to get it out of his mind, but the memory persisted. It didn't help that every moment he was with her, his body ached to hold her. He wanted to kiss her again, to feel the delicious curves of her body rubbing urgently against his, to run his hands over all the intimate places he hadn't gotten to last night.

He couldn't believe how much he still wanted her. No woman had ever aroused him like this. He was in deep trouble—far deeper than he'd first thought. It was going to be damn near impossible to walk away from her when all this was over.

He rolled down the window, needing the cool touch of the wind on his heated face. He had to get through the next day or two without losing his head. The latest report he'd been given when he'd called headquarters earlier had said that someone fitting the description of Mike Stevens had held up a gas station a few miles south of Mellow Springs four days ago.

Which meant that either Stevens had been here in town for a day or two, or he was lying low until things quieted down before making his move.

Narrowing his eyes, Blake scanned the street in both directions. A middle-aged woman stood looking into the window of a jeweler's shop three doors down from the bookstore. Farther along an elderly man stood talking to two young boys, while a woman with a dog crossed the road a few yards away.

He studied the rest of the people on the street. A kid on a bike, a couple of cars cruising down the road, both with women drivers, a delivery van pulled up in front of the hardware store—that was about the extent of it. Nothing suspicious, nothing out of place, nothing to make the tiny hairs on the back of his neck stand up.

Even so, he waited another half hour before climbing out of the car. He left the parking lot, walking at a fast pace, his gaze raking both sides of the street. Twice he stopped and checked out the area behind him in the reflection of a storefront window.

Finally satisfied that Mike Stevens was not in the vicinity, he walked down to the diner. He chose a table at the window where the checkered curtain hid him from view yet gave him a clear shot of the street, and settled down for a long, long wait.

Inside The Book Nook, Polly listened in silence, puncturing it now and again with a sympathetic murmur as Gail briefly recited the story of Frank's murder and Mike's part in it.

"I had no idea," she said, when Gail finally finished the horrifying account. "You poor woman, no wonder you've been acting like a cricket with hiccups. Why didn't you tell me all this before?"

Gail shrugged. "Well, first of all, I didn't think you'd hire me if you knew I was a suspect in a murder case."

"Rubbish," Polly said briskly. "I'm a great judge of character. Anyone only has to look at you to know you couldn't possibly have anything to do with murdering your husband."

Gail uttered a bitter laugh. "Oh, you'd be surprised how many people are ready to believe it."

"Then they're all fools." Polly sent a quick glance over at the door. "You did say the marshal was going to keep an eye on the place?"

"Yes." Gail felt a spasm of guilt. "I'm sorry, Polly. I really didn't want to drag you into all this. To be honest, I don't think Mike would be stupid enough to walk into the shop in broad daylight. He knows the police will be on the lookout for him. I think he's more likely to break into my house and wait for me to get home."

Polly's expression darkened. "Well, I certainly hope you're not going back there. You and Annie are welcome to stay with me until this monster is caught."

Gail felt like hugging the older woman. "Annie's with Darcie. She's going to stay there until this is over. But thanks, Polly, I really appreciate the offer."

Polly studied her with a shrewd look. "What about you?"

"I'll be fine." Gail turned away and pretended to be intensely interested in a pile of calendars on the counter. "As a matter of fact, Blake will be staying in the house for the next few days. Just for protection, of course."

"Of course," Polly murmured, sounding thoughtful. "How do you feel about that?"

"Well, I'll miss Annie, of course," Gail said, deliberately misunderstanding her. "But I'll feel better knowing she'll be safer there." She picked up a leaflet lying beside the calendars. "Is this the new list of trades?"

"Yes, it is," Polly said dryly. "And I'll shut up with the questions. But if you need anything at all, promise you'll let me know."

Gail gave her a grateful smile. "I'll do that."

She thought about Polly's question later, as she stacked some new children's titles on the shelves. The truth was, she didn't know exactly how she felt about being in the house alone with Blake.

On the one hand, it was infinitely preferable to being there alone, jumping at every sound and wondering just when Mike might find his way into the house.

On the other hand, she would find it impossible to relax around Blake. She would have to be on guard the whole time, or she might give him some indication of how she felt about him and the devastating effect he had on her. She wasn't about to make a fool of herself with him again.

All she could hope was that this intolerable situation would be over soon. What with worrying when Mike might turn up, and how Heather was doing without her—not to mention her unpredictable reactions to Blake's every word or movement—if this thing wasn't over within the next few hours, her nerves were bound to snap. She didn't care to dwell on what might happen then.

All afternoon she was on edge, jumping at the slightest sound from the door. Once, when Polly came upon her unexpectedly, she let out a little yelp and backed into the shelves behind her, sending a pile of books scattering over the floor.

"Are you sure you don't want to go home?" Polly asked, as she helped Gail pick up the books and rearrange them on the shelf.

"No, I really don't." She sent Polly a quick glance. "I'm sorry, Polly. I'll try to be less jumpy."

"I'm not surprised you're jumpy. What you're facing is enough to make anyone a nervous wreck. I even find myself checking out everyone who walks past the window."

"I'm sorry," Gail said again, now wishing that she hadn't listened to Blake and told Polly the whole story. "Would you rather I didn't come in tomorrow? There's no sense in you being scared half to death."

Polly made a sound of disgust. "Scared? I'm not scared. I'd just like to get my hands on the bastard, that's all. I'd like to string him up by his heels over a heap of hot coals until he hollered for mercy."

Gail almost smiled at the image of Polly standing over Mike, giving him a piece of her mind. "I don't think it's going to be that easy. Mike is an evil man, and not too stable. There's no telling what he'll do to get what he wants."

Polly patted her arm. "Well, don't you fret, child. Your marshal will take good care of you, I'm sure of that."

Her marshal, Gail thought with a wry smile. That couldn't be further from the truth. If only she could have Polly's confidence that everything would turn out all right. But then Polly didn't know Mike the way she did. Polly hadn't seen the way Mike's eyes gleamed with cruelty, or the way his mouth curled into a vicious grin as he'd explained just what he would do to her when he caught up with her.

Shuddering, she blocked the memories from her mind. She wouldn't let Mike's sleazy threats prey on her imagination, for that would weaken her already shaky confidence. Polly was right; Blake would handle things, and she needed every ounce of her courage not to make things difficult for him.

At last it was time to shut up shop, and Gail put in a call to Darcie before leaving. She was anxious to know how Heather had adjusted to the arrangement.

To her intense relief, Heather seemed quite happy to be staying with her friends, although she sounded wistful when she said, "I wish you could be here, too, Mommy."

"So do I, honey, but it won't be long, I promise, and then you'll be coming home again. If you're really good I'll have a surprise waiting for you when you get home."

After saying good-night to her daughter, Gail pulled on her coat and joined Polly at the door. It was dark outside and snowing heavily. As the two of them stepped out onto the silent street she peered into the shadows, trying to detect anything that might suggest someone lurking in a doorway.

"Where's the marshal?" Polly asked, staring hard at Gail's car across the road.

"I hope he's close by." Gail took her arm. "Come on, I'll walk you to your car first."

They crossed the street at a brisk pace, while Gail's heart pumped furiously. She expected any minute to hear a shout, or to feel a bullet thudding into her back the way one had slammed into Frank's chest at point-blank range.

By the time she and Polly reached the parking spot, her knees felt so weak she was surprised they were holding her up.

"I'll see you in the morning," Polly said, as they stood beside her car. "You will be all right, won't you?"

"I'll be fine." She hoped her voice hadn't sounded as shaky as she felt. She waited, trembling in the cold wind, until her friend had unlocked her car and climbed in. Then, pulling her coat collar higher up her neck, Gail walked as naturally as she dared over to her own car.

The important thing, she reminded herself, was to make everything look normal. If Mike was hidden somewhere, watching her, she didn't want to give him any indication that she was expecting him.

She glanced inside the car, her heart thumping with anticipation. To her utter dismay the front seats were empty. She could see no sign of Blake.

For a moment panic almost overwhelmed her. Visions plunged into her mind of all the movies she'd seen where the car blew up when the door was opened. She took a shaky breath and fought back the fear, willing herself to fit her key into the lock.

It took her a moment or two, but then the lock snapped up. Carefully, she opened the door.

Chapter 8

She hadn't realized how tense she was until she heard Blake's voice speak from the back seat.

"Get in fast and close the door."

She threw herself in behind the wheel and slammed the door shut. "Is he here? Can you see him?"

"No, at least I don't think so. I've been keeping watch all afternoon and I haven't seen anything."

She relaxed her shoulders. "You scared me. I thought he was out there."

"Sorry. I'm freezing to death and I didn't want to let any more cold air into the car."

She couldn't see him in the rearview mirror. He had to be hunched down behind the seat, the way he was when he'd hidden in her car the night before. She switched on the engine and turned up the heater. "Did you get the steaks?" It seemed odd to be talking about such mundane things as food, but it seemed important to hold on to some semblance of normality.

"I got steaks, salad and bread. And I'm starving, so let's go home."

Let's go home. Right then, she couldn't think of anything she would rather do. She pulled out onto the road. Driving slowly in the swirling snowflakes, she cast a furtive glance at every shop doorway on both sides of the street. Once she reached the edge of town she began to relax. If Mike Stevens was in Mellow Springs, he certainly wasn't on Main Street.

Blake must have decided the same thing, as he sat up with a slight groan that told her his cramped muscles were complaining.

She could see him now in the mirror. His gaze was concentrated on the road, and his face looked pinched in the brief glare from oncoming headlights.

"Are you still cold?" She reached for the heater and turned it up higher.

"My teeth have been playing the national anthem for the past half hour."

"I'm sorry." She glanced at him again in the mirror. "Do you have any more news?"

He shook his head. "None. Stevens is either lying low somewhere, waiting for a chance to move, or he's on to me and heading in another direction."

She sighed. "What do we do now?"

"Wait another two or three days, then if nothing goes down we'll have to change our tactics."

That had sounded ominous. She decided to wait until she got home before asking him what he meant.

"Did you check in with Darcie?"

His obvious concern for her daughter was comforting. "Yes, and Heather's fine. Darcie said she's settling down well. I just hope she doesn't get homesick too soon."

"With any luck, this'll all be over before that happens."

He paused, his gaze still on the road. "How did things go with Polly?"

"All right." She wrestled with the wheel at the curve, then relaxed her grip. "I told her the whole story. She was very understanding and sympathetic."

"Good. We could use an ally."

Again she glanced up and this time her pulse leaped when she met his intent gaze. "You really think he'll come here? Or do you think perhaps he changed his mind?"

"I think he'll come. Just about every unit between here and the border is on the lookout for him. He won't get too far without someone spotting him."

"Will the police pick him up if they spot him?"

"They'll notify me first."

She nodded, trying her best to calm the insistent fluttering in her stomach.

"I might as well tell you now," Blake said quietly. "We think he was spotted a few miles south of here at least four days ago. Someone held up a gas station in Bedmonton. It sounded like our man."

"When did you hear this?"

"Last night, when I called in my report."

"Why didn't you tell me?"

"I didn't want to worry you without good reason. They're not really sure it was Stevens."

She felt a flash of irritation. "Well, from now on, I'd appreciate it if you'd tell me everything that's going on. I think I have a right to know."

He was silent for a while, and she fought to control her resentment, aware that her shattered nerves were making her irritable.

"You're right," he said finally. "You do have a right to know. From now on I'll keep you informed of everything I get."

"Thank you." Aware of the frostiness in her voice she

made an effort to thaw it. "Sorry. I guess I'm a little jumpy."

"Understandable under the circumstances. Feel free to yell at me if it will make you feel better."

"It won't, but thanks for the invitation." She glimpsed his flash of amusement in the mirror and felt better.

They finished the trip in silence, while she tried to think how best to pass the evening hours until she could escape to her bedroom. Television seemed the best bet. She wondered what kind of programs he liked to watch. Sports, more than likely.

Football season was over, and it was too early for baseball. She resigned herself to a long evening.

Pulling into the driveway a little later, she switched off the car engine. Some of the tension seemed to be easing from her clenched muscles, but then his next words made her flesh creep.

"I want you to go up to the front door and act as naturally as possible. Don't look around, and don't try to hurry."

She nodded, but his reflection had vanished from the mirror. Aware that he must have slid down behind the seat again, she said quietly, "All right. But what do I do then? Just walk in the house? What if he's in there, waiting for me?"

"No, don't go in. Just open the door then step back. I'll go in first."

She climbed out of the car, feeling as if she were walking along the very edge of a steep cliff. The house watched her in silence, its windows dark and blank. It had never looked so unwelcoming.

Snow covered the front step, and she paused for a moment as she reached it, her ears straining for any unusual sound. All she could hear was the wind in the branches, and the swish of tires on the road behind her.

Bracing herself, she slid the key into the lock and turned it. The click sounded as loud as a gunshot. The door swung open, and she stepped back, pressing herself against the wall of the porch.

She hadn't heard Blake get out of the car, but he slipped past her—a stealthy shadow as silent as the night around her. She waited, leaning against the hard wall, her heart pounding so hard she could feel it in her throat.

The sudden movement from the darkened hallway froze her breath, then light flooded the doorway, making her blink.

"It's all clear," Blake said, reaching for her arm. "Come inside. You look about ready to collapse."

"I'm okay." Glad to see him, she managed a shaky laugh. "I feel as if I'm acting a part in a bad movie." She stepped past him into the welcome warmth of the hallway.

"Sorry, but it's necessary. Wait there a moment. I'll get the groceries." He disappeared, then returned a moment later carrying a sack.

She closed the door behind him, then followed him down to the kitchen, switching on lights as she went. She wasn't entirely convinced by his assurances yet, and the brightness seemed essential to banish whatever might lurk in the shadows.

"I don't know about you but I could use a drink," she said shakily, as Blake set the bag down on the kitchen table.

"I'm way ahead of you." He pulled out a bottle of wine and held it up for her inspection. "I don't usually drink on duty, but I'm always willing to make an exception. Chablis all right?"

"Chablis sounds wonderful." She couldn't help wondering if he'd found it necessary to remind her that he was here in her house for the purpose of carrying out his job and nothing more.

She crossed the kitchen and reached into a cupboard for

a couple of glasses. Setting them down on the counter, she said lightly, "I'll let you do the honors while I take off my coat and get comfortable."

She hadn't meant the comment to sound quite so intimate. Or maybe she was simply overreacting to the situation, seeing pitfalls that weren't really there. Without looking at him to see his reaction, she muttered, "I'll be right back," and escaped to her bedroom.

She changed into jeans and a pale blue sweater, ran a comb through her hair and dashed a lipstick over her mouth. When she returned to the kitchen he was sitting at the table, his jacket draped over the back of the chair and two full glasses of wine set in front of him.

"Sit and relax with this for a moment," he said, as she started to pull things out of the grocery sack.

"I thought you were hungry." She took out the steaks and the bag of salad greens and put them in the fridge.

"I am, but we both need to unwind first."

She wasn't at all sure she would be able to unwind, drinking wine with him in the quiet intimacy of her kitchen. She sat down and picked up her glass. "Cheers. Here's to happier times."

"I'll drink to that."

She watched him take a sip of wine. The beginnings of a beard darkened his jaw, and she could see faint circles under his eyes. Strain had deepened the grooves between his brows and at the corners of his mouth. He looked tired, and just a little ruthless. She could guess how seriously he took the weight of responsibility on his shoulders.

She felt a sudden surge of tenderness, and wished she could just hold him, let him rest his head on her shoulder while she smoothed away the worry lines with her fingers.

Afraid of where that line of thinking might take her, she rested her back against the chair and picked a safe topic of conversation. "How long have you been a U.S. Marshal?"

"Not that long. I was with the DEA until about four years ago."

She raised her eyebrows. "That must have been stressful."

"It was." He grabbed his glass and shot a mouthful of wine down his throat. "Do you mind if I ask you a personal question?"

Aware that he was deliberately changing the subject, she wondered why he was so unwilling to talk about his past. "You can ask," she said, "but I'm not guaranteeing an answer."

He nodded. "Fair enough. I was just wondering why you married Frank Stevens. You don't exactly strike me as the kind of woman who'd be interested in a man like that."

She gave him a wry smile. "I'll take that as a compliment."

"It was meant as one."

"Thank you." She met his gaze briefly, then stared at her glass, slowly twirling the stem between her fingers. "I married Frank because I was looking for a father for my baby."

"Heather's not his child?"

"Oh, yes, she's Frank's child." She struggled for a moment with her own reluctance to share her memories. She had never discussed her past with anyone. Even if she'd been tempted to tell Frank, he'd never shown any interest in her background.

She wasn't sure she wanted to talk about it now. But somehow she knew that Blake would understand. He was hurting from the past, too, she could tell. Much as she hated to admit it, she was intensely interested in knowing what or who had built the wall that shielded him so effectively.

A tiny part of her mind hoped that if she shared her past with him, he might just be encouraged to return the confidence. Although she rather doubted it. He'd locked his past away, apparently, and had no intention of divulging it to anyone—least of all, her.

"I already told you I grew up in foster homes," she began, feeling intensely vulnerable now that she'd made the decision.

"Yes, you did. It must have been rough on you as a kid."

"It was. No matter what the circumstances of your birth, no matter how well-meaning the intentions of your mother, it is never easy to accept the fact that you were given away. The ultimate rejection, I guess, before you've even begun to live. It places a chip on your shoulder that is almost impossible to get rid of."

"I can imagine."

She heard the compassion in his voice, and her pulse leaped. The words were coming more easily now that she felt assured of his sympathy.

"By the time I was six," she continued, "I'd been in three different foster homes. I wanted desperately to be adopted, but I wasn't an easy child to control. According to the nuns at the orphanage, I was rebellious, disobedient and unruly. Not a very good attitude for someone needing a home."

"You were looking for attention," Blake said quietly.

"I was looking for love." She paused to take a sip of wine. "Soon after my sixth birthday, I was sent to yet another foster home. This one was different. Elaine and David Matthews were used to dealing with problem children—they already had eleven foster kids at home."

She sighed, remembering those brief days of peace and happiness. "They were wonderful," she said, her eyes misting at the memory. "For the first time in my life I felt as though I belonged. I slowly learned to let go of the bitterness, and managed to get along reasonably well with the rest of the kids. As for Elaine and David, I absolutely adored them.

"I stopped running away to hide every time something didn't go the way I wanted it to. I stopped pretending I couldn't hear when someone asked me to do something I didn't want to do. I began to behave like a normal human being, instead of like a trapped animal fighting for survival."

She closed her fingers around the glass, her mind slipping away to another time. "But then Elaine got sick and couldn't take care of us anymore. The older children did their best to hold things together, but when the authorities realized what was happening, they took the younger ones away. I was one of those who had to leave."

"God," Blake muttered. "How old were you?"

"I was nine years old. Too young to deal with the pain, too old to escape it anymore. I felt betrayed. I blamed my foster parents bitterly for hurting me. They'd taught me how to love, only to throw me out as soon as things started to go wrong. At least, that's the way I saw things then."

She let out a troubled sigh. "I know better now, of course, but back then all I knew was that it hurt so badly I wanted to die. I made up my mind that I would never let anyone betray me like that again. If that's what happened when you loved someone, then I wanted no part of it."

"Until you met Frank."

She lifted her chin. "Frank? No, I wasn't in love with him. As soon as I was old enough to make it on my own, I left Seattle and moved to Portland. I wanted to start a new life in a new town. And, for a long time, I was very happy living on my own. I was completely independent, free to go anywhere I pleased, do anything I wanted without having to answer to anyone but myself."

"But then you got lonely?"

She shrugged. "I guess."

"I know how that goes."

She looked at him, struck by the irony in his voice. "Is that why you got married?"

He smiled gently at her. "This is your story, not mine."

Feeling frustrated, she went on. "Well, anyway, I woke up on my thirtieth birthday and realized that time was passing me by. I had casual acquaintances, but no real friends. I wouldn't let myself get too close to anyone. I guess I was afraid of being hurt again. But there were times I felt miserable because I didn't really matter to anyone. I could have been struck down by a bus and no one would really have missed me. It became more and more important to me that I mattered to someone before I died."

"So you decided to get married?"

She shook her head. "No, I decided I wanted a baby. I was watching kids play in the park one day, and I realized that what I really wanted was a child of my own. Someone who needed me. Someone who would love me and care about what happened to me."

"And, in order to have a baby, you had to have a man."

"Exactly."

"But why Frank Stevens? You're an attractive woman, with a very warm, generous personality. You must have had better choices."

The unexpected compliment was almost her undoing. She recovered enough to smile naturally. "I guess it was something I drifted into. I'd worked for Frank in the furniture store for five years. His wife had died several years earlier and he seemed lonely. He proposed a couple of times, more in fun than anything, but I began to wonder if perhaps he really wanted to marry me.

"We seemed to get along well, and he was fun to be around. He had a thriving business, and I felt I could offer him companionship in return for the security he could give me and my baby when it came along. The next time he proposed, I accepted.''

''A nice cozy arrangement.''

Again she heard the irony in his voice and looked up sharply. ''All right, so it wasn't the best idea I'd ever had. I didn't know that the Frank who chatted with the customers all day was very different from the real man behind that phony benevolent image. I thought he was strong and protective, when in reality he was jealous and possessive.

''After we'd been married for a while he would fly into a rage if I so much as smiled at a male customer. He wanted complete control of my life, to the point where I had to ask his permission to go somewhere without him. He told me what to wear, what to eat, where I could go and who I could see. If I resisted, he became ugly.''

''So why did you stay with him?''

She waited until the bitterness had ebbed a little before replying. ''By the time I realized what a mess I'd made of things, I was pregnant. I knew I wouldn't be able to provide a decent life for my baby on my own and I was terrified she would be taken away from me—or worse, given to Frank. I decided to stay just long enough to get some kind of security—a better education and a better-paying job.''

''That was six years ago.''

She nodded. ''Much to my surprise, Frank was good with Heather. He adored her. He always bought her gifts and showed her off to the customers. She loved him back, of course. How could I take her away from someone she loved so much?''

Blake shook his head. ''You couldn't, after the kind of childhood you'd had.''

''Right. I knew the pain of being torn from someone I loved. I couldn't do that to Heather.''

''So you were prepared to stay with him.''

"At least until Heather was old enough to be on her own."

"But then along came Mike Stevens."

Gail sighed. "He was always in the picture, right from the start. I always had the feeling that something bad would happen with him, but I never dreamed he would kill his brother."

"Did you know that Frank was involved in dealing in stolen goods?"

She shook her head. "Not until after we were married, and even then I wasn't sure. I never had any real proof, just a sort of hunch. I knew Mike was evil, of course. I didn't know how deeply Frank was involved with him until after he died. He was very good at hiding behind that image. That's why everyone believed I was guilty. The man they knew would never fight with his wife over another man unless there was some truth to it."

She pushed back her chair and got to her feet. "If only I could have made them see what he was really like, I might have had a chance to clear my name. As it is now, there'll always be suspicion about me." She glanced up at the clock. "Now I'd better cook dinner, before we both starve to death."

She felt emotionally exhausted as she prepared to grill the steaks. Talking about her past had brought it all back— all the misery and fear. Some day she would have to bury it and try to forget. Only she couldn't do that while Mike was out there somewhere, doing his best to destroy her life.

She kept the conversation on more mundane topics during dinner. Blake seemed disinclined to talk, appearing to be deep in thought, to the point where she began to worry about him.

He'd promised to keep her informed about everything, but she had the feeling he was holding something back. Something that he didn't want her to know.

"I've got to call headquarters," he finally said, when she stood and began to clear the dishes away.

"You can use the phone in the living room." She carried the plates over to the sink. "You'll have some privacy there."

He hesitated, almost as if he were reluctant to leave her alone, but then he went into the living room and closed the door behind him.

She could hear him talking, but his voice was too muffled for her to hear what he said. The conversation was brief, however, as he returned to the kitchen a short while later.

"Still no news," he said, when she sent him a questioning look. "The way it's snowing out there, I doubt if anyone will move far on these roads tonight. I figure we'll be all right for the night, at least."

She nodded, her nerves tightening at the thought of spending the night alone in her bedroom, listening to every sound. "I hope so."

"Thanks for the dinner. I enjoyed it."

She shrugged. "You bought it."

"You cooked it. That's the tough part."

"Anyone can cook a steak."

"Not me. I'm one of those men who can't boil an egg without messing it up."

She glanced up at him. "You must eat out a lot."

"Or order in. You can't imagine how much I enjoy a home-cooked meal."

"Well, if you're still here tomorrow night, I'll have to try out one of my famous casseroles on you."

"I'll look forward to it."

Maybe it was her imagination again, but she had the distinct impression that Blake was feeling uncomfortable about something. She wondered if he'd heard some news that he wasn't sharing with her. In spite of his promise, she was well aware that in his position, he might not be free to tell her everything.

She turned away from him, reaching up to put the steak sauce back in the cupboard. She must have been even more unnerved than she realized. The bottom of the bottle didn't quite clear the shelf. The blow knocked the bottle from her hand and it fell to the counter with a deafening clatter.

"Darn," she muttered, as the cap fell off and sauce oozed out onto the countertop. "I don't know why I'm so clumsy lately."

She reached for the paper-towel dispenser, and then flinched as Blake closed his fingers over her arm. "Just relax," he said softly. "I'm here to take care of you, remember?"

"I know." To her dismay her voice wobbled and she cleared her throat. "It's just…" She looked helplessly up at him, her throat working, unable to finish the sentence.

He stood very still, his fingers grasping her arm. She could smell the lingering traces of his musky cologne. His eyes seemed darker, softer, almost as if he were pleading with her, although she couldn't imagine why.

The birth of a faint beard shadowed his jaw, and she noticed for the first time a tiny scar at the corner of his mouth. Without warning, the memory of how that mouth had possessed hers filled her mind with hot, suffocating clarity.

From deep within her, a sigh arose and escaped from her parted lips. She heard him draw a harsh breath and fought to breathe naturally herself. She could feel the heat now, gathering momentum, threatening to overwhelm her.

She tried to draw her hand away, but his fingers clamped tighter. Now his eyes burned with the same heat that coursed through her veins. Very slowly, he moved his hand up her arm to her shoulder.

She wanted his kiss as she'd never wanted anything in

her life before. Yet she was afraid, knowing that if he so much as touched her mouth with his lips, she would be lost, helpless to resist the torrent of need already simmering deep inside her.

This time she didn't have Heather sleeping peacefully down the hallway to bring her to her senses. This time, there would be nothing to suppress the mad craving that he so easily aroused in her.

She made one last effort to fight the temptation clawing at her mind. Already she was falling in love with him. If she gave in to this madness, she knew, without a doubt, that she would give much more than her body. She could lose her soul to this man.

If only she could be certain that he wanted her for the same emotional reasons that had driven her into his arms. If only she could be sure that she wasn't just a means of satisfying a physical need. If only he would say something, instead of gazing at her with that little-boy-lost look in his eyes.

At last he spoke, destroying the last of her resistance. "Gail," he muttered, "if you go on looking at me like that, I'm not going to be responsible for what happens next."

All at once she didn't care. So what if he walked away afterward? So what if he broke her heart? All her life she had wondered what it would be like to make love with a man she could really care for—a man who could set her on fire with just the touch of his fingers. A man who could teach her what it was really like to be a woman, in every sense of the word.

This was the man, and now was her opportunity. She could walk away and go on wondering for the rest of her life. Or she could take what was offered and accept the consequences later. At least she would have one hell of a memory to take with her.

Raising her hands, she placed them on his chest. She

could feel his heartbeat through the fabric of his denim shirt. Beneath her fingers lay the very essence of this man, and the knowledge filled her with a bittersweet tenderness. For a little while, at least, he would belong to her.

"Gail." His voice was husky with emotion, and desire burned in his eyes. "You don't know what you're doing."

"Oh yes, I do." Deliberately she slid her hands up to his neck. The movement brought her breasts in contact with his chest, and again she heard his sharp intake of breath.

"Dammit, Gail, I'm not made of stone."

"Then show me what you are made of."

With a groan of despair he cupped her head with his hands and sought her mouth in a deep, lingering kiss. She could feel the impact of it in every pore of her body.

If she'd had any shred of doubt left, it was swept away in the fury of his passion. His hands roamed over her, urgent and demanding, until the tug of need for him grew painful.

She gasped when he lifted the hem of her sweater and dragged it over her head. She closed her eyes when his lips touched the soft swell of her breasts, while his fingers expertly unfastened her bra.

The craving took hold, as every atom of her body came to quivering life. With a quick movement she slipped the straps of her bra down over her shoulders and freed her breasts for him.

Gently he cupped them in his warm hands. "God," he whispered. "I never realized just how beautiful you are."

She wanted to cry at the reverence in his voice. It amazed her that this man, so rugged, so relentless at times, could be so warm and tender, could make her feel so desirably feminine.

With infinite care, she undid the buttons on his shirt and tugged it open. His chest was smooth, and tinted with the light gold of a faded tan. She ran her fingers through the dense triangle of dark hair, then clasped her hands behind his back as she pressed herself against him. "You feel so good," she whispered.

"Gail."

She looked up at him, her breath catching at the searing heat of his gaze.

"I can't make you any promises," he said haltingly.

"I know."

"I want you to understand that, before—"

"I do. I don't need promises, Blake. All I'll ever ask from you is that you are honest with me."

"Always."

She became impatient, determined to ignore what wasn't important right now. She wanted to tell him something. Something she'd never said to any man before. Holding on to him tightly, she looked deep into his gray eyes. "I want you, Blake."

"Oh, Gail, I want you, too."

"Then take me to bed."

"Are you sure?"

She smiled, remembering her words to Darcie. "I've never been more sure." Pulling back, she reached for his belt. Her fingers trembled as she struggled to unfasten the buckle. He waited patiently, although she could feel the tension holding him rigid.

Carefully she eased his jeans down, then waited for him to get rid of his shoes and socks before taking them off entirely. His thighs were thick and solid—the thighs of a trained athlete.

She ran her hands up them slowly, enjoying the feel of hard muscle beneath her palms.

"Do you have any idea what you're doing to me?" he muttered hoarsely.

"Arousing you, I hope."

"I don't think I'm leaving you in any doubt there."

"Then what are we waiting for?" She had never felt such an exhilarating sense of power. This new aggressiveness was so completely opposite to anything she'd experienced before. She liked it—liked the effect she had on this man who had once intimidated her with his own forbidding power and strength.

They finished undressing each other, and when they were both naked, she took his hand and led him into the bedroom.

She left the bedside lamp on, eager to see his body while she explored it. She couldn't help marveling at how he'd managed to instill in her so much confidence and daring. She had never felt quite so reckless.

She soon realized, however, that Blake had no intention of giving up control. His touch was sure and incredibly arousing. Again and again he found new sources of her pleasure, teaching her things about her body she'd never suspected.

He built a fire in her, then slowly stoked it until it consumed her. Her body arced beneath him of its own accord, while she writhed helplessly under his expert hands. He took his time, manipulating her until at last, her control finally snapped.

For the space of a second or two she panicked, afraid of the overwhelming sensation of being completely at his mercy. It scared her to realize the extent of his control over her. Her body tensed, while she gripped his hand.

"Relax," he murmured close to her ear. "Just trust me. Go with the feeling, ride with it. Let it take you where you want to go."

She heard his words dimly through the drumming in her head. Digging her hands into his shoulders, she gave herself up to him, trusting in his touch, striving for the release that seemed so close and yet so unobtainable.

Higher and higher she flew, until it seemed as if her body would explode into a million fiery fragments. She cried out again and again, and then, as she hovered on the brink, she heard him mutter, "Now."

"Yes!" The word hissed through her teeth as the final surge took her even higher. Then unbelievably, magically, she found it. And it was every bit as wonderful as she'd been led to believe.

She floated for a moment or two, marveling again at the sensations rocketing through her body. Then a new urge took over. Now she wanted to give back the pleasure he'd given her. She wanted to hear him moan with it.

She touched him hesitantly at first, then more aggressively as her confidence grew. Aware of his rising excitement, she grew more excited herself. Briefly she wondered where all this assertiveness had come from. Maybe it had always been there, and just needed someone like Blake to nurture it to life. Then she gave up wondering in the heady delight of discovering new ways to give him pleasure.

Finally he'd had enough of her joyful experimentation. With a sharp groan he flipped her onto her back and hovered over her for a breathless moment, his face flushed, his breathing harsh and his eyes burning with urgent need.

His chest rose and fell, gleaming with a thin film of sweat as he lowered himself slowly and entered her. He was gentle at first, but then his passion caught hold. She had thought he'd aroused every conceivable sensation she was capable of, but in that moment she felt an overpowering sense of fulfillment—the ultimate union, the joining of bodies, the final mating of man and woman.

Up until now the pleasure had been mostly physical, but now it was spiritual, as well, and infinitely beautiful. She clung to him as she was swept up in the rising throes of passion, joining with him as he strove for release. When it happened, she was there with him, rejoicing in the conquest, elated to have given him all that she had to give.

She lay quietly in his arms afterward, listening to the steady thud of his strong heartbeat beneath her ear. With her body pressed against the length of his, she felt a tremendous sense of peace. At that moment she felt invincible. Nothing could hurt her. Not even Mike.

Blake was still awake long after she'd drifted off to sleep. His body was at rest, but his mind would not give up. He was acutely conscious of the woman whose naked body lay pressed to his.

Her hair felt silky on his chest, and the gentle rise and fall of her smooth, soft breasts sensuously brushed his skin. She smelled of flowers and the sweet fragrance of sex. He felt a rush of tenderness and tightened his arm about her. She murmured sleepily, snuggling closer to him.

He wanted to protect her, and felt a desperate need to erase the bad memories that must haunt her life. He couldn't take away the pain and loneliness of her child-hood. That was something she would have to deal with in her own way. He couldn't take away the memories of her miserable marriage, either. Time would eventually have to take care of that.

What he could do was to try to erase the stigma left on her by Mike Stevens. One way or another, he was going to catch up with the bastard. And when he did, he would make damn sure that Stevens confessed that he'd been lying about Gail's involvement in the murder.

No matter what it took, Blake promised himself, he would make Stevens admit the truth. Then he would make sure that Gail's name was cleared from the record, officially and publicly.

He turned his head and gently brushed her forehead with his lips. He felt a bittersweet pang as she stirred against his chest. He might not be able to give her the stable home and secure love that she craved so badly. But he would give her back her good name. If it was the last thing he ever did.

Chapter 9

Gail awoke early, before it was light. She knew at once that something was different, but it took a second or two before she remembered. He lay on his side, his back toward her. She could feel the warmth of his body. The full measure of her love seemed to fill her mind, erasing everything else for the moment.

How she loved him. And how she longed to know everything about him. He'd always been so close-lipped about his past. Now that they had finally broken down the barriers, perhaps he would tell her what it was that had hurt him so.

She wanted to take the pain away, to envelop him in her love and make him forget whatever it was that had painted such bitter lines on his face.

Gently, she rolled closer, trying not to disturb him. He murmured, then his body tensed and she knew he was awake. "It's all right," she whispered. "It's only me."

He stirred, reaching back to touch her. "Hey, 'me,'" he whispered back.

She snuggled closer to him, curling her arm across his stomach. "I didn't mean to wake you."

"I can't think of a better way to be woken up."

She skimmed his back with her open mouth and heard his murmur of pleasure. "Maybe I can. How about this?" She moved her hand down his belly.

This time his response was more urgent. He rolled over and pulled her closer to him. "You didn't tell me you were insatiable."

"You didn't ask." She wriggled against him, delighting in the feel of his nakedness.

"I don't know if I have the energy left to go a second round."

"We could have fun trying."

She nipped his shoulder with her teeth and he growled an answer deep in his throat. Flipping onto his back, he pulled her down on top of him. "Okay, lady, do your worst. I'm all yours."

It didn't take her long to bring him to his knees. To her immense satisfaction he found the energy, and to her intense delight and amazement, she found it even more wonderful than the first time.

"Sweetheart," he muttered, as they struggled to catch their breath later, "if I'd known it was going to be like this, I'd have taken you to bed the first day I set eyes on you."

"You'd have had a fight on your hands if you'd tried."

He chuckled. "I don't doubt that. You were so wary of me when I first saw you, I half expected you to thrust a gun in my side and demand to see my credentials before you would talk to me."

"You were pretty intimidating." She sighed. "If I'd known you were a cop, I wouldn't have been so scared of you."

"I couldn't let you know that. I thought you were aiding and abetting an escaped convict."

"And I thought you were aiding and abetting the man who was trying to get my daughter."

"It's a wonder we got together at all."

She smiled and turned her head to look at him. The cold morning light had begun to seep into the room through the drapes, and she could see his strong profile. Very gently, she traced the outline of his nose with her finger. "Even when I was afraid of you, I was fascinated by you."

He reached for her hand and laced his fingers through hers. "Well, you were definitely the most desirable woman I'd ever laid eyes on. It was all I could do to keep my hands off you."

She grinned. "I'm glad I didn't know that. I had enough trouble dealing with you as it was."

He sent her a rueful glance. "That bad, huh?"

"You're just not a very good liar. I had the feeling right from the start that you weren't a real-estate agent from Seattle."

"I pulled that one out of thin air. How was I to know I was dealing with an astute, intelligent woman who just happened to have lived in Seattle?"

"I guess that was a stroke of bad luck for you."

"It wouldn't have been if I hadn't spent so much time with you. Originally the plan was to make contact, then just keep you in sight until you met up with Stevens, nab him and take him back to Portland."

She thought about that for a moment. "Then why did you invite me to dinner?"

He shook his head. "I don't know. It seemed like a good idea at the time. I talked myself into believing that I could keep a closer eye on you if I pretended to be interested in you. The trouble was, I wasn't pretending. The more I was with you, the more I wanted you."

"You did a very good job of hiding it. I was convinced that you were only doing your job."

"I guess I'm a better liar than you give me credit for."
He turned his head, and his expression grew serious. "I
want you to know, I don't make a habit of doing this."

She smiled. "Neither do I."

"I don't want to hurt you, Gail."

A cold finger of apprehension disturbed her fragile contentment. "I'm a big girl," she said lightly. "I know what
I'm doing."

"I hope so."

He turned his head to look back at the ceiling, and his
set face filled her with dismay. Pushing away her unsettling
doubts, she sought to change the subject.

"How did you become a cop?"

"My father was a cop. I never thought about being anything else."

"Are your parents still alive?"

He paused for a moment before answering, as if the subject was painful. "No," he said at last. "My father died
trying to talk a spaced-out kid out of jumping off the roof
of a high-rise. The bastard shot him, then jumped anyway.
The shock of it all killed my mother. She died of a heart
attack a month later."

She squeezed his hand, her heart aching for him. "I'm
so sorry. Were you very young at the time?"

He shook his head. "I was married. It was one of the
things that helped break us up."

"That must have been a tough time for you." She held
her breath, silently willing him to talk about it.

He was quiet for a moment or two, then he let out a long
sigh. "We were both very young. I was a rookie on the
force and was gone a lot of the time. It must have been
hard on her, every time I was late getting home, waiting
for a phone call to tell her something bad had happened to
me. She finally grew tired of it. After my father died, she
stopped waiting around. I'd come home tired and hungry

and she'd be out somewhere. Sometimes she stayed out all night. We fought a lot, and finally she asked for a divorce.''

Gail felt a surge of anger against the woman who had thrown away what she would kill to have. ''That's terrible. Just when you needed her the most.''

He shrugged. ''I couldn't blame her for wanting out. What I do blame her for is not telling me she was pregnant until after the divorce. By the time I found out, she'd married someone else. The guy offered to adopt the baby, and I knew there was no point in fighting it. I had to do what was best for my child. To this day, I've never set eyes on my daughter.''

Now she knew what had caused him so much pain. She remembered the first time they'd had dinner together. What was it he'd said? *''My biggest regret in life is missing out on being a father.''*

She could give him that if he would let her, she thought, with a surge of excitement. Heather adored him, and he seemed to love her just as much. They needed each other, and she couldn't have picked a better father figure for Heather if she had set out to look for one.

Not only that, she could give him children of his own. She had longed to have more children, and a brother or sister would be good for Heather. The thought of bearing his child brought tears to her eyes.

''I'm sorry. I didn't mean to depress you with my sob stories.'' Blake turned on his side and propped up his head with his elbow. ''What were you thinking about so seriously?''

She was so tempted to tell him. Maybe if he knew what she was willing to offer him, he would realize how much they could have together. Before she could answer him, however, the shrill ring of the telephone made her jump.

Instantly alert, she reached for the receiver. Her heart skipped when the curt voice of a stranger answered her.

"Blake Foster."

"Just a minute." She handed him the phone, her new-found peace shattered. "It's for you."

He took the phone from her, and she felt cold when she saw his expression. Tension once more drew hard lines around his mouth, and his eyes reflected his apprehension. "Foster, here."

He listened intently, his fingers curled tightly around the receiver. She saw his knuckles whiten momentarily, then he muttered, "Thanks for letting me know. I'll get back to you."

His colleague must have said something else, as Blake listened some more, then said briefly, "No, I'll handle it." He handed the receiver back, his serious expression telling her that something significant had happened.

"He's here, isn't he?" she said unsteadily.

He nodded. "He's been spotted in the area. The sheriff thinks he's holed up in one of the cabins out at Deep Frost Lake. He says the snow's thick out there, but I should be able to get in and check it out."

She felt as if a giant hand squeezed her lungs. "You're not going alone?"

"It's my job. It's up to me to take care of him."

"But what if he's armed?"

"So am I," he reminded her gently. "Don't worry. If I think I need backup, I'll holler."

She clung to him, burying her face in his warm, smooth shoulder. So this was what it was like to send the man she loved into danger. "Please, be careful," she whispered. "I know what Mike is capable of."

"Don't worry. I've done this before."

"Knowing that doesn't make it easier."

"I know. I'm sorry." He looked at her for a long time, his eyes troubled, then he took her in his arms. "I want you to stay here in the house until this is over."

"No."

He looked as if he were about to argue with her and she laid a finger over his lips. "No, Blake, I'd rather be at the bookstore. At least there I'm on Main Street, and I'll ask Polly to come in this morning and be with me. If I stay here all alone, Mike could easily get into the house and overpower me. I'd be helpless to stop him."

"I could probably arrange protection for you."

"I'd rather be at the bookstore." She kissed him on the mouth. "Please? I'd feel safer there."

He let out his breath in a long sigh. "All right, but I don't like it. I'll be out of touch while I'm on the road."

"If anything happens I'll call 9-1-1," she promised.

"All right. Just promise me you'll be careful, and please don't leave the store until I come and get you, okay?"

"Okay." She held his face between her hands. "You be careful, too, please? I want you back in one piece."

He gave her a faint grin. "I kind of prefer it that way myself."

"You have time for breakfast?"

"If we make it fast. I'm going to need you to take me back to the hotel to get my car."

"Oh, right, I'd forgotten about that." She was already clambering out of bed as she spoke, dragging the comforter with her. She called Darcie first, who assured her that Heather was feeling right at home.

Gail cut off her teasing questions, saying she was late for work. She joined Blake in the shower, then dressed in a warm, salmon pink dress and a black blazer. She poured cereal into bowls while Blake made the coffee, and they ate in companionable silence. By the time they were ready to leave, it had started snowing again.

Several minutes later, Gail pulled up in the parking lot of the Alpine Inn, conscious of a terrible ache of fear. She wanted to cling to him, beg him to stay safe and come back to her. Instead, she managed a shaky smile. "I'll see you when you get back."

He hesitated, then reached for her, pulling her against him while he gave her a long, hard kiss. "Take care," he said briefly, then opened the door to get out.

"You'll call me when you get back?"

"I'll do better than that." He looked back at her over his shoulder. "I'll come to the bookstore and take you to lunch at the diner."

It sounded like such an anticlimax that she actually managed a laugh. "I'll look forward to that."

Turning back to her, he cupped her chin in his warm fingers and kissed her briefly on the lips. "Don't worry, I'll take care of him."

"Just make sure he doesn't take care of you."

He pointed his finger at her in a mock salute. "Count on it."

She watched him crossing the parking lot with an easy stride, the snow swirling around his shoulders and bare head. His shoes left deep imprints in the white blanket that covered the pavement.

He had more to worry about than taking Mike into custody, she thought, as she backed out of the space. If the snow kept up like this, the road to the lake would be tough to travel. She only hoped he wouldn't be stranded out there with his prisoner.

She drove slowly back to town, squinting to see the road through the steadily slanting snowflakes that fell wet and heavy across her windshield. When she reached Main Street, however, the traffic had already churned up the snow, and she made it easily to her parking spot across from the bookstore.

She sat for several seconds in the warmth of the car, hugging her tense body, reluctant to unlock the door and leave her fragile security. As far as she could see, no one stirred on the deserted, windswept street. It seemed as if she were the only person alive here.

Forcing herself to move, she scrambled out of the car, then scurried across the road to the bookstore. Her fingers were stiff with cold, and it took her a while to get the lock open.

Finally she was safely inside, with the door closed securely behind her. There was no answer from Polly's house when she called a minute or two later, but she'd barely gotten her coat off and the cash register opened before Polly rushed into the shop, her hair plastered with melting snowflakes.

"I didn't think you should be alone," she said, when Gail looked at her in surprise.

"You must have read my mind," Gail answered wryly. "I just called you."

Polly's sharp eyes raked her face. "Any news?"

"They think that Mike's out at Deep Frost Lake. Blake has gone to check it out."

Polly pursed her lips. "And you're terrified for him."

Gail nodded, her throat aching.

"Well, don't be. These guys know what they're doing."

Gail smiled. "Thanks for being here with me."

"Well, I needed to do some work in the back office, anyway." Polly hung up her coat and scarf. "How'd things go last night?"

Gail was quite certain her warm flush had told Polly all she needed to know. Turning her back on her, she pretended to rearrange the contents of the gift cabinet. "Fine," she said airily. "He's really a nice man."

"Then you'd better grab him before he gets away." With that, Polly charged off to the office, leaving Gail to regain her composure.

By midmorning the strain of wondering what was happening to Blake had completely destroyed her concentration. She found herself staring out the window, creating appalling images in her mind that made her torment even more unbearable.

To make matters worse, the bad weather kept away potential customers, and with nothing to occupy her time, the hours seemed to drag by. Just to reassure herself she called Darcie again.

"Heather's just fine," Darcie told her. "Stop worrying. If you keep calling you'll unsettle her."

Knowing she was right, Gail resigned herself to waiting until that evening before calling again. By then, all this might be over and she could bring her daughter home. If only she could hang on to that thought, maybe she would get through this terrible day.

Polly had closeted herself in the office, and Gail was reluctant to disturb her. In any case, there wasn't much she could do to help. It was just a matter of waiting for news, and praying that Blake had safely recaptured Mike.

Pacing back and forth in front of the window, Gail understood how it must have been for Blake's young wife. This was how it would be for her, too, if she were with him all the time—constantly worrying if he was going to make it home, dreading that the phone might ring with bad news.

It would be worth it, she was convinced of that. She would suffer a thousand agonies like this, if it meant she could spend the rest of her life with him.

By lunchtime the snow had stopped, although the skies still looked gray and swollen with clouds, and a cold wind had whipped up drifts against the door. Blake still hadn't appeared, and Gail felt physically sick with anxiety.

When the phone rang, she felt as if the entire world had just come to a standstill. She stared at the jangling instrument, struggling to find the courage to answer it. It couldn't be bad news about Blake. It just couldn't be.

The ringing cut off and she realized Polly must have picked it up. She waited, heart pounding furiously, her eyes fixed on the door. After what seemed an eternity it opened, and Polly stuck her head out.

"It's for you."

She wanted to ask her who it was, but Polly had already withdrawn her head. She reached out a shaky hand and picked up the receiver. "This is Kate."

The voice that answered her chilled her blood. "Really? Sounds more like Gail to me."

Mike. Her fingers clamped down on the receiver and she pressed it to her ear. "Where are you? What do you want?" *Where was Blake, for God's sake?*

She was terrified at the thought of what Mike might have done to him. She wanted desperately to ask him, but knew that would be stupid. If he wasn't aware of Blake's presence, she certainly didn't want to warn him.

"Well, it's funny you should ask." Mike gave one of his evil chuckles, and her blood ran cold. "I was just about to tell you. I'm at Landings' gas station on the edge of town, freezing my balls off in a telephone box, if you want to know."

"I wouldn't hang around there too long," Gail said, wishing she had a separate line to call the police. "The cops are looking for you."

"Yeah, I figured that." Mike chuckled again, as if he were enjoying some huge practical joke. "Not too smart, these cops around here. I've been here for three days already, and they haven't spotted me yet."

"They'll catch up with you sooner or later."

"Maybe. Right now, though, I'm looking for a ride."

A quiver of fear shook her body. "So call a cab." She had plenty of time to call the cops when she hung up, she assured herself. If he was out at Landings' station, it would take him a while to get to the store. She could be long gone by then.

"Very funny." Mike's voice hardened. "I think you should know, I'm not alone. Someone you know is keeping me company."

Gail closed her eyes. He had Blake. Dear God, let him still be alive. Surely fate couldn't be so cruel as to let her find a man she could really love, only to snatch him away from her again?

She forced her mind to stay clear. If she wanted to know what had happened, she would have to play his game. She did her best to sound indifferent. "Okay, so who are you with?"

"Well, she's around three feet high, has short curly hair and blue eyes, and answers to the name of Annie. Though that's not her real name, of course."

Shock slammed into her, making the room swim. She must have cried out, for she could hear the echo of it around the bookshelves. "Damn you," she muttered. "If you've hurt her I'll find a way to kill you."

Behind her she heard the office door open, but she paid no attention. All of her concentration was focused on the insidious voice coming from the phone.

"She's okay, so just calm down, will you? She's just fine."

"Then let me talk to her."

"There's no time for that." Mike's voice had turned ugly. "You get out here fast if you want to see her again. And no cops. I see the slightest sign of a cop, or anyone else for that matter, and I'll make sure this pretty little face is cut up so bad you won't recognize your precious daughter when I'm done with her."

"Where—?" The phone clicked, cutting off her reply. She felt sick now, and the drumming in her head seemed to vibrate down the length of her body. Vaguely she was aware of Polly coming toward her, a worried look on her face. She was saying something, but Gail wasn't listening.

Frantically she punched out Darcie's number and waited, praying that Mike's call was a bluff. She heard the ring at the other end—once...twice...three times... She knew Darcie wasn't going to answer. God, what had he done to her? She couldn't think about that now.

Polly was looking at her, reaching for her arm.

"Call the cops," Gail said urgently. "Send them over to Darcie's."

Polly's eyes widened and she covered her mouth with her hand. "Oh, no, not Annie!"

"That's what I'm going to find out," Gail said grimly, making a grab for her purse. She dragged her coat from the rack and headed for the door.

"Where are you going?" Polly demanded.

For a split second she was tempted to tell her she was heading for Landings' gas station. But she would be gambling with her daughter's life. She shook her head. "I'll call." She was out the door before Polly finished answering her.

Racing across the road, she skidded to a shaky halt at her car. Cursing at her fumbling fingers, she finally got the key into the lock and dragged the door open.

She made mental trade-offs with God if he would only spare her daughter as she aimed the car at the road and hit the accelerator. The compact bucked and slithered around, then the studded tires gripped and she roared down Main Street, churning up clods of snow with her wheels.

She knew the gas station; it was the one Blake had stopped at on the way back from the mountains. On the heels of that thought came a flash of revelation. Why had Mike chosen to call her from that particular station? Was it possible he'd seen them stop there on the way back from the mountain? Had he been following them that afternoon?

If so, neither of them had noticed. That wasn't too reassuring.

She pressed her foot down on the accelerator pedal as hard as she dared. Her heart ached for her daughter. She must be terrified. Although Heather knew Mike, she had never liked her uncle very much.

Gail didn't want to think about the effect it would have on Heather if she'd seen Mike use violence on Darcie to get what he wanted. She wouldn't even consider the possibility that Heather might be hurt herself.

Poor Darcie, Gail thought in despair. At least her kids would still be in school. The police would take care of them if something bad had happened to their mother, at least until their father got home from work.

Oh, God. She closed her eyes briefly in despair. What a mess. What trouble she'd brought down on the heads of so many innocent people. How was she going to face anyone after this?

She clenched her teeth, leaning forward to peer through the driving snow as a dark shape loomed up on her right. It was the old abandoned millhouse that stood on the edge of the Three Forks Creek. She was about half a mile from the gas station.

She saw the pumps as soon as she rounded the bend. The station looked deserted, but as she drew closer she saw a battered gray Chevy parked to one side. She saw the hanging fender the minute she drove into the station. She'd seen it before, on Main Street...how many days ago? She couldn't remember.

She slammed on the brakes a little too hard and skidded past the first pump. The lights were on in the office but she couldn't see anyone inside. She was afraid to open the door, exposing herself as a clear target, but she was more afraid to sit there wondering what had happened to her daughter.

She bent low as she opened the car door, using it to

shield her. Still bent double she raced for the office, her feet now secure on the dry pavement beneath the overhang.

When she reached the door and looked in, she knew why she hadn't seen anyone there. The gas attendant, a young man with straight blond hair and wearing stained overalls, lay on the floor.

Feeling her stomach rise into her throat, Gail took a closer look. His eyes were closed, and an ugly gash on the side of his head seeped dark blood, but she could hear his shallow breathing. She was trembling with shock by the time she straightened and looked outside.

An eerie silence seemed to settle all around her, cutting her off from the outside world. Nothing moved, not even a car passing on the road outside. She stood in the doorway and scanned the area as far as she could see.

A faint squeaking sound caught her attention and her muscles contracted in a classic pose for flight. Her gaze flew to the sign that hung above the pumps, but she could see no movement from it.

She looked the other way and felt a jolt of fear. The door to the rest room stood open and swung ominously back and forth in the wind.

She couldn't make her feet move. She knew she would have to look inside that dreadful room and was terrified of what she might see. Her teeth began to chatter, and she clamped them together. She took a hold of herself, urging her feet forward. One step. Then another.

She was almost at the door when the sudden sharp toot of a horn jarred her. Swinging around, she looked across at the Chevy, then her stomach gave a sickening lurch. Staring at her from the front passenger seat of her own car were the vicious dark eyes of her brother-in-law.

She didn't know whether to run for the rest room or the car. While she was still dithering, Mike rolled the window down and stuck out his greasy black head. "Hi there, gorgeous. It's been a long time."

Snapping out of her confusion, Gail marched over to the car. For a moment she'd hoped she would see Heather sitting in the back seat, but one glance told her that Mike was alone. "Where the hell is my daughter?" she demanded, grinding her teeth in her fury.

Mike's eyebrows lifted. "My, my. Your temper hasn't improved since you've been away."

"Either you tell me where she is right now," Gail said evenly, "or I'll take great pleasure in tearing you apart with my fingernails." She raised her hand, her fingers curled, ready to strike.

Mike shook his head, lifting his hands to shield his face. "Hey, hey, gorgeous, take it easy. I didn't bring her with me. I figured this wasn't the kind of weather to bring a kid out in."

"Then where is she?"

"Don't worry. She's perfectly safe."

She wanted so much to believe him. Yet knowing him, she knew she dared not take anything he said for granted. Still painfully aware of the rest-room door swinging open behind her, she tried not to imagine what might be lying inside. "I want to know where she is," she said, her teeth clamped tight. "And I want to know now."

He uttered a dry laugh. "Calm down, will you? I said she's okay. I'll take you to her."

Slowly, Gail lowered her hand. Staring hard at his face, she tried desperately to read his mind. "I'm not going anywhere with you until you tell me where she is."

"I said I'll take you to her. Now get in the damn car. It's colder than ice out there."

She fought with indecision, her eyes never leaving his face. The last thing she wanted to do was get in the car with him, putting herself at his mercy. Yet it might be her only chance to find her daughter.

Mike scowled back at her, obviously losing patience. "I'm telling you, babe, unless you get in this damn car and drive where I tell you, you'll never see your daughter again." He sat back and lifted his shoulders in a contemptuous shrug. "It's your choice, gorgeous."

When it came down to it, she didn't have a whole lot of choices. Gritting her teeth, she climbed in behind the wheel and started the engine. "Where to?"

Mike settled back in his seat. "That's better. You know, you haven't even said how glad you are to see your lover again."

His breath smelled of stale beer, and he reeked of body odor. Judging by the rough stubble on his chin, he looked as if he hadn't shaved or showered, for that matter, since he'd escaped from prison. "I wouldn't take you for a lover if my life depended on it," she said evenly.

"Well, it might very well come to that."

His coarse laugh made her feel like throwing up. She knew he was playing on her nerves. He was good at it. She'd lost count of the number of times his tormenting words had threatened to drive her into a blind rage.

For a moment a vision of Blake rose in her mind and her throat ached. Would she ever see him again? What would he do when he found out she'd gone?

Now she could feel the fear clawing at her stomach. Up until now, she'd been afraid for her daughter. Now she was afraid for herself. "Are we going to drive, or are we going to sit here all night?" she said harshly.

"Okay, drive. Take a right out of here."

She drove, closing her ears and her mind to the taunts he threw at her as they sped down the road. She concentrated on the driving, following his curt directions, doing her best to memorize the route they were taking. If she had to walk back with Heather, she wanted to know the shortest route to town.

She ached to see her daughter again. To hold her small body tight in her arms and never let her go again.

"So, what have you been doing since you hotfooted it out of town?" Mike said, with a sneer in his voice. "No, don't tell me. You found a new boyfriend. That wasn't nice, sweetheart. You know you belong to me."

Gail felt a jolt of dismay. So he must have seen Blake with her. How long had he been following her, for pity's sake?

"Quit the silent treatment, Gail. I never did like to be ignored."

She flinched when she felt the barrel of a gun poke into her side. "I'm concentrating on the road," she snapped, "so quit bugging me."

"Well, you can concentrate on me at the same time. I'm getting bored talking to myself."

"Tell me where my daughter is, and maybe I'll feel more like talking."

The gun snaked up her side and rested against her breast. Her skin crawled, and it was all she could do not to slap his hand away.

"I said I'd tell you when we got there. How many times do I have to repeat myself?"

She forced herself to stay calm. "Okay, but if you don't want us to end up in a ditch you'd better get that gun off me." She waited an agonizing second or two before he removed the gun and sat back.

"So tell me about your new boyfriend. I bet he's a tiger in bed."

She flicked a glance at his face. His evil eyes stared back at her and she said carefully, "I haven't got the faintest idea what you're talking about."

He lifted the gun and jammed it painfully into the side

of her neck. "I'm talking about the jerk who stayed with you last night, that's what I'm talking about. I stayed awake long enough to see the bedroom lights go out."

The pressure of the cold steel against her neck nauseated her. She moistened her dry lips. "Just how long have you been following me around?" As she'd hoped, he was only too happy to tell her how clever he'd been.

"I've been right on your cute little tail for three or four days." He lowered the gun again. "I figured something cozy was going on when I saw lover boy pick you up the other morning."

"How did you know where to find me?"

"That was easy. I got good connections." He leaned forward, peering through the mist of snow. "Take this left fork here."

She knew where they were going now. The report Blake had received that morning had been right on the button. She was on the road to the lake.

Hope flared like a flickering candle in the dark. Maybe Blake was still there. Maybe he'd found the cabin where Mike had holed up and was waiting even now for him to come back. Maybe she could dare to hope that Heather was with him, unharmed and unafraid while he assured her that everything was going to be all right after all.

She kept glancing at the rearview mirror, hoping against hope that a cop might have been on the lookout and spotted them. Not that it would help her much. With the snow falling this hard, it would be impossible for them to see inside her car unless they were right on top of it, and hers was just another car on the road. Unless they had set up a roadblock on the road in to the lake.

At least Mike hadn't realized that Blake was a cop. If it came down to a fight, he wouldn't expect Blake to be armed. She closed her eyes briefly, praying that this would soon be over and they would all survive somehow.

The drive seemed endless, slowed as she was by the thick snow that threatened to bog down her tires. She was terrified that they might be stranded out here on the road somewhere, leaving Heather to the mercy of wherever he had left her.

She could be outside in the snow, slowly freezing to death. Or locked in a cabin and starving to death. What if she tried to escape and fell into the lake?

Her fear was like a physical thing, grabbing at her throat and cutting off her breath. She made herself stop creating scenarios in her mind. She had to concentrate on driving, and do her best to get where they were going as fast as humanly possible.

"Pull off here," Mike said sharply, as she was skirting the woods that surrounded the lake.

She saw the narrow trail he'd pointed out and headed the car onto it. So much for a roadblock on the lake road. Obviously, Mike had thought of everything.

The snow was lighter, the ground sheltered by the thick branches of the firs. The compact car made it easily on the narrow path between the massive tree trunks, and before long the shortcut brought them out to the edge of the lake.

"Stop here," Mike ordered, before they were clear of the trees.

She slammed on the brakes, tipping him forward so that his shoulder slammed into the dashboard.

Cursing at her, he rubbed his shoulder and peered out the window. "Get out and scout around. See if anyone else is out there."

"What will I do if they see me?"

"Make sure they don't." He leveled the gun at her, and her blood ran cold when she stared into the cold, black hole of the barrel. "I'll have this baby trained on you all the time. One wrong move and little Heather will be an orphan, just like her mommy was."

Tight-lipped, she gave him a curt nod, then slipped away from the car, keeping to the shelter of the trees. A blue jay screeched at her, and something scrabbled away in the undergrowth as she peered around the trunk of a massive cedar.

The lake appeared to be deserted. The snow filtered through the branches of the trees, which were weighed down with a thick, white coat of frosting. The cabins were strung out around the icy water's edge. They must all be empty, she realized, since she could see no columns of smoke floating up from the chimneys.

If Heather was inside one of them, she had to be freezing. She wondered what clothes Darcie had put on her this morning—a frivolous thought, considering the circumstances. Chances were it might no longer matter what her daughter was wearing.

Chapter 10

Gail pushed the grisly thought away, and a violent shudder shook her body. Heather was all right. She had to believe that, or she would go mad. She sent one last searching glance around, then trudged back to the car.

The warmth felt wonderful after the keen chill of the wind off the lake. She rubbed her hands together to get the circulation back in them, and brushed snowflakes from her damp hair.

"Well, did you see anything?" Mike demanded roughly.

"No, I didn't. There isn't anyone else here but us." *And Heather,* she prayed silently.

"Okay. Drive around to that first cabin on the end. The one with the green sign over the door."

She put the car in gear and pulled out onto the trail around the lake. "Is that where you left my daughter?"

"Park around the back of it," Mike ordered, ignoring her question. "Park it behind the trees, so it can't be seen from the lake."

She was shaking uncontrollably, the combination of fear and cold making her teeth chatter. She drove with infinite care through the piles of snowdrifts around the cabin and parked under the trees at the back of the ramshackle building.

The second she'd shut off the engine she stumbled out of the car. The curtains at the windows were drawn and she couldn't see inside.

Rushing up the steps, she shouted Heather's name. Before she could call out again, a cruel blow between her shoulder blades sent her staggering forward.

"Keep your big mouth shut, you stupid bitch," Mike muttered. "Every damn cop in the neighborhood can hear you."

She came up hard against the door, bruising her shoulder. She barely felt it, with all her attention focused on getting inside the cabin to her daughter.

She rattled the handle, and to her horror, the door opened easily. With a frantic cry she rushed inside. The damp, musty smell of neglect and decay was overpowering. The bitter cold seemed to eat at her bones. Although a pile of logs had been stacked next to the potbellied stove in the corner, no fire had been lit in it. She noticed a gleaming brass gas lighter hanging from a hook on the wall. It looked ridiculously out of place in the primitive surroundings.

Her glance raked the room, over a rickety table and four chairs standing against one faded wall. Threadbare, once-blue curtains covered the windows, and in front of them a long demised plant rotted in a clay pot. A small pile of tattered paperbacks lay scattered on a coffee table in front of a sad-looking couch, and beyond it a door leading to a bedroom stood open.

"It ain't much, but it's home," Mike said, chuckling as he closed the door behind him.

Paying no attention to him, Gail raced across the room

to the bedroom. She found two bunk beds with bare mattresses lurking in one corner, while a double bed with a rumpled blanket took up almost all the remainder of the room. A cheap oil lamp stood on the beat-up-looking bedside table, and a chest of drawers leaned drunkenly against one wall.

"Cozy, ain't it?"

He'd spoken from directly behind her, and she whirled on him, fury giving her a reckless courage. "Where's Heather? What have you done with her?" She raised her hand, her fingers curled into claws. "If she's hurt, I'll—"

He grabbed her wrist and twisted it, causing her to cry out in pain. "You'll what?" Cursing viciously, he dragged her back into the living room. "Look around. You don't see her, do you? Wise up, stupid. She ain't here."

"Then where is she? For God's sake, Mike—"

"Will you stop whining about the damn kid? She's all right. She's still with that dumb broad who's looking after her."

Gail blinked, wary of accepting this new hope he offered her. "She's with Darcie? But I called her. There was no answer. Her answering machine wasn't on. I thought—"

"You thought I'd iced her. Jesus, I'm not that stupid. All I did was cut the phone line to your baby-sitter's house. If you know the right line to cut, the caller still hears it ringing. Otherwise you'd have a maintenance crew turning up to see what's wrong. I tell you, the kid's all right."

Bewildered, she stared at him, wanting desperately to believe him.

"You still don't understand, do you?" He turned away from her and flung himself down on the couch. The springs creaked noisily under his weight. "I never wanted to hurt the kid. Kids are not to blame for what their parents do."

He looked up at her, his eyes burning with hate. "It's you I want. Ever since you turned me in. I can promise you, sweetheart, your new boyfriend ain't gonna want you once he sees what I've done to you.'' He raised the gun in his hand and squinted along the barrel, aiming at her face.

She eyed the door, trying to hide her sudden rush of fear. At least Heather was safe. She believed him now. Heather was simply a means of getting to her. Now that he had her in his clutches, he had no further use for her daughter. Now all she had to do was find a way to get out of this alive.

''Forget it, gorgeous,'' Mike said, reading her mind. ''I'd drop you before you'd taken two steps. You wouldn't get far with a smashed shinbone.''

She shot a quick glance at the window. Maybe, just maybe, Blake was out there somewhere, still checking on the cabins. There was just a chance he'd seen them come in. He could even now be hanging around outside, waiting for the right moment to rush in and grab Mike.

''The window doesn't open,'' Mike said, anticipating her thoughts once more. ''It's painted shut.''

Her best bet was to keep him talking, she decided, clutching at the fragile hope. If she could hold him off long enough to give Blake time to find them, or at the very least give herself a chance to make a break for it, she just might get out of this alive.

She rubbed her arms with her hands. ''It's cold in here,'' she said, with a genuine shudder. ''We'll freeze to death if we don't build a fire.''

Mike's laugh was full of contempt. ''And tip off anyone skulking around that we're here? I don't think so. No dice, gorgeous. You'll have to be a little more clever than that.''

''I'm not trying to be clever. I'm cold and I'm hungry.'' She looked around the stark room. ''Don't you have anything to eat?''

''You're not going to need food where you're going.'' He grinned at her, his uneven teeth yellow against his swarthy skin. ''As for me, I'll knock over another gas station when I leave here." To her dismay he leaned forward and pushed himself lazily to his feet. "You won't mind if I take your car, will you? After all, you won't be needing that, either."

She struggled to think clearly through the silent screaming in her head. "Mike, this is stupid. I can help you get out of here. I can do the driving while you rest. You look exhausted. We can go up to Canada. With me alongside you no one will question you at the border. We can stay there until things quiet down. They won't go looking for you up there."

He nodded slowly, tucking his gun into his belt. "Great speech. Now she's being nice to me." Without warning he reached out and grabbed her arm. "Why couldn't you be nice to me before, huh? How come you told the cops I killed Frank? You were damn glad to be rid of him. That's why you came on to me, wasn't it? So I'd kill my own brother."

"That's not true, Mike, and you know it," Gail said evenly. "I never encouraged you for one second."

"Yeah, well, that's your story." He twisted her arm, bringing his face close to hers. "I tell you something. I'm glad he's dead. He was always ramming it down my throat how much better he was than me. He had it all—looks, money and a gorgeous, sexy wife, and he never shut up gloating about it."

"I'm sorry. I know Frank could be...hurtful at times, but—"

Mike made a sound of disgust in his throat. "Our old lady was right. She always said that Frank would make it and I would rot in hell. Well, she should be happy now that she's got her best son up there with her. I finally did something to make her happy. I sure as hell couldn't do it while she was alive."

For a moment she could almost feel sorry for him. She

knew what it was like to grow up feeling lonely and unloved. "Mike," she said quietly, "let me help you. I know some people.... I'm sure we can work this out and no one has to get hurt anymore."

He didn't seem to hear her. "You should've been happy that Frank's dead. He certainly wasn't giving you what you wanted, was he? I could see it in your eyes, in the way you looked at me."

"Mike—"

"Shut up." He twisted her arm again, sending a shaft of agony up to her shoulder. His voice hardened to a snarl. "I thought you cared about me. I thought you and me could be good together. You shouldn't have done that. You shouldn't have told the cops. Now I'm gonna have to make you pay for that."

He grinned, a grimace dark with evil that filled her with dread. "First, though, I'm gonna take what's been coming to me for a long, long time. Ever since you twitched that cute little butt in front of me the first day I set eyes on you, I've been waiting for the chance to show you what a real man can do for you. I've got tricks I bet your new boyfriend never even dreamed of."

All at once she lost it. Panic swept her up in a swirling cloud of fear. She tugged her arm, frantically striving to break free of his cruel grip. "Let me go, you bastard!" she yelled. "I'll die before I let you touch me."

He laughed, the sound thick with derision. "You ain't got a say in it, gorgeous."

Again she jerked her arm, her fear exploding into fury. With a desperate cry, she drove her knee forward and up, aiming for his groin.

She wasn't quite fast enough. He sidestepped her, then twisted her around, so that her arms were trapped at her sides and his forearm jammed against her throat.

She felt the gun in his belt pressing into the small of her

back. If only she could reach it. Even as the hope flickered, she knew it was useless. The pressure on her throat was tightening, cutting off her breath. She could hear the blood roaring in her ears. "You're choking me," she muttered painfully.

"Oh, you can bet I'm gonna choke you. I'm gonna squeeze every last breath out of that pretty throat of yours. Just as soon as I've torn off your clothes and taught you a few new tricks. And just in case you have any ideas about fighting me, I'm gonna hog-tie your hands and feet together. So say your prayers, gorgeous, because very soon now, you're gonna be reunited with your dear, departed husband."

Heather, she thought. What would her daughter do without her? Would she end up in foster homes, just like her mother? *Dear God, Blake. Help me.*

He'd felt this sense of urgency before. He hoped to God that it didn't mean the same thing. He'd screwed up once, and badly. He would never be able to live with himself if he screwed this one up now.

The wheel jerked in his hands as he took a curve too fast. He made himself slow down. She was at the store, he told himself. He was worrying over nothing. *Stay calm. Just get there in one piece.*

He entered Main Street, ignoring the speed limit that warned him to slow down to twenty-five miles an hour. Slamming on the brakes, he slithered to a halt in front of The Book Nook. One look across the street and his worst fears were realized. Her car wasn't in the usual parking space.

She'd gone out to lunch, he told himself. She'd been too hungry to wait for him. She was most likely in the diner, waiting for him to join her. Flinging himself out of the car, he prayed that he wasn't nursing a false hope.

He slammed the door and leaped across the mounds of snow to the slippery doorstep. The bell jangled in protest as he flung open the door, and Polly looked up from behind the counter, her eyes wide with apprehension behind the rimless glasses.

"Where is she?" he demanded hoarsely.

Polly's hand went to her throat. "I don't know. She left here almost an hour ago."

"She didn't say where she was going? You didn't ask her?"

Polly shook her head. "I asked, but she didn't stop to tell me. She rushed out of here so fast. All she said was to call the police and send them to Darcie's house. I thought she was on her way there, but—"

"What happened to Darcie? Is Annie—?" The fear was painful, burning in his gut. Not Heather! Damn, where had he gone wrong?

"Annie's fine," Polly said, sounding frightened. "The police called here a little while ago. Apparently Darcie's phone line has been cut, but everyone's fine there. She didn't even know her phone was out. I asked the officer about Gail but he hadn't seen her. He wouldn't tell me anything else and I can't call Darcie...."

Blake took a deep breath. "Polly, this is important. Did Gail say anything, anything at all, about where she was going when she left?"

Polly shook her head. "Not a word. I'm sorry Blake. I wish I could help. What about the police? Can they help?"

"I hope so." Blake passed a hand across his eyes. "Look, I don't have time to talk to the cops. I want to get back there as fast as I can. Call them for me, will you? Tell them I found evidence of someone staying in one of the cabins. I'm pretty sure it's Stevens. Tell them he wasn't there when I got there, but I think he might have kidnapped Gail and taken her back there. At least, I hope that's where he's taken her. Tell them I'm on my way back there right now."

Polly glanced up at the clock. "Please hurry, Blake. She's been gone over an hour. Anything could have happened by now."

"Don't I know it. Damn this snow. It'll slow everyone up. Just tell the cops to meet me out there." He was out the door again before she could answer.

The engine coughed, spluttered and died when he tried to start the car. Cursing viciously, he jammed his foot down on the accelerator and tried again. After two more tries, the engine fired, and he let out the brake. His wild U-turn took him up onto the empty sidewalk and then he was off, his hands gripping the wheel, his face creased in concentration.

He had to drive as he'd never driven before. He had to push the big car to the limit and pray that he could keep it on the road, for something told him that time was running out for Gail, and he could lose again. And if he lost this time, he would lose much more than his self-respect.

Gail struggled to breathe in the cruel grip of Mike's hands as he dragged her across the floor to the bedroom. Faced with the horror of his crude and offensive promises of what he would do to her, she was desperate enough to try anything. She would die now, she told herself, rather than submit to this disgusting monster. If only she could get her hands on the gun.

Bracing herself, she waited until he'd shoved her up to the doorway of the bedroom, then she jammed her knee against the door frame. The pain made her cry out, but it was enough to jostle Mike off balance.

He stumbled, and for a moment, loosened his grip on her throat. Using his momentum, she grasped his arm and hauled him forward. Cursing, he sprawled on the floor in front of her.

He made a grab for her foot, but she sprang back. Her foot hit the floor and she twisted around, then hurtled for the cabin door. The handle turned easily and she hauled the door open, just as deafening bang exploded behind her and a bullet thudded into the woodwork above her head.

With a squeak of fright she raced down the steps. She heard Mike's angry bellow behind her and knew she had no time to get to the car. With an agility she never knew she had, she plunged across the clearing and into the trees.

Leaping and stumbling, with her hands and face scratched and torn by the undergrowth, she ran until she could run no more. She fell in a sobbing, panting heap into a mound of wet snow and lay there, fighting for air. When she could finally breathe without pain again, she carefully sat up and listened.

The forest buzzed with noise. Squeaks, chirps and chattering echoed in the majestic firs, accompanied by endless shifting and rustling among the undergrowth. A twig snapped nearby and she was instantly alert, her heart palpitating with anxiety.

As quietly as she could manage, she slid farther into the undergrowth, sheltering behind a thick, prickly shrub. She couldn't feel her feet, her hair hung in damp strands across her face and she couldn't seem to stop shaking.

She waited as the seconds ticked by, fearful of hearing the sound of Mike's footsteps. After a while her muscles screamed out to move as the cold slowed down her circulation.

Was it her imagination or was it growing darker? The thought of being alone in the cold, wet forest after dark filled her with dread. Yet, her common sense told her that the darkness would give her the protection she needed.

She wasn't going to be able to move, however, if she didn't get the circulation back into her limbs. Painfully, easing up an inch at a time, she climbed to her feet. Her toes felt as if a thousand bugs were crawling over them as she stamped them on the ground to get some warmth back in them.

Her coat felt heavy on her shoulders, and she knew it was wet through. She had to do something. She couldn't just sit there and freeze to death.

She tried to figure out in which direction the road lay. In her mad dash through the trees, she'd lost all sense of where she was heading. The heavy storm clouds gave her no hint of where the sun might be. She would have to find the lake, she decided, and get her bearings from there.

Following one of the trails seemed to be the best bet, and she set off through the trees, hoping she could spot a trail beneath the snow. She realized then that it had stopped snowing. At least that was something.

She remembered reading somewhere that it was possible to smell water. She lifted her nose and breathed in the cold air. She could smell nothing but damp pine and rotting wood. She turned around, hoping to detect something different from another direction. Without warning, a man stepped out from the trees a few yards ahead of her.

"Hey, gorgeous," Mike said, "it's about time you came home."

Her reaction was entirely automatic. She whirled around and started running. The first bullet whizzed into the trees to her left. She heard it ricochet twice.

Stumbling over a protruding root, she fell to her knees. The second bullet zinged by, far too close to her ear.

"The next one's gonna open up your head if you don't stop!" Mike roared.

She scrambled to her feet, but even as she did so, she knew she was too tired to run anymore. She waited, with a dull sense of resignation, for him to reach her. When he grabbed her arm and twisted it she made no sound. She was beyond protest now. Beyond hope.

Mike gave her a shove, sending her stumbling forward. "We're going back to the house," he said, his voice harsh and grating, "and then you're gonna give me what I want."

She willed her feet to move, feeling as if she were watching her own actions from a long way off. No matter what she did now, it wasn't going to help. She was going to die out here, and Heather would have to grow up without her.

"Get a move on, bitch," Mike snarled, giving her another jab in the back. "Too bad your boyfriend isn't here to see this. I could really make him squirm."

"Is that right," a deep voice said, almost at her elbow.

She thought at first that she was hallucinating. She froze, afraid to trust her fragile senses. She heard Mike swear, and slowly, not daring to believe, she turned around.

Mike stood with his hands in the air, the gun dangling uselessly from his fingers. Blake stood right beside him, his feet braced solidly apart, his own gun pressed securely, and none too gently, against Mike's temple.

He shot a glance in her direction. "Are you all right? If he's so much as touched you, I'll—"

"I'm okay." She was crying, silently, the tears rolling down her cheeks and falling into the trodden snow. With the possible exception of her daughter's birth, she had never seen a more beautiful sight in her entire life.

With a swift movement of his hand, Blake reached up and took the weapon from Mike's unresisting fingers. "You're going to be real sorry you did this," he said, sounding every bit as vicious as Mike had earlier.

"How did you f-find me?" Her teeth were chattering so badly she could hardly form the words.

"We have mastermind here to thank for that," Blake said grimly, sending Mike stumbling past her with a savage thrust. "He was so eager to take potshots at you, he advertised his exact location." He gave Mike another violent shove. "Lucky for you those damn bullets missed, you bastard, or you'd be talking out of a hole in your head right now."

"Yeah?" Mike muttered sullenly. "Then you'd go down for murder, lover boy."

"I don't think so." Blake glanced at Gail, who was doing her best to mop up her face with a wet tissue. "I see you didn't tell him."

She managed a shaky smile. "He didn't ask."

His answering wink did more to warm her than a raging fire.

"What the hell are you nattering about?" Mike demanded. "You'd better watch out, lover boy. You could be in real trouble, waving that piece around. It's against the law, you know."

"Not if you're a cop," Blake said cheerfully.

Mike looked stunned, then uttered a terse oath. "I should've frigging known."

Blake handed his gun to Gail, who took it in her trembling fingers. "Shoot him if he makes a move."

It was the first time she'd held a gun. It felt smooth, warm and almost comforting in her hands—a very different prospect from when she'd stared down the barrel of Mike's revolver.

She leveled both hands around the grip and pointed it at Mike's belly. "It will be my pleasure," she said evenly. She enjoyed the sudden look of apprehension in Mike's eyes.

She watched Blake fish out a pair of handcuffs from his jacket pocket and snap them onto Mike's wrists. Now, at last, she could really begin to relax. All at once she felt incredibly weary, as if her eyelids were made of lead.

Blake took the gun from her, which was just as well, she thought, since she wasn't at all sure she would be able to use it. He started off through the trees, roughly propelling Mike ahead of him.

Listening to the solid crunch of their footsteps in the snow, she marveled at how silently he had come up behind Mike on the trail. Following directly behind him, she let out her breath as the lake suddenly came into view. She'd been so close. Another few yards and she would have found it.

Darkness was closing in rapidly now; she could barely see the outline of the cabins. She thanked God for the comforting presence of Blake striding along in front of her. She could just make out the shape of a car in front of the cabin where Mike had taken her. It had to be Blake's car.

She wondered if he would let her ride with him back to town, and perhaps return for her car in the morning.

Suddenly remembering, she said urgently, "Blake, he hurt the young man in charge of Landings' gas station. He was lying on the floor unconscious when I left him."

Blake looked grim. "One more thing he'll pay for," he muttered. "What do you think we should do with him? It would save us all a lot of trouble if we just dumped him in the lake."

"Hey, you can't do that," Mike said, beginning to stutter. "I've got rights."

Blake laughed, a hollow sound that echoed eerily among the silent trees. "Rights? The only rights recognized out here in the wilderness are the ownership of territory and the power to defend it. I'd say you were a little short in both respects, wouldn't you?" His tone was so unpleasant, it even made Gail's flesh creep.

"What are you talking about?" Mike jerked his head around to look at him. "You lay a hand on me and I'll shout police brutality so loud you'll hear the echo for weeks."

"What makes you think I'm going to take you back to town?" Blake halted, dragging Mike to a stop at the edge of the lake, just a few yards from the cabin. "What's to stop me from pumping you full of bullets and dropping you into the lake? Who's going to know, except Gail? And you can bet she's not going to tell anyone after what you did to her.''

Gail edged around him, drawing closer to the cabin. She wasn't sure what was going on, either. Blake was making her nervous. Much as she hated Mike, and wanted to see him pay for what he'd done, she couldn't agree to cold-blooded murder. She couldn't imagine Blake doing something like that. If he did carry out his threat and kill Mike, then she didn't know him very well, after all.

Mike was beginning to panic. She heard it in his voice when he blabbered, ''You're a cop. You can't ice me.''

Blake took a step toward him, forcing him closer to the shore of the lake. ''I'm a marshal,'' he corrected coldly. ''And I can do anything I damn well please.''

''They'll find out. They'll know it was you.'' He stumbled back as Blake moved forward again, placing him precariously close to the ice-covered water's edge.

''It's more likely they'll figure it's one of your cronies upset with you. An escaped con on the run doesn't have too many friends. You don't deserve friends after what you did to Gail.''

Mike's voice rose. ''I didn't touch her. I swear I didn't. Tell him, Gail. Tell him I didn't lay a finger on you.''

Blake moved forward once more. ''Yeah, tell me, Gail. Tell me what he did to you. Why don't you lie to me, just like he lied to the cops about you helping him murder your husband.''

Gail's pulse leaped. Now she knew what he was doing. And she loved him even more for it.

''I didn't mean to, Gail,'' Mike stammered, on a note of desperation. ''Honest, I didn't. I was pissed because you turned me in. I had to tell them something, so I told them you helped me.'' He backed away, his feet moving onto the ice. It creaked ominously beneath him.

"But she didn't help you, did she, Mike? You made it all up, just to get even.'' Blake lifted his hand. The gun gleamed black against the backdrop of snow and ice.

Still backing away, Mike shook his head and yelled, "All right, you bastard! She didn't do it. She had nothing to do with it. I planned it all myself. Now tell him, Gail. Tell him I didn't touch you.''

It seemed to happen all at once. Blake turned to look at Gail—at least, she thought he was looking at her, but he might have been looking at the three deputies who had suddenly appeared from behind the cabin.

Even as she noticed that they were there, Mike let out a howl and took off, slithering and sliding on the ice.

Blake started after him. His yell rang out across the frozen lake. "Come back, you damn fool! You'll go in!''

Mike paid no attention. He just kept running. The deputies reached the shore and yelled to Blake to let him go. The ice creaked louder, then snapped, with a sound as sharp as a gunshot.

Gail screamed as Mike seemed to stumble sideways. He slithered for several yards, his cuffed hands waving above his head. Then, in slow motion, he sank from view. His cry of horror was cut off by abrupt silence.

Now the ice cracked and popped in all directions. Blake turned and headed for the bank. Gail screamed again as she saw his feet disappear beneath the surface of the black water.

"Jump, man, jump!'' one of the deputies yelled.

She saw him gather himself for the leap and launch himself into the air. Her heart stopped as he seemed to fall back. Then, with a loud grunt, he flung himself forward and his fingers grazed the edge of the shore. Within seconds the deputies hauled him onto dry ground. Water poured

from his wet clothes as he swept his dripping hair back
from his face with his hand.

With a cry, Gail flung herself at him and clung to him,
closing her eyes as his arms folded around her. The deputies had started off at a run around the lake, searching for
a sign of Mike. She shivered, knowing what the icy water
would do to him.

"I want you to go into the cabin," Blake said, gently
holding her away from him. "See if you can find something
to light a fire. Then bolt the door and stay there, get yourself dried out."

She looked up at him, at his face pinched with cold.
"What about you? You'll freeze to death in those wet
clothes."

"I'll be there in a few minutes."

She clung to him, reluctant to let him go.

"I promise." He leaned down and kissed her cold lips.
"Now go on."

She backed up the steps, watching him jog into the darkness, until she couldn't see him anymore. Then she went
inside the cabin and bolted the door.

She felt her way in the darkness to the bedroom and
found the oil lamp. Shaking it, she was relieved to hear the
fuel sloshing around inside. At least she wouldn't have to
sit in the dark.

Feeling for the gas lighter, she found it, and flicked it
without much hope. The tiny flame flared, and she uttered
a soft cheer. She lit the lamp, and found a pile of old news-
papers underneath the logs, which she crumpled up in the
stove.

After making a pyramid of the chunks of wood over the
paper, she set them alight, then sat back to watch her hand-
iwork. Within seconds the logs had caught, crackling and
popping sparks up the chimney.

The warmth felt like heaven as the glow slowly filled

the small room. She tried not to think about what was happening outside. Instead, she thought about Heather and how worried her daughter would be that she hadn't called. Polly, too, must be out of her mind with worry. She would have to call as soon as she got back home.

She thought longingly of her cozy house, yearning for a hot shower, clean dry clothes and a cup of hot coffee. Now that she was warm and beginning to dry out, she could deal with everything that had happened in the last few hours.

She shuddered when she thought about how close she'd come to dying in this miserable hole. If it hadn't been for Blake, she could have been dead by now, probably lying in the lake beneath the ice.

Restlessly she got to her feet and went to the window.

Pulling back the curtains, she peered outside. She could see nothing but her reflection in the dusty panes. Wandering back to the stove, she squatted down in front of it.

She longed to open the door, but was afraid to unbolt it. With her own eyes she had seen Mike sink into the depths of the lake. There was always the chance, however, that he could have escaped, and eluded the deputies and Blake in the dark. She wouldn't feel safe until she knew he was in custody again.

But she still wouldn't feel totally secure, even then. There would always be the chance he could escape again, or eventually be paroled. Or, as he'd threatened to do, he could send someone else after her.

Knowing Mike as she did, he wouldn't give up. He wouldn't forget, and he wouldn't be satisfied until he'd paid her back for her betrayal. She would always have that fear, not only for herself, but for her daughter. For she was quite sure that if Mike couldn't get to her, he would find a way to get to Heather.

Gail sighed, as her eyelids drooped again. She was so tired. The warmth was making her lethargic, drowning her mind of coherent thought. She moved away from the stove and sat down on the couch, trying not to remember Mike sitting there just an hour or two ago.

Soon, she thought hopefully, it would all be over. Mike would be back in jail, and she could go home. Only where was home? Now that Mike knew where she lived, Mellow Springs would no longer be safe for her and Heather.

Slowly she got up from the couch and went over to the stove. She picked up a log and threw it on the fire, then closed the little metal door. She could hear the flames roaring all the way up the metal chimney.

She would have to find somewhere else to live, start a new life all over again for herself and her daughter. The thought depressed her.

She sat down on the couch again, then froze as footsteps sounded on the steps outside. The door shook as someone pounded furiously on it. "Gail? Let me in. It's freezing out here."

With a cry of joy she leaped to her feet and sped across the room. The bolt slid back in her impatient fingers and then she had the door open. A blast of cold air made her gasp as she reached out to Blake, who stood shivering on the doorstep, his lips blue with cold.

"Quick, come inside," she urged, as she stood back to let him pass. She looked out into the darkness, expecting to see the deputies, but the lake was deserted once more.

"The deputies are going back to town," Blake said, as he crossed the room to the stove. "They're taking my car with them. I thought we'd go back together in yours."

Even as he spoke, she heard the roar of a car engine bursting to life from somewhere behind the cabin. Another one joined it a moment later.

"Good. I didn't fancy the idea of driving back alone in this snow." Gail slammed the door shut and shot the bolt.

Turning to look at him, she asked quietly, "Did you find him?"

Blake gave a brief shake of his head. "No, not a trace of him."

She tried to hide her dismay. She must not have succeeded, as he gave her a bleak look.

"I'm sorry, Gail."

She wanted to ask him for details, but decided that could wait. He looked about ready to collapse. Instead, she hurried over to him and laid her hand on his shoulder. "Blake, you are soaking wet and cold as ice. You have to get out of those clothes and dry them before we drive back to town. There's a blanket in the other room. It's not spotless but it will keep you warm while your clothes dry."

He nodded, looking unutterably tired. He struggled out of his jacket and she took it from him.

"I'll get the blanket," she said, as she draped the soggy coat over the back of a chair.

Leaving him to get out of his clothes, she hurried into the bedroom. The blanket was a thick one, and she dragged it off the bed, thankful to have something warm to offer him.

When she went back into the living room, he was still standing where she'd left him, gazing moodily at the stove, his hands outstretched to warm them.

"I'll air this out while you take off the rest of those wet clothes," she said, holding the blanket up close to the hot stovepipe.

She kept her face averted while he stripped. After everything they'd shared she was aware that she was being a little ridiculous, but somehow she just couldn't be blasé about the man she loved stripping naked in front of her.

To break the awkward silence, she asked quietly, "Do you think he's dead?"

He sounded defeated when he answered her. "He could be. We just can't be sure."

She pulled in a shaky breath. "So what you're saying is that there's still a chance he got out."

She knew, by his long pause, that he hated having to admit it. "I'm sorry, Gail. I've seen too many scenarios like this to take anything for granted. Until we find the body of Mike Stevens, we have to assume he is still alive—and extremely dangerous. It's not over yet."

Chapter 11

The blanket shook in Gail's hands. Blake was right. It wasn't over yet. Maybe it would never be over. "It's unlikely anyone would survive for long in that water," she said, in a vain effort to reassure herself.

"True. We did manage to string out across the ice to the hole where he'd gone in. There was just no way to see him. It was dark, the water's deep right there, and it was impossible to see under the ice. It was breaking up pretty quickly, so we got out of there fast."

She glanced at him, shocked by what he'd done. "You could have all drowned out there."

He crossed his arms over his head and grabbed hold of his T-shirt. "We couldn't just leave him there to die."

She watched him draw the T-shirt over his head, baring his chest. A tingling began low in her belly and spread rapidly up to her breasts.

"You risked your life to save a cold-blooded murderer," she said unsteadily. "A man who'd killed his brother. A man who planned to rape me and then kill me, too."

The look on his face was hard to define. He dropped the T-shirt on the floor, and then reached for the buckle of his belt. "It's my job, Gail."

For some reason she was angry, although she wasn't sure why. Maybe it was the thought of how close she could have been to losing him. Or maybe it was his lack of regard for his own life, and for the feelings of those who loved him.

Her voice shook when she answered him. "How could you do that? How you could risk the lives of yourself and three men for the sake of a black-hearted criminal who'll spend the best part of his life in jail? That hardly seems like a fair trade to me."

His mouth tightened into a thin line. "I don't expect you to understand." He flicked open his belt and unzipped his jeans.

He was silent while he took off his shoes and socks, then dropped his jeans and stepped out of them.

What she couldn't understand was how she could be so angry at him and want desperately to make love with him at the same time. Deciding that her mixed-up feelings had a lot to do with the terrifying events she'd been through, she held the blanket out to him. "Here," she said, with an attempt at a smile. "This should be aired out now."

He took the blanket from her and wrapped it around his shoulders. She turned away while he removed his shorts, and kept herself busy hanging the rest of his clothes over the chairs.

"I wish I could offer you something hot to drink," she said, when she judged it safe to look at him again.

Draped in the blanket, his shorts in his hand, he still managed to look formidable. "I'll survive." He hung the shorts over the last chair and huddled in front of the stove.

She felt guilty now, for taking her tension out on him. Trying to figure out how to make amends, she picked up a log to put on the fire. "Do you really think there's a chance that Mike is still alive?"

Clutching the blanket closed with one hand, he reached for the log and took it from her. "There's always a chance—though we searched the entire area around the lake. I'd say you're right, and it's unlikely he got out of there, considering the temperature of the water, and the fact that he was cuffed."

She opened the door of the stove and waited for him to throw the log onto the flames. "I wish I knew how that poor man is at the gas station. Someone must have helped him by now, don't you think?"

"I asked the deputies to look in on their way back."

She didn't want to talk about Mike now, but she needed more reassurance. "You think Mike's still in the lake, then?"

"I think his body's trapped somewhere under the ice. We won't know for sure until tomorrow, when we can mount a search in daylight. If he did get out—he's probably miles away by now."

She nodded. "I know I shouldn't say this, but my life would be so much simpler if he were dead."

"Yes." Blake moved over to the couch. "It would simplify a lot of things."

"What if you don't find him?" She sat down next to him, weariness once more creeping over her.

He leaned back and closed his eyes. "I'll worry about that if it happens. My job is to find him and bring him back, and it's not over until I do, whether he's dead or alive. But right now I have to grab a couple of minutes sleep before we drive back."

And then what? she wanted to ask. But his deep, even breathing told her that he'd fallen asleep.

She felt like going to sleep herself. The room had grown

very warm, almost suffocating, in fact. The little stove was more efficient than she'd thought.

She leaned back and let her tired muscles relax. She couldn't ignore the depression that was creeping over her. Something was different between them; she could feel it. It was a subtle change, nothing she could really put her finger on, but it was there, lurking like an insidious disease waiting to strike.

She tried not to think about it, tried to tell herself that it was a reaction to everything she'd been through that day. She closed her eyes and listened to the logs popping and snapping in the stove. Until the sounds faded away and she knew no more.

Blake awoke suddenly, with a jerk that shook his entire body. He opened his eyes and blinked, wondering for a moment where he was. It was dark, and he could see nothing at all in the room, except a thin glow of red in one corner.

Memory came crashing back fast. The red glow was what was left of the fire behind the door of the stove. He was still in the cabin, naked under the scratchy blanket, and Gail was asleep with her head on his shoulder.

The jolt of his body had disturbed her. She muttered something, shifted closer to him, and relaxed again. He eased an arm from under the blanket and curled it around her shoulders.

She murmured again, and moved her head to the center of his chest. His body responded at once, hardening and tensing as the hot flame of desire licked at his loins.

Damn, he wanted her. Now that he was rested, warm and undeniably naked, his natural urges were once more taking over. He could feel the curve of her breast against his side, and he fought the urge to reach down for the tempting mound of soft flesh. He couldn't do this to her—or to himself. Not again.

Once more she stirred, and this time she whimpered. He was instantly alert. He knew by the change in her breathing that she was awake. "What is it?" he asked sharply. "Are you hurting?"

"My shoulder." She shifted away from him and groaned. "Ouch. And my knee. I must have bruised them."

"I think the lamp ran out of fuel." He stood. She must have been anchoring the blanket underneath her, as it pulled away from him, dropping away in the dark. "Damn," he muttered.

"What is it?"

She'd sounded frightened and he hurried to reassure her. "It's okay. I dropped the blanket, that's all."

"Oh. Here, I'll get it."

His eyes were beginning to adjust to the darkness, but he could barely see her outline as she sat up. Apparently she still couldn't see him, as she put her hand out in front of her, smack in the middle of his belly.

The touch of her cool fingers on his heated skin shut off his breath. He heard her soft gasp, then she said faintly, "Oh, sorry."

He fought for a second or two longer while the blood roared in his head and his body throbbed with need. Then, with a muttered, "Oh, what the hell," he reached for her and dragged her to her feet.

She came willingly, all arms and lips and thrusting body. He couldn't see her properly, but he could sure as hell feel her. And right then, that was all that mattered.

No woman had ever destroyed his control so easily. The hot clamoring in his body demanded to be satisfied, and only she could quench the flames. He wanted her with a fervor that could not, would not, be denied.

She was struggling to get out of her clothes, her impatience matching his. That was what he found so irresistible—her eagerness, her uninhibited enjoyment of both giving and receiving the pleasures of lovemaking. She excited him to fever pitch, driving him wild with her questing fingers and searching mouth.

She was like a drug—the more he had of her, the more he wanted. Warning bells were going off in his head, but he paid them no heed. She was naked now, and pressed against him, belly to belly and breast to chest, and all he could think about was tasting her again, and sinking himself into her until the ache in his groin was appeased.

He pushed her down on the couch and fell on top of her. She writhed beneath him, making those little moaning sounds that fired his mind with excitement. He could feel her fingers digging into his buttocks, creating little rivers of molten heat as he found her breast at last.

She moaned again as he pulled on the taut nipple with his lips. "That is so…good."

Her hand caressed him before he expected it and he grunted with surprised pleasure. "Damn it, woman, what are you doing to me?"

She laughed—a low, musical sound that caused a shiver down his spine. "Mister," she whispered softly, "you ain't seen nothing yet."

She started wriggling beneath him, sliding under him, her mouth traveling down his chest, his belly…

His breath exploded out of his lungs as the waves of sheer pleasure rocked his very soul. Never in his life had he felt such exquisite torture. He reared above her, his head thrown back, and gave himself up to the intense, almost-painful delight.

When he could stand it no more he reached for her, roaming her body with his lips, his teeth and his tongue, until she pleaded with him to take her.

He was only too happy to oblige. Ravenous for the relief

only she could give him, he drove into her with an urgency that shook him to the core. The thunder in his head erupted in a furor of excitement as her body merged with his. He could feel her striving with him as he arced and bucked, and then her name was torn from his lips in a desperate plea as he crashed through the barriers into the cool, peaceful calm beyond.

He lay for a long time with her, covered by the blanket, content just to listen to her breathing. He would not allow himself to think beyond this moment. This was now, and it was beautiful. Moments like this were rare in his life, and he was determined to savor every second granted him.

When she finally stirred, he felt a deep, inexplicable sadness.

"What time is it?"

Her voice held a dreamy quality with which he could easily identify. He felt as if he were dreaming himself. He lifted his arm and peered at the pale green numerals on the face of his watch. "It's almost eight."

"I have to get home and call Heather. Everyone must be frantic wondering what's happened to me." She gave a little gasp. "I can't call Darcie. Mike said he cut her line."

"I asked the deputies to get a message to Darcie. I told them to tell her you were fine and that you'd call her later. By the time we get home, her line will probably be repaired. I also asked them to call Polly. I figured she'd be worried about you, too."

He felt her raise her chin. "You had it all figured out, didn't you? If I didn't know better, I'd say you deliberately jumped in that lake as part of an intricate and devious plan to seduce me this evening."

He smiled wryly in the darkness. "I can promise you, honey, I'd figure out an easier plan than that." He turned his head and nuzzled her neck. "You didn't exactly offer much resistance, you know."

She sighed. "I know. I find you utterly irresistible."

"The feeling's mutual, believe me." He found her mouth and gave her a long, deep kiss. "I guess we'd better be making tracks for home."

She murmured her reluctant agreement. "Can I just ask you something first? Something that's been niggling at me for a while."

He felt a pang of wariness. "Okay. Shoot."

"The day we took Heather to the children's museum, I asked you what you did before you were in real estate. I know that was a cover for you, but you said you used to be a teacher."

He could feel his muscles slowly tensing. "Yeah, I remember."

"I was just wondering how true that was, or if it was part of the cover."

He thought about it for so long he was surprised she didn't comment on his silence. Except for the official reports, he hadn't talked about it since that day. For some reason, he wanted to talk about it now. That surprised him.

No, it was stronger than that. It stunned him to realize that he wanted her to know, that it seemed important to him that she know. "It was true in a way," he said at last.

"I thought so."

Amazed at her intuition, he said quietly, "It was while I was with the DEA. I was in charge of training undercover agents."

"And something bad happened. I know. You don't have to tell me if you'd rather not."

He stirred, knowing he was going to tell her, and wondering how to put it into words so that she would understand. "It was my job to teach them the danger signals, to know when their cover was blown and when to get out. It's always a tough call. You want to finish the job, especially if you've put months of work into building a case."

She sounded subdued when she said, "I can imagine."

He pulled in a breath and let it out slowly. "Anyway, one of my units, three very eager, very dedicated young guys, took on a particularly tough case with me. The drugs were coming over the border from Mexico, and we were following up on a lead from an unknown source. After a while, I sensed that something wasn't quite right. It's not anything you can explain in so many words. It's more like a gut feeling, something you get with experience. I ordered them to pull out."

"What happened?"

He could hear her apprehension now. He closed his eyes, dreading the memory yet knowing he had to face it one more time. "They begged me to finish it. We'd sweated blood for months, taken terrible risks, and put in untold hours of living on the edge. They told me I was overreacting, being too cautious. They accused me of losing my nerve. I began to wonder if they were right."

She stirred in his arms. "I can understand how you felt. It's so easy to believe what others say about you."

He couldn't stop the bitterness from creeping into his voice. "We were so close, and I knew only too well how much they hated to give up everything we'd fought so damn hard for. They were young and eager to show what they could do. They needed to prove themselves. They weren't about to lose their first big one. And I wasn't about to let them blame me for it if they did."

He paused for a moment, waiting for the ache in his throat to subside. "I let my personal feelings get in the way. I went against my better judgment and I gave them the go-ahead."

He could feel the tension in her body, which matched his own. He forced himself to go on. "We were ambushed. All four of us left for dead. I was lucky. The bullet that got me grazed my skull. The others didn't make it."

She shuddered, drawing closer to him.

"You know the toughest part?" He blinked, willing his voice not to break. "It was trying to explain to their wives what had gone wrong. I'll never forget the faces of those women as long as I live. I can't tell you how much I wished I could trade places with any one of those dead men. I asked myself over and over, why was I the one who survived? Why Blake Foster, who had nothing to lose, instead of three dedicated young men with families who loved them and needed them? It didn't make sense. It still doesn't."

Her arm tightened about him. "I'm sorry. I shouldn't have brought all this up."

"No." He hugged her closer. "I wanted you to know. I left the squad, of course. I couldn't deal with the nightmares. Six months later I took on the job of marshal. That was something I could handle without messing up someone else's life."

She shifted restlessly beside him. "It wasn't your fault, Blake, you must know that. You did what you thought was best at the time. Those men didn't die because of you. They died because they were doing a dangerous job. They must have known the risks."

He uttered a bitter laugh. "Yeah—well, no matter how many people say that to me, I can't convince myself of that."

"No one is perfect." Her lips brushed his cheek. "No one expects you to be."

He turned his head and met her lips with his own. She was doing her best, he knew. But the forgiveness he sought would have to come from a higher power.

"Come on," he said, giving her a light smack on her rear. "Let's go home. I'm starving."

The skies had cleared, but Gail could feel the rear wheels of the compact car slipping every now and then on the packed snow as they drove home. Blake was unusually quiet, his face set as he stared at the road ahead, his hands gripping the wheel as if he were afraid to ease up on it.

She stole a glance now and again at his forbidding profile, wishing she hadn't been so curious about his past. She'd sensed there was something else there, something he hadn't wanted to talk about, but she hadn't dreamed it would be so devastating, or how much impact the tragedy had wrought on his life.

She longed to heal that part of him, to give him the reassurance he needed. If only she could find the right words to say what was in her heart. If only she could reach that part of him that he guarded so tenaciously.

She was relieved when they reached town. She hadn't eaten since breakfast, and her stomach ached with hunger. Maybe they would both feel better, she thought wistfully, once they had some warm food inside them.

She called Darcie as soon as she was in the house.

"What happened?" Darcie demanded, the moment she heard Gail's voice. "The cops wouldn't tell me anything except that you were all right. What's this all about?"

"I had some trouble with my ex-brother-in-law," Gail said, skimming over the truth. "I'm sorry you got involved. Is Annie all right?"

"She's fine," Darcie assured her, although she still sounded anxious. "She wanted to stay up and talk to you, but she fell asleep so I put her to bed."

"I can't thank you enough, Darcie," Gail said, swallowing her disappointment at missing the chance to speak with her daughter.

"You can thank me by telling me what's going on."

"I can't explain it all now, but I promise I'll tell you everything just as soon as I can."

"Does this have anything to do with Blake? He's not your brother-in-law, is he?"

Gail smiled. "No, he's not. I swear, Darcie, I'll tell you everything...soon. Can you just keep Annie for tonight?"

"As long as you want. Just make sure you fill me in on the all the mystery."

"I promise." Gail hung up and looked at Blake, who sat slumped in an armchair, his chin resting on his hands. "You do think Heather will be all right there, don't you? I mean, Mike knows where she is now and—"

Blake looked up at her, his eyes bleak and full of a sadness she didn't understand. "She'll be fine. Even if by some miracle Stevens got out of the lake, he could walk all night and not reach Mellow Springs until late tomorrow. By then the sheriff will have picked him up."

"He could get a ride into town."

"He couldn't take the chance. Not with his hands cuffed." He frowned. "Gail, the chances of him coming out of that water are very slim."

"I know. I just won't feel safe until I know he's been found, one way or another." She glanced at the clock. "Shower first or food?"

"Definitely food."

"I was hoping that's what you'd say." She went into the kitchen and started opening cupboard doors.

After a moment or two, he followed her in and sat down at the table. "I could take you out to dinner."

She shook her head. "I'd rather eat at home. I look a mess."

"You look pretty good to me."

She pulled a face at him. She knew what she looked like. Hair matted and tangled, probably full of twigs. She'd rinsed off her face and hands before calling Darcie, but she hadn't had time to tackle any more than that.

"How about sloppy jocs?" she suggested, taking a quick survey of her cupboard. "Or I could defrost some chicken in the microwave."

"The way my stomach is hollering for food, dry toast would taste good right now."

"Sloppy joes, then. It'll be faster."

She could feel his depression all the way across the room. She crumbled hamburger into a pan and wondered if he was blaming himself again for what had happened at the lake. If so, they needed to talk about it.

She waited until she had set the steaming burgers in front of him and joined him at the table before bringing up the subject. "You didn't tell me how you knew where to find me this afternoon," she said, watching him take a huge bite of his sandwich. "Were you there when I drove in?"

He shook his head. "I went to the bookstore. Polly told me you'd left without saying where you were going, but that you'd sent someone to Darcie's house. The officer called back and told Polly that you hadn't been to the house. I guessed Stevens was involved somewhere. I'd already found the cabin and figured he'd been there. I banked everything on the hope that he'd taken you back there with him."

"Thank God you did." She shuddered. "I'd hate to think what would have happened if you hadn't turned up when you did. You saved my life, Blake. How do I thank someone for saving my life?"

"I got you into this mess in the first place. If I'd taken better care of you he wouldn't have grabbed you."

So he had taken the blame. She let out a sigh of exasperation. "When are you going to stop blaming yourself for everything that goes wrong? What if you hadn't found out he was coming to Mellow Springs? He would still have found me, and I would be dead by now. Maybe Heather, too. We both have you to thank for our lives."

He looked at her, and the warm gleam in his eyes made her forget how hungry she was. "You're one heck of a woman, Gail Stevens," he said softly. "I'm real glad I met you."

She smiled. "I'm glad I met you, too. Now eat your supper."

"I will if you'll eat yours. Then we'll take that shower you talked about earlier."

"Together?" She grinned. "Hmm, I like that idea." She tilted her head to one side. "You are going to stay, aren't you? Tonight, I mean?"

He nodded without looking at her. "I'm not leaving your side again until I know Stevens is either dead or behind bars. I'm not taking any more chances."

It wasn't the answer she wanted, she thought ruefully, but it would have to do for now.

He helped her with the dishes, and then led her to the shower. She climbed out of her clothes for the second time that day, and stepped with him into the wonderful, healing torrent of hot water. He shampooed her hair for her, and she did the same for him.

When he took the soap in his hands and worked up a lather, she waited in breathless anticipation, then shivered with delight as he gently and thoroughly smoothed the foam over her entire body. Then it was her turn, and she took her time, savoring the feel of his hard, smooth muscles beneath her fingers, and the sound of his harsh breathing.

"I would have taken an even bet," he muttered when she was finished, "that I was too wiped out for you to do this to me again tonight."

Smiling in triumph, she slid her wet body slowly back and forth across his stomach. "That just goes to prove, Marshal, that you don't know your own strength."

His hands slid down her back to her bottom. "Maybe not," he muttered thickly, "but I get the distinct feeling that I'm about to find out."

She slept in his arms that night, exhaustion and a strange

feeling of contentment blocking out the hours until daylight awakened her.

She opened her eyes, knowing at once that she was alone. She lay quiet for a moment, and listened for the sounds of him moving around. She could hear nothing but the scratch of frozen shrubs against the bedroom window.

She slipped out of bed, and snatched a white terry-cloth robe from the closet. She didn't wait to put on slippers, but padded out barefoot to the kitchen.

Relief washed over her when she saw him sitting at the kitchen table. She'd thought for a moment that he'd left without waking her. He was fully dressed, in jeans and a dark multicolored sweater. He sat with the morning paper in front of him, although she could see he hadn't turned the pages.

Disappointed that he hadn't waited for her to wake up, she fastened the belt of her robe and headed for the coffeepot. "How long have you been up?" she asked casually.

"A couple of hours. I put in a call to the sheriff's office but there's no news yet."

She nodded. His job. Always his job. She pushed back the resentment. After all, her life was in possible danger until they knew what had happened to Mike. She was his responsibility.

She tried to feel happy about that, but she couldn't. She didn't want to be a responsibility. She didn't want him there because he had a job to do. She wanted him there because she loved him, and above all, she wanted him there because he wanted to be with her.

She filled the coffee machine with water and switched it on. "How long do you think it will be before we know?"

"Any time now, I guess. They're out there dragging the lake."

"What if they don't find him?"

"Then we start tracking him down again. He's not going to get far wearing cuffs."

She reached in the cupboard for a couple of coffee mugs and set them on the counter. Her stomach felt as if it had a cold, hard knot in it. He'd withdrawn from her again.

Gone was the warm gleam in his eyes, and the sensuous smile. His voice was no longer soft and husky with emotion. His words were clipped, and so far he'd avoided meeting her gaze.

Was he simply immersing himself in his job, she wondered, to the extent of shutting her out? Or was there something else, something that he still hadn't told her? Something that kept intruding into their private little world and destroying the beautiful, fragile bond between them—a bond that was much too new to be tested yet.

If only she knew what was really going on in his mind. Just when she thought she'd reached him, just when she thought she was beginning to understand him, he would disappear again into that remote, obscure region where she was forbidden to follow.

She was afraid. Not of Mike anymore; she was reasonably sure that Mike had died under the black ice of Deep Frost Lake. She was afraid for herself. Afraid of what would happen to her if Blake had simply been amusing himself while he did his job.

The coffee began to drip into the pot, filling the kitchen with its enticing fragrance. "I have bacon and eggs if you're hungry," she said, tossing the words over her shoulder.

"That sounds great. Thanks." The newspaper rustled as he turned the pages.

Again she had to fight back the resentment. Men reacted differently than women in these situations. She was just put out because he wasn't filled with the same romantic glow that enveloped her. Maybe she was being unreasonable to expect him to feel the same heady excitement she felt whenever she set eyes on him. But then, she'd never been in love before.

She poured him a cup of coffee and set it in front of him. He smiled up at her, but she couldn't see it reflected in his eyes. The knot in her stomach tightened. "Breakfast will be ready in a minute."

"Thanks. Can I help?"

"No, you finish reading the paper." She summoned a smile of her own and went back to the stove to cook his breakfast. In spite of the tantalizing aroma of the sizzling bacon, she didn't feel in the least bit hungry. She cooked some for herself anyway. She remembered him saying how much he hated eating alone.

She could see the stress in his face as he ate, although he made a valiant attempt to cover up his tension. "It looks as if the snow has gone for a while," she said, determined not to eat in silence.

"I hope so. It will make things easier out at the lake."

She thought she knew what was bothering him. "Would you rather have been out there? I'll be fine here if you want to go out and see what's happening."

He shook his head. "No, they'll call me if there's any news." His gaze wandered around the kitchen, almost as if he was looking for something to comment on. He finally found it.

"Did Heather draw that picture on the fridge?"

She nodded. "In kindergarten. She's drawn several of them, but that one's my favorite."

He gazed for some time at the crude drawing of children sliding down the mountain on brightly colored disks. Then he said quietly, "She does a good job."

She remembered it then. "Just a minute," she said, "I have something to give you. Heather drew a picture for you the day we went to the mountain. She was going to give it to you that night, after you told her the story, but she fell asleep. She made me promise to give it to you, but with everything that's been going on I forgot."

His expression remained impassive, but she could swear she saw grief in his eyes. "That's sweet," he said, his voice catching just a little.

"I'll get it." She turned to go, but just then the phone rang—a shrill sound that brought her to a full stop. She felt sick as she watched Blake get up and reach for the wall phone.

"Foster." He listened for a moment, his head slowly nodding, his expression unreadable. "Thanks. I'd appreciate that," he said at last, and replaced the receiver.

She felt cold, then hot, then light-headed. "What happened?"

He walked back to the chair he'd just vacated and stood behind it, resting his hands on the back of it. "They found Stevens," he said, his gaze intent on her face. "He's dead."

Her relief was almost overwhelming. It was over. It was finally over. She held out her arms to him, and after a moment's hesitation he strode toward her and gathered her against his broad chest.

She didn't even realize she was crying until he stroked her hair, murmuring, "It's all right, it's over now."

She buried her nose in the warmth of his sweater and blinked back the tears. He felt so good. He smelled so good. She had forgotten how much she liked the spicy cologne he wore.

"We got the bastard," Blake muttered, above her head. "He can't hurt you anymore. I'm just glad we got him to clear your name before he died."

Her pulse quickened as she absorbed the full implication of his words. Her name had been cleared. She could go anywhere with her head held high. She had nothing to hide anymore. She could even go back to Portland if she wanted to.

Now that it was possible, she wasn't at all sure she wanted to go back. There were too many unhappy memories there, and both Heather and she had been happy in Mellow Springs. They had built a new life, a good life, far from the evil and misery of the past.

The air was clean and smelled so pure, and life was simple in Mellow Springs. It was such a friendly town, and now that she no longer had a reason to hide her past, she would be free to make more friends.

No, she decided, with a quickening of her pulse, she didn't really want to leave Mellow Springs and go back to Portland. There was only one reason she would go back. And that was if Blake asked her to go, to be with him. She would go anywhere in the world with him.

She raised her head to look up at him. "I never thanked you for clearing my name," she said shakily. "I hope you know how much that means to me."

He smiled down at her, but made no attempt to kiss her. She would have given anything for his kiss right then. "It was the least I could do. You deserve to have the truth known. I'll make sure it's put on public record."

"Thank you." She pulled back from him, and hunted in her pocket for a tissue.

Immediately he dropped his arms and moved away. The room seemed to turn suddenly cold. She watched him reach for the empty plates, trying desperately to read his expression.

"The sheriff's office is going to handle the body," he said, as he stacked the dishes one on top of the other. "They will probably want a report from you, and they might ask you to sign the release of the body since you are a relative."

Still avoiding her gaze, he carried the dishes to the sink and laid them on the counter.

"All right." She glanced over at the clock. "I'm going to take a shower. I want to go over to Darcie's and collect my daughter. I feel as if I haven't seen her in weeks, instead of a couple of days."

She hesitated. Then, when he didn't answer her she added, "Would you like to come with me? I know she'd love to see you."

"Gail—" He looked up, and now she could see his expression.

She had seen that look of hopelessness once before, on someone else's face. A long time ago. The day she'd been torn from the arms of Elaine Matthews.

Now Blake had that same look on his face, and she could guess what it meant. She lifted her chin, waiting for the blow to fall, determined that no matter what he told her, he wouldn't see her cry.

Chapter 12

"I have to go back to Portland, Gail."

"Of course." She gave him a bright smile. "When are you leaving?"

"Right away. I need you to take me to the sheriff's office to pick up my car. I'll stop by the hotel on my way out of town."

She nodded, afraid to trust her voice.

Moments ticked by while he seemed to be searching for the right words. Then he added quietly, "I'm sorry, Gail. I did tell you I couldn't make any promises."

Her throat ached with the effort to keep her voice steady. "I understand, Blake."

"I don't think you do."

Her cold fury came from nowhere, swift and uncontrollable. "I'm not totally naive. I was one of the perks that go with the job, right?"

Pain slashed across his face as if she'd slapped him. "Damn it, Gail, don't make this any harder for me than it already is."

"Of course not," she said, her voice brittle. "I'll make it easy for you. Goodbye, Mr. Foster. Thanks for a great time. It was fun while it lasted. Have a good life."

She turned to leave, but he grabbed her from behind, his fingers gripping her arm. She tried to twist out of his grasp, but he held on, turning her so that she faced him.

"I'm not going to let you walk out of here until you've heard what I have to say."

"What gives you the idea I'm interested in what you have to say?"

"Whether you're interested or not, you're going to hear it." He pushed her toward her chair. "Now sit down."

She glared at him, prepared to resist to the death.

"I said, sit down!"

He was mad, too. She could see it snapping in his eyes. Shrugging, she dropped onto the chair, her face rigid with rebellious anger.

He stood towering over her for a second or two, as if making sure she would stay put. Then he moved around the table and slumped into the other chair. Leaning his elbows on the table, he ran the fingers of both hands through his hair in a gesture of frustration.

"I quit the force," he said, his voice muffled so that she could barely hear him. "After the ambush, I quit. I spent six months trying to decide what I was going to do with the rest of my life. I started drinking. Heavily. Nights at first, then daytime, as well, when the pain and the guilt wouldn't go away."

He lowered his hands, lifting his chin to look at her. "It was as if I'd lost all sense of direction. I couldn't eat, and I couldn't sleep without drinking myself into a stupor. I lost all my self-respect. And I didn't care anymore. Until I woke up one morning in a motel room and couldn't remember how I got there. I realized then where I was heading. I knew I had to take back my life.

"Thanks to an understanding colleague who had some influence, I was offered the post of U.S. Marshal, and I accepted. I never looked back." He thrust his hands onto the table, his fingers clenched into fists. "I need to be a part of law enforcement, Gail. It isn't something I do, it's who I am. It's been a part of me ever since I was born. Without it I have no life. It wasn't until I faced that fact, and did something about it, that I finally pulled myself out of the hole I'd dug."

She frowned, striving to understand. "No one is trying to take that away from you, Blake. Least of all me."

He shook his head, his gray eyes reflecting his determination. "I can't have both, Gail. I wish to God I could, but it just isn't possible. I saw what my father's death did to my mother. What the deaths of my unit did to their wives. I couldn't face the thought of bringing that kind of suffering down on someone who might love me."

He shoved his chair back and stood. "As long as it's only myself who's involved, I don't think about the risks. If I had to consider someone else, someone who would suffer if something happened to me, I would lose my edge. I've seen what happens when I let personal feelings sway my judgment. I just couldn't do my job if I worried about the risks. And without my job, I couldn't live with myself."

She didn't need to look at his face to know how useless it would be to argue; it was in his voice. He'd had to make a choice between her and his job. And his job had won. Slowly, she got to her feet, feeling as if she were facing a long, dark and endless tunnel. "I'm going to take a shower," she said wearily. "And then I'll drive you to the sheriff's office."

Gail managed to make small talk on the way there. He answered her in monosyllables, looking almost as unapproachable as he had that first day he'd walked into The Book Nook.

It wasn't until they'd pulled up at the curb that he finally looked at her. "If you ever need me—for anything—please don't hesitate to call. The number's listed in the book under U.S. Justice Department.''

She nodded, meeting his eyes briefly before switching her gaze back at the road. The sun sparkled on the packed snow, dazzling her, and she wished she'd brought her sunglasses. If she had, she could have hidden behind them to take that last, long look at his face.

"Have you decided what you're going to do? Will you be going back to Portland now that you don't have to worry about Stevens?"

"No, I don't think so. This is my home now, and Heather hardly remembers Portland anymore. I prefer to keep it that way."

"Tell her goodbye for me. Tell her—" He paused. "Tell her I'll never forget her."

"I never did give you the picture she drew for you."

"Mail it to me?"

"Of course I will."

"Thanks."

They were talking like strangers, she thought sadly. No one would ever guess that they had shared something so beautiful, so damned meaningful. At least, it had been beautiful and meaningful to her.

She wanted to yell at him, to strike out at him, to let him know how badly he had hurt her. She had given him her heart and her soul, and he'd thrown it all back at her.

I can't make you any promises. She hadn't asked for promises. All she'd asked for was honesty. But he hadn't been honest. He'd let her believe that he really cared for her. And all the time he'd known that he belonged to his job. He'd never belonged to her. He never would.

She would never be able to understand the complex emotions that drove him. She only knew that she'd lost him. But dammit, she would let him go with as much grace and composure as she could manage. Afterward, when she was alone, she could give in to the rage.

"I guess I'd better get going," he said, his voice thick with regret.

He would never realize what it cost her to turn to him and smile. "Have a good trip back."

"Thanks. You take care, okay?"

"I will. You, too."

"And look after that cute little daughter of yours. She's going to be just as beautiful as her mom, some day."

"I'm counting on it," she said evenly.

He nodded. Reaching for the handle, he eased the car door open. He looked back at her, and for just a moment she saw a flicker of emotion in his eyes; then it was gone. "Goodbye, Gail."

"Goodbye, Blake."

She watched him climb out. The door slammed shut, and he stepped back, touching his forehead with his fingers in a gesture of farewell. Then he turned and hurried up the steps of the building. He went through the door without looking back, and it closed behind him, shutting him out of her life.

She took off with a squeal of tires and drove up the street, heedless of the speed limit. She needed to be alone, just for a little while, before she collected her daughter. She needed time to accept the fact that for the second time in her life, she had dared to love and had lost it all.

She drove until the tears forced her to pull over, onto a winding lane that led to an open field. There she parked, and laid her head on the steering wheel until the tempest had passed and she was exhausted.

When she finally lifted her head, only a dull ache remained, instead of the tearing agony of loss. She still had Heather, she told herself as she mopped up her face as best she could. And when Heather was grown and no longer needed her, God willing, there would be grandchildren to enjoy.

Maybe a dog, she thought, as she drove slowly back to Darcie's. Heather would like that. Her spirits rallied a little at the thought of her daughter. Now she was anxious to see her. Now she couldn't wait to hold that wiry little body and hug her tightly.

She pulled up at the traffic light at the edge of town, and deliberately shut her mind to the memories. Later, much later, she might be able to face them again, but not now. Now she wanted to forget.

After a few minutes she pulled up in front of Darcie's house. The door opened immediately to her knock and a small body hurled itself at her in a flurry of arms and legs.

"Mommy, where have you *been?*"

For a moment she was afraid she would cry, then she collected herself. Hugging the little girl closer she murmured, "I've been on a long trip, but I'm back now." She looked up to see Darcie in the hallway, a look of deep concern on her face.

"It's good to see you, Kate. We missed you."

"I drew lots of pictures for you," Heather announced, and grabbed hold of her hand to pull her inside.

Gail managed a tight laugh as she met Darcie's intent gaze. "You wouldn't have a pot of coffee on, would you?"

"Don't I always? Come on in and sit down. You look as if you haven't slept in a week."

"I feel as if I haven't slept in a week." Gail sank wearily into a chair in Darcie's comfortable family room and stretched out her feet. She listened as Heather brought her up to date on every minute detail of her life for the past three days, while Darcie busied herself in the kitchen.

"Here," she said, coming back into the room a few minutes later. "Coffee and a bagel."

"Thanks, but I'm not hungry."

"Eat it anyway." She tilted her head to one side and studied Gail's face. "Have you come to take Annie home?"

Gail nodded. "I figure you must have had enough of her by now."

"I'll never have enough of her. She's a good kid." Darcie patted Heather on the head. "If you're going home you'd better collect all those pictures you've been drawing."

"Okay." Heather scrambled to her feet. "You wanna look at them, Mommy?"

Gail smiled. "I'll see them when we get home. We'll have lots of time to look at them then." Too much time, she thought dismally, then banished the depressing thought.

Heather left the room, presumably to collect her pictures. As soon as she had gone, Darcie pulled her chair closer to Gail. "Okay, shoot," she ordered.

Gail sighed. "It's a...little complicated."

"Okay, so tell me about Blake first."

She told her the entire story. Hesitantly at first, then with growing confidence as Darcie listened, enthralled. She left out her feelings for Blake. She wasn't ready to talk about that yet, if ever. She skipped over the time she'd spent making love with him; that was something she would always keep locked away in her heart.

Darcie's expression changed so rapidly as the story progressed that Gail almost smiled. Especially when she got to the part when Mike called her to tell her he had Heather.

"My God," Darcie whispered, when she had finished the story. "You must have been out of your mind."

"I was."

"Weren't you terrified of meeting that monster in that lonely spot?"

"I didn't have time to be afraid. Not for myself, anyway." Blake had said something like that, she remembered. *"As long as it's only myself involved, I don't think about the risks."*

"So what happens now?"

Gail shrugged, doing her best to look indifferent. "Not much, I guess. I'll have to answer some questions. The sheriff will take care of the rest."

"And Blake?"

"He's gone back to Portland." Just like that. So easy to say, and so damn difficult to understand.

Darcie looked disappointed. "I thought there was some big romance budding here. Or are you planning on going back there, too?"

Heather chose that moment to rush back into the room, much to Gail's relief. "No," she said, rising to her feet. "We're not going back. This is our home, and we're going to stay."

Darcie smiled. "I'm glad."

Maybe one day, Gail thought, as she left the warmth of the baby-sitter's home, she would be glad about it, too. Right now, the prospect seemed as bleak as the clouds that were blotting out the sun.

Heather chatted happily on the way home, and seemed more than content to be back in her own room, surrounded by familiar and loved possessions. If she missed the company of Darcie's children, she didn't mention it.

Gail found it hard to go to sleep that night. Although she did her utmost to banish all thoughts of Blake, his image insisted on intruding into her mind. She wondered how long it would take for the pain to ease, and the memories to fade. She wondered if he was lying awake, too, thinking about her. She rather doubted it.

The next morning she dropped Heather off at the kindergarten and then drove to The Book Nook. Polly greeted her warmly, and although obviously curious, refrained from asking her too many questions.

Gail was relieved about that. The less she talked about it, she decided, the sooner she would forget.

Unfortunately, in the days that followed, that theory proved unfounded. No matter where she went, the memories haunted her. Long after Heather had stopped asking about Blake, Gail would see his image everywhere she went.

She could no longer enjoy meals in the diner, and every time she passed the Alpine Inn, she felt the acute ache of loss. She made excuses when Heather begged to go back to the mountain, or to the children's museum in Parkerville.

The entire town of Mellow Springs seemed to grow smaller and more confining every day. Her work at the bookstore suffered, and more than once she caught Polly staring at her, her face wrinkled with concern.

Finally, as the snow gradually melted and the crocuses and daffodils brightened the front yards, Gail faced the truth. She would never be rid of the memories as long as she stayed in Mellow Springs. The town no longer seemed a haven; it seemed like more like a prison, shutting her away from the outside world.

For days she struggled with indecision. She could go back to Portland, but that would mean risking the chance of bumping into Blake. She couldn't bear that. Although the pain never quite left her, she was beginning to heal. She could go for an entire day or two without thinking about him. Without wondering where he was and what he was doing. Without worrying that he might be in danger, aware that she would never know if something bad had happened to him. Or good, for that matter.

To go back now, knowing he was so close, knowing that the possibility of seeing him was always there would only drag out the agony of getting over him. No, Portland wasn't the answer.

The day she finally made her decision was bright with sunshine and soft breezes that brought with them the promise of spring. She'd dropped Heather off at the kindergarten and was driving along Main Street, trying not to think about the first day she'd had lunch with Blake.

The idea grew slowly, but the more she thought about it, the more she liked it. Seattle. She was familiar with the city, although it had grown considerably since she was there as a child. But she liked the openness of it, the waterways, the proximity of the ocean, the climate that was so similar to Portland's.

Heather would love it—there was so much to do there,

so much to see. The opportunities for growth, a broader education and exposure to a variety of cultures were all readily available compared to the limited resources of a small town like Mellow Springs. And best of all, the memories she had of the city were of another life, another time—before she even knew that Blake Foster existed.

Excited now by the prospect, she told Polly what she intended to do.

Polly listened gravely, then nodded her head in resignation. "I've been expecting it," she said. "And you're right, it's time. You've spent way too long pining away in this piddling little town. You need to get back where you can enjoy some excitement in your life."

Gail pulled a face. "I've had more than enough excitement lately. I just think it's time I took charge of things and did what's best for me and my daughter. I've been running away all my life, taking the easy way out, instead of taking risks and running toward something. This time I'm going to make plans for the direction I want to take, and do my best to make them work."

"Good for you." Polly gave her a hearty slap on the shoulder. "You've come a long way from that frightened little thing who came looking for a job a few months ago."

"Yes," Gail said wryly. "I certainly have."

Heather didn't seem at all happy about the move at first. "I'll miss all my friends," she said, as Gail tucked her into bed that night. "I'll miss Miss Thompson, and Darcie, and Janice and—"

"You'll make new friends," Gail said firmly. "And you can write letters to everyone here. We'll call now and again, and even come to visit if you like."

Heather pouted. "Don't want to go."

"You'll be missing a lot if you don't. Boat rides in the summer, amusement parks, the zoo, train rides—there's an even bigger children's museum there, and we'll still be fairly close to the mountains."

Heather thought about that. "Can I take my dolly's house?"

Gail smiled. "You can take every one of your toys. We'll buy new ones, as well. Maybe we'll even buy a dog."

"I think I'm going to like Seattle," Heather said sleepily.

So would she, Gail thought hopefully, just as long as she could leave all the memories behind in Mellow Springs.

Blake had made a mistake and he knew it. The truth of it hit him from every direction, everywhere he turned. In his lonely apartment, when he returned to it at night, he kept imagining her sitting next to him on the couch, laughing at something on the television, while a blond, curly-haired child played at their feet.

He heard her laughter in the wind, and her whispers in the dark. He couldn't take a shower without remembering her wet, smooth body sliding across his, her mouth eager and hot on his bare skin. He ached for her, with a deep-seated pain that would not let up.

He wouldn't even look at a bottle of beer. He was too afraid that once he started drinking, he wouldn't stop. He analyzed his thoughts and his emotions until his mind whirled in crazy circles of denial.

When he'd first arrived back in Portland he'd been assigned a desk job for a while, taking care of the assets seized from the profits of illegal drug operations. Then the day he'd dreaded had arrived, and he was handed another field assignment. Another prison escape—this time two inmates, both known to be savage killers.

He was assigned a deputy, an excitable young man on his first big case. In the beginning things went smoothly—the initial investigations, the reports, the follow-ups. But then, when the first fresh lead came in and he knew it was time to take action, he had to face the truth.

He was no good without her.

He couldn't concentrate. He'd lost that keen edge, that

sixth sense, that gut responsiveness that could only come with experience, and which could mean the difference between living and dying.

If he'd had just himself to worry about, he would have taken a chance. But he would not, could not risk the life of an associate again. He handed in his resignation.

When he tried to explain, haltingly, the reason he wanted to quit, Paul Richmond, his superior, interrupted him.

"You don't have to tell me what's wrong with you," he said, giving Blake a direct stare from across his wide, antique desk. "It's written all over you. You're still wallowing in guilt over the loss of your men."

Blake started to deny it, but again, Paul interrupted with a swift movement of his hand. "It happens to most of us, sooner or later. This is a tough job we're in, and sometimes things go wrong. It goes with the territory, and every man knows that when he accepts the job. You are not responsible for the deaths of those men. The bastards who shot them are responsible. The problem is, Blake, you're waiting for someone to forgive you. It doesn't happen that way. You have to forgive yourself. You won't have any peace until you do."

It took him another month of wrestling with his conscience before he made the trip north. He wanted to be sure he could offer her a stable future. He would not disrupt her life again unless he was certain that he could give her what she wanted—a comfortable home, reasonable security, and above all, his everlasting love.

The sun was shining on Main Street when he drove down it a few days later. The mountains welcomed him, their white peaks stark against a clear blue sky. The sun warmed the car enough to have the window down, and the breeze rustled his hair, while the scent of pine brought back the sharp memory of the night at Deep Frost Lake.

He smiled, his heart leaping with excitement at the thought of seeing her again. And he wondered if Heather had grown, and if she would remember him. Children forgot so fast.

She'd never sent him the picture that Heather had drawn for him. He hoped she still had it. He wanted to keep it, as one of his most treasured possessions.

His pulse quickened when the bookstore came into view. His gaze went eagerly to the parking space opposite. Only one car stood there, and it wasn't hers.

His stomach took a nosedive, but then he glanced at his watch. It was a little past noon. She was probably at lunch. He was tempted to stop at the diner, in case she was there. He wanted to walk in and surprise her. But he didn't want to waste the time if she'd gone somewhere else for lunch. Polly would know where she was.

He pulled into the space next to Polly's car and shut off the engine. His heart was pounding now, vibrating throughout his entire body. Just looking at the bookstore gave him goose bumps. It looked different than he'd remembered, without the snow banked along the curb, and the sign looked as if it had a coat of fresh paint.

He opened the car door and climbed out, wondering just how much she'd told Polly. Had she talked about their relationship? What if she were no longer interested in him? That possibility had occurred to him a couple of times on the drive up, but now that he was minutes away from seeing her, the enormity of the question and its consequences hit him full force.

She had to still care, he told himself as he crossed the road. If not, he would make her care again. He would work at it for the rest of his days, if need be.

The bell on the door jangled as he opened it, evoking the sharp thrust of memory. Polly stood yards away, poised in the act of placing a book on the shelf. He could see at once by her expression that she wasn't happy to see him. His spirits dropped.

"Hi," he said easily. "Remember me?"

"Indeed, I do, Marshal." She placed the book on the

shelf with extreme care, as if she wanted to give herself time to collect her thoughts. "What can I do for you?"

"I came to see Gail. Is she out to lunch?"

Polly came forward slowly, her eyes wary behind her rimless glasses. "Gail no longer works here," she said quietly.

He tried to ignore the swift rise of panic in his gut. "Oh? Where is she working, then?"

"I really wouldn't know." She moved behind the counter and began sorting through a stack of mail, her movements slow and deliberate.

He clamped down on his impatience. "Come now, Polly, this is a small town. You must know where she's working."

There was no mistaking the hostility in Polly's eyes when she looked at him. "Gail doesn't live here anymore. She and Annie left Mellow Springs a few weeks ago. They won't be coming back."

His disappointment was so acute he couldn't speak for a moment. "I see. Where did she go? Back to Portland?"

He half expected Polly's answer.

"I really can't say."

"Can't, or won't?"

Polly's eyes narrowed. "Don't bring your dang police tactics in here, Mr. Foster. Gail has left to begin a new life. The best thing you can do for her is leave her alone."

He managed to control his spurt of anger. "Don't you think that's up to her to decide?"

Polly lifted her chin. "She has decided," she said evenly. "She asked me not to disclose her whereabouts…to anyone."

The sun threw sparkling rows of diamonds on the waters of Lake Washington as Gail drove over the floating bridge from Mercer Island. Summer was at its height, and a light haze hung over the Seattle skyline.

In just a matter of weeks, Heather would be starting first grade, Gail thought, as she slowed behind the line of traffic at the light. She would have to start using her lunch hours to buy her daughter some new clothes.

Minutes later she parked beneath the small shopping mall. After the brightness of the sunshine, the underground parking lot seemed dark and dismal. She'd been working at the mall bookstore for several weeks now, but still couldn't rid herself of the eerie feeling she got every time she had to walk through the lonely rows of cars to the elevator.

The hollow echo of her footsteps followed her, and she resisted the temptation to look over her shoulder. She was slowly overcoming her irrational fears. After living with them for so long, they'd been harder to conquer than she'd anticipated.

A small group of people waited at the elevator, and she relaxed. She had nothing to fear anymore. She was safe. Heather was safe. She'd found a nice house to rent, close to the school where Heather would go in the fall, she had a job she liked and she was beginning to make new friends. Heather had settled down, and their lives were slowly but surely taking shape.

And if, now and again, the bittersweet bite of nostalgia disturbed her peace, she knew it was only temporary and would pass, given time. All in all, she was reasonably happy.

The bookstore was always busy on Saturdays, and today was no exception. Gail hardly had time to stop for coffee as the customers streamed in to browse and invariably left with purchases. It was a long way from The Book Nook in Mellow Springs.

Gail rarely thought about Polly these days. She'd sent a couple of postcards, and Polly had responded, filling her in on all the local gossip. No real news. Nothing unusual had happened in town since she'd left, Polly had assured her. Darcie, who had confessed to being notoriously bad at writing letters, hadn't answered her last one. Gail had made a effort to put Mellow Springs out of her mind, so she didn't really miss the correspondence.

By the end of her shift, Gail was exhausted. She worked until nine on Fridays, leaving Heather at her new baby-sitter's until she could pick her up on the way home. It was the only night she worked late, and she was always tired at the end of it.

The thing she disliked most about the late hour was the walk through the parking lot to her car. It was bad enough in the daytime, but at night it felt positively creepy.

The elevator was empty when she stepped into it, and she punched the button for her floor, wishing she had some company. Irritated with herself, she wondered when she would be completely free of her ridiculous hang-up of feeling uneasy whenever she was alone.

The elevator jerked to a creaky stop, and the door slid open. The dim lights of the parking area only served to increase the shadows that lay in wait for her.

She hurried to the car, trying not to listen to the echo of her footsteps. She'd done this every week for months, she reminded herself. She was perfectly safe.

Her fingers were actually turning the door handle of her compact when a shadow detached itself from the thick stone pillar a few feet away.

She stared at the figure moving toward her, shock sending protests screaming through her mind. It wasn't possible. He couldn't have found her. Yet deep down, she'd always known that he would.

"Hello, Gail," Blake said, in the husky tone she remembered so well.

He stepped out of the shadows, while her fingers curled painfully into her palm. She felt a jolt when she saw his face. In the cold, green-tinted light from the fluorescent lamps, he looked drawn and immeasurably tired.

"How did you find me?" she demanded. In spite of herself, she felt a twinge of compassion when she saw the pain in his eyes.

"I was hoping you'd be glad to see me. You weren't easy to track down."

She looked down at her car, and reached for the handle again. "I'm sorry, Blake. I wish you hadn't come." It was still there, after all—the pain; the deep, tearing need. She'd thought she'd finally buried it, but all it had taken was one look at him, and she found she hadn't buried it at all.

"I had to come. I had to see you. I need to talk to you."

"I think we said all we had to say the last time we met." *Go away!* her mind screamed. *Haven't you done enough?*

"I quit the force, Gail."

She froze, her hand gripping the handle. Her heart had stopped leaping around like a startled rabbit and was now throbbing—a slow, steady beat of hope. She moistened her lips. "Why?"

A car's engine roared to life across the aisle, making her jump.

"Can we go somewhere and talk?" He moved closer, and the trembling started, deep inside her.

"I have to pick up Heather." God, how she wanted to go with him. *No, no! Don't listen to him. He'll hurt you again.*

"You can call, can't you?"

She fought with herself, angry over her inability to resist him.

"Please, Gail. This might be the most important decision of your life. Of both our lives."

Of both our lives. She was afraid to believe, afraid to hope. *Damn him! Why did he have to come back now?* She couldn't answer him, for fear she would betray her own convictions.

"I understand. I can't say I blame you."

She looked up, and saw him turning away. "I'm not going to let you hurt me again." Her voice trembled, in spite of her best efforts to prevent it.

He paused, but didn't look back at her. "I know. I hurt myself, too. I have to live with that the rest of my life. I'm sorry that I waited too long to find out that I love you, Gail. That the only important thing in my life is you...and Heather.''

The words seemed to fill every pore of her being—soothing, healing, melting away the pain. She drew a long, shaky breath. "Did you really quit?"

He uttered a dry laugh. "Yeah, I did. I guess I'm a three-way loser."

She hesitated, knowing she was a fool, yet helpless to stop the torrent of love that refused to die. "There's a bar around the corner," she said carefully. "I'll call the sitter, but I can only stay a few minutes."

He turned back to face her, thrusting his hands into the pockets of his jeans. He wore a pale cream shirt with a banded collar, and had rolled the cuffs back to his forearms. He looked thinner, defeated and carefully controlled. She had never loved him more in her life.

She led the way and he followed in silence, his footsteps now echoing with hers. The bar had tables outside on the sidewalk, and she spotted an empty one in the corner. "Grab that one," she told him. "I'll be right back."

She made the call, asking if Heather could stay the night. She needed time to deal with this, no matter how things turned out.

When she came back to the table, he'd ordered her a glass of wine. She sipped at it without tasting it, conscious of his eyes on her.

"You look great," he said, when she found the courage to meet his gaze.

"Thank you. I feel pretty good."

"And Heather?"

"She's fine. She starts grade school in the fall. She talks of nothing else."

"I've missed her so much. I've missed you."

Careful, she urged herself. *Take it slowly.* "Why did you quit the force?"

He let out his breath in a long sigh, dropping his gaze

to the beer glass between his fingers. "It wasn't working. It didn't mean anything anymore. I found myself thinking about you, when I should have been worrying about the whereabouts of the escaped cons I was supposed to find."

"Blake—"

"No." He looked up, and the passion burned so bright in his eyes that she wanted to cry. "Let me say this. I just hope I can say it right. I was a fool. I should never have walked away from you. I told myself it was for the best. I convinced myself—and you—that it was because of my job. When all the time I knew that it was more than that."

He tilted his head back and looked up at a night sky carpeted in stars. When he lowered his chin again she could swear he had tears in his eyes. "I couldn't forgive myself for losing those three men, Gail. The reason I felt so compelled to stay in law enforcement wasn't because it was my life, it was because I was trying to make amends for what I'd done. I was looking for forgiveness.

"You and Heather represented everything I've ever dreamed about, but no matter how much I wanted you, subconsciously I felt that I didn't deserve you. How could I be happy with a home and family, when I'd destroyed three other families?"

She searched his face, needing so much to understand. "And now?"

"It took me a while. A good friend pointed out where the problem lay, but it took a lot of soul-searching before I finally accepted the fact that in order to live my life, I had to let go of the guilt. If I really wanted to make amends for what happened, I could do it best by spending every waking moment doing my damnedest to make someone else happy."

He reached across the table and enclosed her hands in his strong fingers. "I love you, Gail. I love Heather. Nothing means anything to me without you both—not the job, not my life or anything in my future. I need you. I have some money put away. I've been wanting to start my own security business and settle down somewhere. Anywhere. Mellow Springs, if you like, or here in Seattle. I don't care where it is, just as long as I'm with you. Marry me, Gail. Marry me, and give me back my life.''

Now she was crying—tears of happiness slipping heedlessly down her cheeks. There had never been any real doubt in her mind. ''On behalf of Heather and myself,'' she said unsteadily, ''I joyfully accept.''

His smile was beautiful to see. He lifted her fingers to his mouth and kissed them. ''I love you, Gail.''

''I love you, too,'' she said softly. ''Now...let's go home.''

* * * * *

New York Times bestselling author

LINDA HOWARD

Was this the man she'd married…or a total stranger?

When Jay Granger is escorted by the FBI to the bedside
of her injured ex-husband, she is unprepared for her
own reaction—something is different about him.
Although he doesn't remember anything, his effect on
her is intense…sensual…uncontrollable. And each day
as he grows stronger, he gains back more of his life.
Including Jay.

Linda Howard delivers a suspenseful and emotional
story of love and deception…

WHITE LIES

Available in May 1997 at your favorite retail outlet.

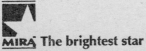

MIRA **The brightest star in women's fiction**

Take 4 bestselling love stories FREE

Plus get a FREE surprise gift!

As seen on TV!
Free Gift Offer

With a Free Gift proof-of-purchase from any Silhouette® book, you can receive a beautiful cubic zirconia pendant.

This gorgeous marquise-shaped stone is a genuine cubic zirconia—accented by an 18" gold tone necklace.

(Approximate retail value $19.95)

Send for yours today...
compliments of ▼ *Silhouette*®
TM

To receive your free gift, a cubic zirconia pendant, send us one original proof-of-purchase, photocopies not accepted, from the back of any Silhouette Romance™, Silhouette Desire®, Silhouette Special Edition®, Silhouette Intimate Moments® or Silhouette Yours Truly™ title available in February, March and April at your favorite retail outlet, together with the Free Gift Certificate, plus a check or money order for $1.65 U.S./$2.15 CAN. (do not send cash) to cover postage and handling, payable to Silhouette Free Gift Offer. We will send you the specified gift. Allow 6 to 8 weeks for delivery. Offer good until April 30, 1997 or while quantities last. Offer valid in the U.S. and Canada only.

Free Gift Certificate

Name: _____

Address: _____

City: _____ State/Province: _____ Zip/Postal Code: _____

Mail this certificate, one proof-of-purchase and a check or money order for postage and handling to: SILHOUETTE FREE GIFT OFFER 1997. In the U.S.: 3010 Walden Avenue, P.O. Box 9077, Buffalo NY 14269-9077. In Canada: P.O. Box 613, Fort Erie, Ontario L2Z 5X3.

FREE GIFT OFFER   084-KFD
ONE PROOF-OF-PURCHASE
To collect your fabulous FREE GIFT, a cubic zirconia pendant, you must include this original proof-of-purchase for each gift with the properly completed Free Gift Certificate.

084-KFD

Intimate Moments is proud to bring you an unforgettable miniseries.

BEVERLY BIRD

The Wedding Ring

Wrapped in the warmth of family tradition, three couples say "I do!"

LOVING MARIAH
(Intimate Moments #790, June 1997)
Adam Wallace searches for his kidnapped son...which leads him to the Amish heartland and lovely schoolteacher Mariah Fisher.

MARRYING JAKE
(Intimate Moments #802, August 1997)
Commitment-shy Jake Wallace unravels the ongoing mystery of stolen babies and helps Katya Essler learn to believe in love again.

SAVING SUSANNAH
(Intimate Moments #814, October 1997)
Kimberly Wallace needs a bone marrow donor to save her daughter's life. Will the temporary nanny position to Joe Lapp's children be the answer to her prayers?

INTIMATE MOMENTS®
Silhouette®

This summer, the legend
continues in Jacobsville

Diana Palmer

A LONG, TALL TEXAN SUMMER

Three BRAND-NEW short stories

This summer, Silhouette brings readers a special
collection for Diana Palmer's LONG, TALL TEXANS
fans. Diana has rounded up three **BRAND-NEW**
stories of love Texas-style, all set in Jacobsville,
Texas. Featuring the men you've grown to love from
this wonderful town, this collection is a must-have
for all fans!

*They grow 'em tall in the saddle in Texas—and
they've got love and marriage on their minds!*

Don't miss this collection of original Long, Tall Texans
stories...available in June at your favorite retail outlet.

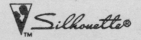